On the
Naughty List

On the Naughty List

Lori Foster

Carly Phillips

Beth Ciotta

Sugar Jamison

St. Martin's Paperbacks

This is a work of fiction. All of the characters, organizations, and events portrayed in this novel are either products of the author's imagination or are used fictitiously.

ON THE NAUGHTY LIST

"Christmas Bonus" copyright © 2000 by Lori Foster. Previously published in 2000 in the anthology *All I Want for Christmas*.

"Naughty Under the Mistletoe" copyright © 2001 by Karen Drogin. Previously published in 2001 in the anthology *Naughty or Nice?*

"Some Kind of Wonderful" copyright © 2013 by Beth Ciotta. Previously published as an eBook in 2013.

"Have Yourself a Curvy Little Christmas" copyright © 2013 by Sugar Jamison. Previously published as an eBook in 2013.

For information address St. Martin's Press, 175 Fifth Avenue, New York, NY 10010.

ISBN: 978-1-250-07129-3

Printed in the United States of America

St. Martin's Paperbacks edition / October 2015

St. Martin's Paperbacks are published by St. Martin's Press, 175 Fifth Avenue, New York, NY 10010.

10 9 8 7 6 5 4 3 2 1

Table of Contents

Christmas Bonus

Lori Foster

One

Eric Bragg heard the even staccato clicking of her designer high heels coming down the polished hallway. He straightened in his chair as anticipation thrummed through him, matching the quickened beat of his heart.

He knew the sound of Maggie's long-legged, purposeful walk with an innate awareness that exemplified his growing obsession with her. He could easily identify the sound of her stride apart from that of all the other employees. Mostly because when he heard it, he felt the familiar hot need, mixed with disgruntled dismay, that always seemed to be a part of him these days wherever Maggie Carmichael was concerned.

He remembered a time not too long ago when her footsteps would have been muted with sneakers that perfectly matched her tattered jeans and oversized sweatshirts. A time when she was so anxious to visit the office, she wouldn't have bothered to measure her stride and she would have forgotten her now impeccable good manners in her excitement at the visit. She used to hurry up and down the hallways with all the enthusiasm of a nineteen-year-old woman-child, almost old enough, almost mature enough.

Eric shifted, trying to settle himself more comfortably in his large chair while his muscles tightened and his pulse quickened.

Unfortunately for Eric, Maggie had stepped right out of college and into the role of boss, a circumstance he had never foreseen. Perhaps if he had, he wouldn't have bided his time so patiently, waiting for the differences in their ages to melt away under the influence of experience and maturity. Ten years wasn't much, he'd always told himself, unless you were tampering with an innocent daydreamer still in college. *The boss's daughter—and now the damn boss.*

But who would have guessed that her father would pass away so unexpectedly with a stroke? Or that he would have left Maggie, fresh-faced and uncertain, in charge of his small but growing company, rather than Eric, who'd served as his right-hand man for many years?

Deliberately, Eric loosened his hold on the pen he'd been using to check off items on a new supply order and placed it gently on his cluttered desk. Every other year, at just about this time, Maggie had visited him. She'd be out of school on Christmas break and she'd show up wearing small brass bells everywhere. They used to be tied in the laces of her shoes, hanging from a festive bow in her long, sinfully sexy hair, on ribbons around her neck. She loved Christmas and decorating and buying gifts. Eric reached into his pocket and smoothed his thumb over the engraved key ring she'd given him the year before.

This year, everything was different. *This year, he'd become her employee.*

Sprawled out in his seat, pretending a comfort he didn't feel, Eric waited for her. But still, he caught his breath as Maggie opened his door without knocking and stepped in.

There wasn't a single bell on her person. No red velvet ribbons, no blinking Santa pins. She was so damn subdued these days, it was almost as if the old Maggie had never existed. The combination of losing her father and gaining the responsibility of a company had changed her. Her glossy black hair had long since been cut into a chic shorter style, hanging just to the tops of her breasts. When she'd first cut it, he'd gotten rip-roaring drunk in mourning the loss of a longtime fantasy. Her slender body, which he'd become accustomed to seeing in sporty, casual clothes, was lost as well, beneath a ridiculously boxy, businesslike suit. It was drab in both color and form—but it still turned him on.

He knew what was beneath that absurd armor she now wore, knew the slight, feminine body that it hid.

And her legs . . . oh, yeah, he approved of the high heels Maggie had taken to wearing. They'd helped him to contrive new fantasies, which he utilized every damn night with the finesse of a masochist, torturing himself while wondering about things he'd likely never know. He went to sleep thinking about her, and woke up wanting her.

He was getting real used to surviving with a semi-erection throughout the day.

He felt like a teenager, once again caught in the heated throes of puberty. Only now, groping a girl in the backseat of his car wasn't about to put an end to his aching. Hell, an all-night sexual binge with triplets wouldn't do the trick. He wanted only Maggie, naked, hot, breathless, accepting him and begging him and . . .

Damn, but he had to get a grip!

"Maggie." He ignored the raw edge to his voice and eyed her still features as she stared at him. There was a heated quality to her gaze, as if she'd read his thoughts. "You're flushed, hon. Anything wrong?"

Maggie looked him over quickly, her large brown eyes widening just a bit as her gaze coasted from the top of his head to the toes of his shoes. Unlike Maggie, he hadn't trussed himself up in a restricting suit. But then, he never had. From the day he'd been hired, he'd made do with comfortable corduroy slacks or khakis—a true concession from his preference of jeans—and loose sweaters or oxford shirts. Ties were a definite no-no. He hated the damn things. Her father had never minded, and evidently, neither did she.

Maggie shut the door behind her and lifted her chin. She was a mere twenty-two years old, yet she managed to imbue her tone with all the seriousness of a wizened sage. "We need to talk."

Eric smiled the smile he reserved just for Maggie. The one with no teeth showing, just a tiny curling at the corners of his mouth, barely noticeable, while his eyes remained intent and direct. He knew it made her uneasy, which was why he did it, cad that he was. Why should he be the only one suffering? Besides, seeing Maggie squirm was like refined foreplay, and he took undeniable satisfaction in being the one who engineered it. These days she was so set on displaying confidence, on proving herself while fulfilling the role her father had provided, it was a major accomplishment to be the one man who could put a dent in her facade.

He relished the small private games between them, the subtle battle for the upper hand. He wanted the old Maggie back, yet was intrigued by her new persona.

Eric leaned forward, propping his elbows on his desk amid the scattered papers. He did his job as well as ever, and managed to contain his nearly uncontainable lust. There surely wasn't much more she could ask of him. "What is it you think we need to talk about, Maggie?"

Her indrawn breath lifted her delicate breasts beneath the wool jacket. When he'd first met her several years ago, he'd thought her a bit lacking in that department. Then she'd shown up one hot summer day, braless in a college T-shirt, and the air-conditioning had caused her nipples to draw into stiff little points—which had caused various parts of him to stiffen—and since then he'd been mesmerized by her delicacy. He wanted to hold her in his hands, smooth her nipples with his thumbs, then his tongue, tease them with his teeth . . .

Her jaw firmed and she pushed herself away from the door, catching her hands together at the small of her back and pacing to the front of his desk in a grand confrontation. "I want to talk about your attitude and lack of participation since I've stepped into my father's position."

Eric eyed her rigid stance. She was such a sweet, inexperienced woman that she'd at first misinterpreted his lust for jealousy. She'd assumed, and he supposed with good reason, that he resented her instant leap into the role of president of Carmichael Athletic Supplies. Most men would have. Eric had worked long and hard for Drake Carmichael, and under his guidance, the close personal business had grown. It was still a friendly company with a family atmosphere and very loyal employees, but the presiding stock Maggie inherited had doubled in worth from the year before—thanks to Eric. Because of that, Eric wasn't the only one who had assumed he was next in line for the presidency.

But in truth, Eric didn't give a damn about his position

on the corporate ladder, except that he didn't like the idea of having Maggie for his boss. It put an awkward slant to the things he'd wanted with her, throwing the dynamics of a relationship all out of whack. Maggie wasn't a woman you messed around with; she was the marrying kind. Only now, if he pursued her for his wife, some might assume he was still going after the company in the only way left to him. That not only nettled his pride, it infuriated his sense of possessiveness toward her. He wouldn't let anyone shortchange her worth.

So he'd assured her immediately that he had no desire to be president, no desire to usurp her new command. She'd looked equally stunned by his declaration, and bemused.

Still, he had hoped Maggie might tire of being the boss. She had always seemed like a free spirit to him, a woman meant to pursue her interests in the arts and her joy of traveling. She was a very creative person, fanciful, a daydreamer who had only learned the business to please her father, or so he'd assumed. Eric thought she'd merely been going through the motions when she worked first in the stock room, then briefly on the sales floor, before eventually making her, way all the way to the top—at her father's request.

But he had to give her credit; she knew what she was doing. Like, all new people, she needed a helping hand now and then in order to familiarize herself with how operations had already been handled, but she was daring enough to try new things and had enough common sense not to rock too many boats at one time. The employees all respected her, and the people they dealt with accepted her command.

He'd do nothing to upset that balance, because contrary to his predictions, she hadn't gotten frazzled and bored with corporate business. She'd dug in with incredible determination and now, within six months of taking over, Maggie had a firm grasp of all aspects of the company.

Eric, in the meantime, suffered the hellish agonies of unrequited lust and growing tenderness.

Shoving his chair back, Eric came to his feet and circled his desk to stand in front of Maggie. This close, he could inhale her scent and feel the nearly electric charge of their combined chemistry. Surely she felt it, too—which probably explained why she'd begun visiting his office more often. Eric got the distinct feeling that Maggie *liked* his predicament.

Tilting his head, he asked, "Why don't you drop the president aura and just talk to me like you used to, Maggie?" Six months ago, when her father had first passed away, Maggie had clung to him while she'd grieved. Eric had settled her in his lap, held her tight, and let her cry until his shirt was soaked. The emotions he'd felt in that moment had nearly brought him to his knees.

Nothing had been right between them since.

Eric crossed his arms over his chest and watched a faint blush color her cheeks.

He loved how Maggie blushed, the soft rose color that tinted her skin and the heat that glowed in her eyes. She blushed over everything—a good joke, a hard laugh, a sly smile. He could only imagine how she'd blush in the throes of a mind-blowing climax, her body damp with sweat from their exertions. . . . *Down, boy.*

"How long," Eric asked, trying to distract himself, "have I known you, honey?"

A small teasing smile flitted across her mouth. "I was seventeen when Daddy hired you."

"So let's see . . . that's five years? Too damn long for you to traipse in here and act so impersonal, wouldn't you say?" If he could only get things back on a strictly friendly basis, maybe, just maybe, he could deal with the powerful physical attraction between them.

"Yes." She sighed, letting out a long breath and clasping her hands together in front of her. "I'm sorry, Eric. It's just . . . well, since taking over, so many people have been watching me, waiting for me to fall on my face. I feel like I'm under constant scrutiny."

"And you think I'm one of those people?"

She met his gaze, then admitted slowly, "I don't know. Despite what you've said, I know you thought—*everyone* thought—that you'd be the president, not me." There was an emotion in her face that seemed almost . . . hopeful. No, that couldn't be.

"I already explained about that, Maggie."

"I know." She gave a long, dramatic sigh. "But you've been so . . . I don't know, *distant,* since I took over."

And she'd been so damn beguiling.

Eric had done his damnedest to come to terms with a radical chink in his plans. He wanted her. Looking at her now with her hair pulled sleekly to one side by a gold clip, her clothes too sophisticated for her spirit, her heels bringing her five-foot-eight-inch height up enough to make her within kissing level to his six-foot-even length . . .

God, but he wanted her. She had her back to the desk and he could have gladly cleared it in an instant, then lowered her gently and parted her long sleek thighs. The thought of exploring her soft female flesh, of coaxing her to a wet readiness, made him shake. He knew without the slightest doubt how well they'd fit together.

He cleared his throat as he thrust his hands into his pockets and tried to inconspicuously adjust his trousers. "It's the holiday season, hon," he said with a nonchalance he didn't feel. "Lots to do, not only at work, but at home, too. You know that. If you need anything—"

She waved that away. "You've been very helpful here, Eric. I never could have made the transition so smoothly if you hadn't been giving me so much assistance."

That made him frown. "Nonsense. The transition was smooth because you worked hard to make it so. Don't shortchange yourself, Maggie. Drake would have been damn proud if he could see how you've filled his shoes without a hitch."

A short laugh escaped her, even as she began to relax. She stared out the window to the left of his desk. A gentle swirl of snowflakes softened the darkening day. "Daddy's wishes," she said quietly, while sneaking a somewhat shy peek at him, "might not have been as clear as you think."

Eric frowned at those cryptic words, sensing she meant to tell him something, but having no idea what it might be. "You want to explain that, Maggie?"

"No." She shook her head, determination replacing the vulnerability he'd witnessed. "Never mind."

"Maggie . . ." he said, making it sound like a warning.

She sighed again. "There've been plenty of hitches, Eric. Believe me."

A feeling of menace invaded Eric's muscles, making him tense. "Has someone been giving you a hard time?" He stepped closer, willing her to meet his gaze. He'd specifically warned everyone that if they valued their jobs, they'd better work with her, not against her, or he'd personally see them out the door.

"No!" She reached out and touched his biceps in a re-assuring gesture. Her touch was at first impersonal, and then gently caressing. God, did she know she was playing with fire?

She drew a shuddering breath. "No, Eric, it's nothing like that. We have the very best employees around."

Eric barely heard her; his rational mind stopped functioning the moment her small hand landed on his arm. She was warm and soft and her scent—that of sweet innocence and spicy sexuality—drifted in to him. He inhaled sharply, and she dropped her hand, tipping her head to study him.

"The problem," she said, now watching him curiously, "is that I've been ultra-popular since taking over."

A new feeling of unease threatened to choke him. "What the hell does that mean?" He propped his hands on his hips and glared. "Have the guys here been hitting on you?"

"Yes, of course they have." Her simplistic reply felt like the kick of a mule, and then she continued, oblivious to his growing rage. "Not just the guys here, but the men we deal with, men from neighboring businesses, men from—"

"I get the picture!" Eric paced away, then back again. It was bad enough that the female employees had, for some insane reason, decided he was fair game and had been coming on to him in force. But the males were hitting on Maggie, too? Forget the holiday spirit of generosity—he wanted to break some heads!

"You realize," he growled, deciding she could do with a dose of reality, "that it's not your sexy legs and big brown eyes they're after?"

She blinked at him and that intriguing blush warmed her skin. "You think I have sexy legs?"

Eric drew back. Damn, he hadn't meant to say that. Just as he didn't mean to glance down at her legs, and then not be able to look away. Her legs were long and slender and shapely and they went on forever. He'd seen her in jeans, in shorts, in miniskirts. He'd studied those long legs and visualized them around his hips clasping him tight, or better yet, over his shoulders as he clasped her bottom and entered her so deeply. . . .

"Eric?"

He shook his head and croaked, "You have great legs, sweetheart, really. But the point is—"

"And my eyes?"

She watched him, those big dark eyes consuming him, begging for the words. "You have bedroom eyes," he whispered, forgetting his resolve to keep her at a distance. "Big and soft. Inviting."

"Oh."

His voice dropped despite his intentions. "A man could forget himself looking into your eyes."

Her face glowed and she primped. "I had no idea."

Eric locked his jaw against the temptation to show her just how lost he already was. "The point," he said in a near growl, "is that many of the men hitting on you are probably only after the damn company."

"I'm not an idiot. I know that already."

"They think if they . . . What do you mean, you know?"

"That's what I was talking about," she said with a reasonableness Eric had a hard time grasping. "I've been in or around this business for ages—as I already said, since I was seventeen. Most of the men ignored me. I mean, I realize I'm kind of gangly and people saw me as a little too flighty. No," she said when he started to argue with her, appalled by her skewed perceptions of herself. "I'm not fishing for more compliments. I'm a realist, Eric. I know who and what I am. But the point is that men who have always ignored me or only been distantly polite suddenly want to take me to the Bahamas for a private weekend winter getaway, or—"

"*What?*"

"—or they want to give me expensive gifts or—"

"Who the hell asked you to the Bahamas?"

"It doesn't matter, it's just—"

"It most certainly does matter!" Eric felt tense from his toes to his ears. He was forcibly keeping away from her, refusing to involve her in an affair, and equally opposed to making her the object of speculation and office gossip. He'd be damned before he let some other bozo—especially one with dishonorable intentions—cozy up to her. "Who was it, Maggie?"

She touched him again, this time on his chest. "Eric." Like a sigh, she breathed his name, and once again her eyes were huge. "I appreciate your umbrage on my behalf, really I do. But I don't need you to play my white knight."

His tongue stuck to the roof of his mouth. Ridiculous for a thirty-two-year-old man to go mute just because of a simple touch. And on his chest, for God's sake. Not any-place important. Not where he'd really love for her to touch him.

But he'd wanted her for five long years, and then been denied her just when he'd thought his waiting was about over. He mentally shook himself out of his stupor and framed her face in his hands. Her skin was so warm, so smooth, his heartbeat threatened to break his ribs. "If anyone—and I do mean anyone—insults you in any way, Maggie, I want you to promise to tell me."

Her eyes darkened, and she stared at his mouth. "Okay."

"Your father was one of my best friends." *Good,* he thought, *a tack that makes sense, a reason for my unreasonable reaction.* "Drake would have expected me to help take care of you, to watch out for you."

Just like that, the heat left her eyes. She gave him a withering half smile, patted his left hand, and then pulled it away from her face. Stepping back, she put some space between them and propped her hip on the edge of his desk.

She once again wore her damn professional mien that never failed to set his teeth on edge.

"I appreciate the sentiment, Eric, but I'm a big girl. I know that even though you don't want the company, others do, and they're not above trying to marry me for it. But I can take care of myself."

Goddamn it, *he* wanted to take care of her. But he couldn't very well say so without running the risk of sounding like all the others. If only he hadn't been so noble, if only he'd told her from the beginning how much he wanted her. But she had been so young. . . .

Eric nodded his head, feeling incredibly grim. "Just keep it in mind."

Her smile was a bit distracted. "It's almost time to call it a day, so I'd better get to the point of my visit, huh?"

"All right." Eric watched her as she stood and began edging toward the door.

"The annual Christmas party. I heard from Margo that you don't plan to attend?"

Margo had a big mouth; he'd have to talk to her about that. "I haven't decided yet," he lied, because he had no intention of forcing himself into her company any more than he had to.

"Margo said you turned her down."

Eric rubbed the back of his neck. "Yeah, I didn't . . ."

"I understood that you'd turned everyone down. Margo, Janine, Sally . . ."

"I know who I've spoken with, Maggie. You don't need to remind me." Hell, half the female employees had asked him to the party. He wondered how Maggie knew that, though.

She stared him in the eye. "You, uh, aren't dating anyone right now, are you?"

Eric frowned at her, wondering what she was getting

at. It wasn't like her to get involved in his personal life. "No, I'm not dating anyone right now." Despite the female employees' efforts, there was no one he wanted except Maggie, so he'd been suffering a self-assigned celibacy that was about to make him crazed.

"Excellent." She lifted her chin with a facade of bravado and announced boldly, "Then you can go with me. I . . . I need you, Eric."

Two

Maggie watched as Eric gave her his most intimidating frown. Good Lord, the man was gorgeous. Her father had accused her of an infatuation, calling her obsession with his right-hand man *puppy love*. Granted, at seventeen, it could have been nothing else. But she was twenty-two now, and there was nothing immature or flighty about her feelings for Eric Bragg.

She was getting downright desperate to get his attention, and her New Year's resolution, made a bit early out of necessity, was to seduce him. It would be a Christmas present to herself. At least an office fling would give her something, if not what she really wanted. And perhaps, with any luck, once she'd made love to him, he'd begin to see her as a woman, rather than the boss's daughter.

Eric looked dazed. His broad shoulders were tensed and his legs were braced apart as if he had to struggle for his balance. Hazel eyes narrowed, he rasped, "Come again?"

Being cowardly, Maggie inched a tiny bit closer to the door and escape, should Eric's response prove too humiliating to bear. Admittedly, she lacked experience. But she felt certain that he'd been giving her mixed signals. Sometimes he patted her head like she was still seventeen, and then every so often he'd throw her for a loop, like his comment on her legs, accompanied by a certain hot look in his eyes. . . .

"I need you," she blurted again. It was easier saying it the second time, but not much. "I want to attend the party. As the boss, I'm pretty much obligated to go. But so many of the male employees and associates have asked me, and I wasn't sure how to refuse them without causing a personal rift—so I lied and said I already had a date. You."

"Me?"

Nodding, she added, "It's just for pretend. I mean, you won't be expected to spend any money on me or dote on me or anything. But I might as well come clean and tell you that everyone also assumes you're helping me organize the Christmas party."

"Maggie . . ."

He sounded choked and she didn't know if it was anger or not. If he was mad, she'd have to scrap the second step of this evening's plan. That is, if her lack of courage didn't cause her to scrap it anyway. She reached behind her and felt for the doorknob. "Don't worry about it. I've got everything under control, so you don't have to really do much for the party. Except make others think you're helping me." Which she hoped would force them into some isolated time together. She bit her lip with the thought. "I'll give you a . . ."—she had to clear her throat—"Christmas bonus for helping out."

"I don't want a goddamned Christmas bonus from you," he growled, and started toward her with a dark frown.

Maggie felt her mouth drop open when he stopped a mere inch in front of her. Her entire body was zinging with awareness, the way it always did whenever Eric was close. His hazel eyes were intent and probing and they made her feel like he could see right into her soul.

She'd often wondered if he looked at a woman like that while making love to her.

She swallowed audibly with the visual images filling her brain.

"You're mad?" She wanted it clarified before she went any further.

"With your assumption that you need to reward me for helping. You're damn right."

"Oh." Well, that was good, wasn't it? Definitely. "Okay, so you *will* help?"

He gave an aggrieved sigh. "Yes."

So far, so good. "Will you also accompany me to the party?"

Flattening one hand on the door, Eric leaned toward her. Despite his dark frown, there was something else in his eyes, something expectant. He looked at her mouth, and his jaw clenched. "Yes."

She licked her lips, saw his eyes narrow, and shivered. "The thing is," she said, sounding a bit breathless, "I have to give you a bonus. I'm giving everyone a bonus, so if I don't, the employees might begin to talk."

He stilled, then leaned away from her again, shoving his hands deep into his pants pockets. He scowled. "That would bother you? If they talked, I mean?"

She didn't want anyone to say anything negative about Eric! Her possessiveness over him had amused her father, but he'd promised never to say a thing to Eric, and as far as she knew, he hadn't.

What her father had done instead was worse, because

it had backfired in a big way. "I just think we should avoid gossip whenever possible."

Looking resigned, Eric nodded. "What do you want me to do for the party? Hell, I don't even know what goes into planning a party. I've never done it before."

Maggie tried a nervous smile. "As I said, most of it is taken care of. But I had those offers from the guys . . . so I said you were helping. That's okay?"

He gave a sharp nod, distracted by some inner thought.

"The hall and caterers are taken care of. And I've already started to . . . well, decorate the offices a little."

Some of the rigidness left Eric's shoulders. She loved his body, how hard it was, how tall and strong. He did nothing to emphasize his muscular bulk, but his leisurely attempts at style managed it anyway. He always rolled his shirtsleeves up to his elbows, displaying his thick wrists and solid forearms. Even the look of his watch on his wrist, surrounded by dark crisp hair, seemed incredibly sensual and masculine. And his open shirt collar, which showed even more hair on his chest, made her feel too warm in too many places. She imagined he was somewhat hairy all over, but she wanted to know for sure. She wanted to touch him everywhere.

His walk was long and easy, his strength something he took for granted. His corduroy slacks appeared soft and were sometimes worn shiny in the most delectable places—like across his fly.

She forced herself to quit staring and met his gaze. "Why are you smiling?"

"Because I like seeing you enthused about something again."

Her eyes nearly crossed in her embarrassment. He knew how enthusiastic she was about his body?

Eric chuckled at her startled expression. "I remember

how excited you used to get over Christmas." He reached out and touched her gold barrette with one long, rough finger. "What happened to those cute little bells you used to wear, Maggie?"

Cute? She'd assumed that she was far too immature for Eric, what with her silly holiday dressing. So she'd tried to look more sophisticated, more mature, in order to get his attention. But every day it had seemed like additional distance had come between them.

Her father had thought the lure of the company would be enough to get Eric to notice her. The letter he'd included to her in his will had stated as much. He was giving her a chance at the man she wanted, and she loved him so much for his well-meaning efforts. But instead of having the desired result, Eric wanted less to do with her than ever.

He'd said he didn't want the presidency. Evidently he didn't want her, either. Yet. But she was working on it.

Maggie pulled the door open and prayed he wouldn't notice the mistletoe until it was too late. "I'm not eighteen anymore, Eric. And I'm the boss. I can't be caught dashing up and down the hallways, jingling with bells and disturbing everyone."

He stepped into the doorframe with her. "You never disturbed me, hon." His eyes darkened and his mouth tilted in a crooked, thoroughly endearing smile. "At least, not the way you think."

Maggie had no idea what he meant by that, and besides, she needed all her concentration to screw up her daring. She drew a deep breath, smiled, and then said, "Oh, look. We're under the mistletoe."

Eric faltered for just a heartbeat, but she moved too quickly for him. Grabbing his neck with both hands, she pulled him down as she went on tiptoe. She heard his indrawn breath, felt the heat of his big body, and then her mouth was smashed over his and lights exploded behind her eyelids.

She moaned.

Eric held very still. "Uh, Maggie?" he whispered against her lips.

"Hmmm?" No way was she letting him go yet. This was very, very nice.

She felt the touch of his right hand in her hair, then his left was at her waist and he said in a low, rough rumble, "If we're going to do this, baby, let's do it right."

Maggie's eyes opened in surprise, but slowly sank shut again as Eric drew her so close that their bodies blended together from hips to shoulders. Her breasts, feeling remarkably sensitive, flattened against the hard wall of his chest. Her pelvis cradled his, and she became aware of his erection, which literally stole her breath away.

He wanted her? He liked kissing her?

His large hand opened on the small of her back and urged her closer still, until she felt his every pulsing heartbeat in the most erotic way possible. With a subtle shifting of his head, his mouth settled more comfortably against hers and he took control of the kiss. And wow, what a kiss it was!

He left her mouth for a brief moment to nuzzle beneath her ear. "Relax, Maggie."

What a ludicrous suggestion! She felt strung so tight, her body throbbed. "Okay."

She gave him all her weight and sighed as every pleasurable sensation intensified. His open mouth left a damp trail from her throat to her chin to her lips. She shivered. His tongue slid over her lips, teasing, and then into her mouth. *Oh, God.* She tried to stay calm, but it was so incredible, so delicious, that her breath came faster and her nipples tingled into hard tips and a sweet ache expanded low in her belly.

Eric growled low, a primitive response that thrilled her. His tongue, damp and hot, stroked deeply into her, over her own tongue, tasting her, exploring her.

Her hands knotted in his shirt, she arched into him, and then—she heard the tiny twitter of a feminine laugh.

Stunned when Eric suddenly pulled away, Maggie would have stumbled if he hadn't kept her upright with one strong arm wrapped around her waist. He glared over his shoulder, and there stood his secretary and two male employees.

Mortified heat exploded beneath Maggie's skin, making her dizzy. Everyone stood in heavy silence.

She was the boss, Maggie told herself, she had to take control of this small turn in events. Clearing her throat even as she stepped out of Eric's reach, Maggie said, "Well. I thought everyone had gone home already." She raised a brow, silently asking for an explanation.

"We were just about to leave," his secretary, Janine, informed them.

Eric dropped back to lean against the doorframe and crossed his arms over his chest. He seemed either oblivious or unconcerned with the fact that he had a very noticeable erection. Despite the impropriety, it thrilled Maggie, because at least that meant he was interested.

Of course, she had been rubbing up against him rather thoroughly, and that could account for the physical reaction. Mere friction?

Maggie stepped in front of him, shielding him with her body, and pointed up. "Mistletoe," she explained to her audience.

The secretary smiled like a damned cat and glided forward, her intent plain. "So I see. How . . . fortunate."

Not about to let anyone else touch Eric now that she'd gotten him revved up, Maggie stationed herself in front of him like a sentinel. When the secretary merely looked at her, Maggie made a shooing motion with her hands. "Go on home, Janine. I'm not approving any overtime today. Go on."

Janine barely bit back a smile. "But . . ."

Eric, sounding on the verge of laughter, said, "I think it's just the mistletoe she's after, Maggie, not more pay."

Maggie sent him a quelling glance over her shoulder, before addressing the woman again. "There's more down the hall," Maggie assured her, trying to shoo her on her way. "I put some in all the doorways. You two," she added, pointing to the men, both of whom had been pursuing her earlier, "go with her. Find some mistletoe. Go."

The men, displaying a sense of discretion, hid their amusement and escorted the willing secretary out. Maggie glared at them until they were completely gone from sight, mumbling under her breath about pushy women.

"You want to explain that?" Eric asked.

"Hmmm?" Maggie turned to face him. "Explain what?"

"Why you turned into a ferocious amazon just because Janine wanted to kiss me. I mean, kissing is the purpose of mistletoe, right? And you're the one who hung it in my doorway."

"Well." Of course kissing was the point, but she wanted to be the only one taking advantage of it with Eric.

Maggie couldn't quite look at him as she tried to figure out how to get things back on track. Which meant getting his mouth back on hers, his hands touching her again. "I put you in that awkward situation by kissing you," she muttered, thinking it out as she went along, "so I didn't want you to feel . . . obligated . . . to kiss anyone else. I was . . . protecting you."

"So you don't personally care if Janine kisses me? I

mean, if the mistletoe stays there, I assume she'll take care of it in the morning."

It was hard to speak with her teeth clenched. "No," she ground out, nearly choking on the lie. "If you want to kiss Janine, that's certainly your business."

His eyes narrowed. "I see." In the next instant he surprised her by plucking the mistletoe down and shoving it into his pants pocket.

Maggie gave a silent prayer of relief. But when she peeked up at him, she felt doubly foolish for the confusion and annoyance on his face.

"I don't want to kiss Janine," he explained.

"Good." *Get it moving, Maggie.* "I mean, then since that's settled, perhaps . . ."

"Maggie?" When she pretended a great need to straighten her jacket, Eric reached out and tilted up her chin. "Why did you kiss me, sweetheart?"

She gulped. He wanted explanations? Good grief, she hadn't expected that. She'd planned on carrying things through should he prove agreeable, or slinking away if he rebuffed her. But not once had she considered an interrogation, for crying out loud.

Men, in her limited experience, were either interested or not, but they never wanted to talk about it!

"I . . . ah, I was trying to get you into the Christmas spirit."

Eric released her and frowned thoughtfully. "You're embarrassed?" She denied that with a shake of her head, so he pointed out, "Your face is red."

She was horny. Turned on. Aroused. All hot and bothered. "I'm not embarrassed."

He quirked one brow.

"It was just a simple kiss, after all." And at twenty-two,

she'd had as many kisses as any other woman her age. *But none like that. None with Eric.* Oh, it was different, all right, just as different as she'd always known it would be. "We've both been kissed plenty, right? No big deal."

His frown turned fierce, and she figured she'd managed to tick him off after all. "All right, then." She clasped her hands together and gave him a beatific smile. "Since you agreed to help me with the Christmas party, I guess we're all settled."

She started away, bent only on retreat before she blew it completely, but Eric's voice stopped her. "When do we start, Maggie?"

She hesitated. "Uh . . . how about tomorrow? At my place? That is, if you don't already have a date for the weekend. . . ."

"I'll be there at two o'clock."

Two? In the afternoon? She'd really been hoping for something toward the evening, when she'd be able to light some candles, put a fire in the fireplace, set the mood for seduction. . . .

She realized Eric was waiting, staring at her in speculation, and she smiled as if she had not a care in the world. If he got suspicious, if he guessed at everything she wanted to do to him, he might not come at all. "Two is just fine. I'll see you then."

Eric managed to wait all of five minutes before curiosity got the better of him and he made his way to Maggie's office. If he'd read her right—and he was fairly certain he had—she wanted him. Not as much as he wanted her: that was impossible. But while he'd made a resolution not to seduce her, he hadn't figured on her trying to seduce him!

Despite everything he'd told himself about how disastrous a relationship would be, he knew damn good and well he wouldn't be able to resist her now that she'd shown some interest. She was lucky he'd let her walk away at all, much less promised to wait until two the next day. If he'd been thinking clearly, he'd have pulled her back into his office, locked the door, and made use of the desk as he'd envisioned earlier.

He told himself it didn't matter that all they could have was an affair. Maggie had already made it clear what she thought about someone chasing her for the company. If he tried to take things beyond an affair, she'd forever wonder what he'd really wanted. And then, too, there'd be the jokes about him trying to screw his way to the top. The idea was intolerable. Especially since she didn't want any gossip. Marrying the boss, which was what he really wanted to do, would certainly stir up the speculation.

Damn, he didn't have many choices.

When Eric opened her office door, he knew right away that she was already gone. All the lights were out and, as usual, her desk was neatly cleared of all the day's work. Maggie was tidy to a fault.

Then he noticed a paper on the floor.

Evidently she'd been as rattled as he after that killer kiss. Perhaps she'd left in a hurry, anxious to get home to the same cold shower he now anticipated. Although actually, looking out the window toward the frozen winter landscape, he realized that just getting to his car was liable to cool down his lust.

Knowing he was condemned to a lonely night of erotic frustration made Eric want to howl. Unlike Maggie, he wasn't in a hurry to head home, where the solitude would cause him to dwell on all the sensual things he wanted to do to Maggie Carmichael, and all the explicit things he wanted her to do to him.

But the cleaning crew, who came by every Friday evening, would be arriving soon. He had no choice but to be on his way. He stepped forward to retrieve the piece of paper in case it was anything important, meaning to simply place it on her desk.

One typed word, about midway through the text, seemed to leap right out at him. *Thrust*. He leaned against the edge of her desk and read the sentence: *She was hot and wet and his fingers thrust into her easily, eliciting a cry from deep in her throat.* Eric nearly dropped the paper.

He locked his knees as his pulse quickened and his body reacted to that one simple sentence. Quickly, his gaze flicked up to the header on the paper and he read: *Magdelain Yvonne, Heated Storm, pg. 81.* Magdelain Yvonne? That was Maggie! Magdelain Yvonne Carmichael.

Maggie had written this?

Numb, moving by rote, Eric pulled out her desk chair and sank into it, his eyes still glued to the paper in his hand. A small lighted ceramic Christmas tree, situated at the corner of her desk, provided all the illumination he needed. He started at the top of the page and began reading.

It was by far the most sensual, erotic, explicit passage he'd ever read outside of porn. But porn was unemotional and there was nothing unemotional in the deeply provocative love scene his Maggie had written.

When the paper ended—right in the middle of the female protagonist experiencing a gut-wrenching orgasm thanks to the guy's patience and talented fingers—Eric nearly groaned. His own hand clenched into a fist as he considered touching Maggie in just that way, watching her face while he made her come, feeling her body tighten around his fingers, feeling her wetness, her heat, and hearing her hoarse cry.

Where the hell was the rest of it?

Frantically he looked at her desk, moving papers aside and lifting files, but it was all business-related things. He opened a drawer and peeked inside, feeling like a total bounder but unable to stop himself. The drawer had only more files and notations in it. So he tried the others. Finally, in the drawer at the bottom of her desk, hidden beneath a thick thesaurus, he found the rest of the manuscript.

With no hesitation at all he slipped page 81 into place and settled back in the chair to read from the beginning. He was still there when the cleaning crew arrived. He'd just reached the end—which wasn't the end at all. Maggie needed several more chapters to finish the story, but already Eric could tell that she was very talented. He'd gotten so absorbed in the story he'd almost forgotten it was written by Maggie, and simply began enjoying it.

When he had remembered it was written by Maggie, he'd been hit with such a wave of lust he broke out in a sweat.

He'd never read a romance. He'd had no idea they were so good, so full of fast-paced plot and great characterization. Just like his mystery novels, only with more emphasis on the emotional side of the relationship. And lots more sex. *Great sex*. He liked it.

The only problem, to his mind, was the physical descriptions of the characters. The blond female was voluptuous, with large breasts and generously rounded hips and a brazenness that Eric had to admit was sexy as sin. She in no way resembled Maggie.

So why the hell did the male character so closely resemble him?

Maggie had given him the same height, same eyes, same dark hair. Even some of the things the guy said were words right out of Eric's mouth. And his wardrobe . . . well, he had the exact same clothes hanging in his closet at home.

The only major difference was that the guy in the story

had finally gotten the heroine naked and in the sack for some really hot action. Hell, not only that, but he'd come three times thanks to the heroine's enthusiasm, something Eric wasn't even sure was possible.

Yet Eric was going home each night to an empty bed.

Well beyond the crazed stage, Eric was highly affronted, and jealous, that his fictitious character could take what he'd denied himself.

Was this, perhaps, what Maggie really wanted?

His heart pounded with both excitement and resentment. Ha! He was on to her now. It made his insides clench to realize she wasn't nearly as inexperienced as he'd always let himself believe. No way could she have devised such graphic sex scenes out of the depth of imagination.

In hindsight, he admitted Maggie was too sexy, too vivacious, to have stayed inexperienced for long. His nobility in attempting to wait had come back and bitten him in the ass. But that was over with now. She wanted him, had made love to him in fiction, and no more would he play the gallant schmuck, giving her plenty of time and space.

If Maggie wanted to write about sexual satisfaction, he'd show her sexual satisfaction! She'd started this tonight with her damned mistletoe and her teasing and her invitations.

His little Maggie was in for a hell of a surprise.

Despite Eric's heated plans, it bothered him immensely to put the book back in her drawer, where anyone might be able to find it. He'd have to talk to her about that—after he showed her that no fictitious character had anything on him when it came to reality.

He buried the manuscript under books and papers, just as she'd had it, then piled in a few more things, trying to be extra cautious. He was aware of a fine tension in his muscles, a touch of aroused excitement.

Eric glanced at his watch, saw that it was seven o'clock, and by the time he could reach Maggie's, it'd likely be eight. But that wasn't so late, and now he had a damn good reason to call on her tonight. He felt for the mistletoe he'd put in his pocket, and grinned when his fingers closed around it.

Maggie was a writer. A very talented, very erotic writer. And she wanted him; he had no more doubts about that. If he couldn't have Maggie for a wife, at least he could have this, and if all went as planned, she'd be his, not in matrimony, but in a basic, physical way that was even more binding.

For the first time in six months, things seemed to be getting back on track.

Three

Maggie hurried out of the shower when she heard the doorbell peal. The pizza she'd ordered must have arrived early, so she trotted out of the room even as she pulled on her oldest, thickest robe. Her wet hair was wrapped in a towel, turban-style, and her bare feet left damp indentations in the plush carpet.

On the way to the door she made certain her cloth belt was securely tied and grabbed money for a tip. She ordered so many pizzas that the owner of the small restaurant let her run a tab, which she paid at the end of each month.

She wrenched the door open just as the doorbell chimed again. "Sorry, you got here quicker than . . . I . . . thought. . . ."

Eric stood there, snowflakes clinging to his midnight hair, his cheeks ruddy from the cold, his gaze blazing with some emotion that she couldn't begin to decipher. At the sight of her, his eyes narrowed and did a slow study of her from head to toe. She felt it like a tactile stroke, flesh on flesh. Ignoring her mute surprise, he stepped in, which forced her to step back. Holding her gaze, he pushed the door shut.

Maggie shivered. A cold blast of winter air had preceded Eric, but that wasn't what caused the gooseflesh to rise on her damp skin. No, Eric brought with him the scent of the brisk outdoors, his delicious cologne, and his own unique smell, guaranteed to make her melt. She never failed to react to it with a delicate shudder and a hungry tingling inside.

He looked so good, and here she stood looking her worst! Her makeup was gone, her hair in a towel, and her robe was so ratty it would had been generous to describe it as broken-in.

"You expecting someone?"

There was a growled undertone to his words that Maggie didn't understand. She pressed her hands to her warm cheeks even as she began to explain. "I thought you were the pizza guy."

The frown disappeared. With a small predatory smile, Eric looked her over once again, and there was so much heat, so much satisfaction in his gaze, she suddenly felt too warm for the thick robe. "Do you always greet deliverymen dressed like this?"

"No." She pulled the lapels of her robe together at her throat, a five-dollar bill clenched in her fist. "I thought he was early. Usually I have plenty of time to shower and change. I could have just let him leave the pizza outside the door, but I wanted to tip him. It is almost Christmas, and the weather isn't the best. . . ."

Eric reached out and slowly plucked the money from her hand. In the process his knuckles grazed lightly over the top of her breast, across her chest and throat. "Sweetheart, if you answer the door that way, you won't need any further tip, believe me."

Mouth hanging open, she blinked at him, dazed by what she assumed—*hoped*—was a compliment. Eric gazed briefly at her mouth before abruptly turning away. Maggie watched as he laid the money on the entry table and then looked around her home with frank interest. She cleared her throat. "I . . . I didn't expect you tonight."

"I know." He said the words gently, and with some great, hidden meaning. "I changed my mind about waiting until tomorrow. Am I interrupting any plans?"

None that she would mind having interrupted. She'd hoped to work on her book for a few hours, which was why she'd ordered the fast food. Whenever she typed, she ate. The two just seemed to go hand in hand, which, because she was always pressed for time since taking over for her father, was a blessing. Heaven knew she rarely had time for a sit-down meal. "I was just going to get some . . . work done."

"Ah." He gave her a wicked, suggestive grin. "Maybe I can help?"

She got warm with just the thought. Eric help her with her writing? She didn't think so. For now, she was still a closet writer, not telling any of her non-writing friends. As the president of the company, she couldn't imagine how her business associates might react to the fact she wrote very racy romance novels. She wasn't ashamed of what she did, but she simply didn't need the added hassle of speculation. At various conventions, she'd heard all the jeers and jokes about how a romance writer researched. For her, research on the love scenes was simply daydreaming about Eric. There were parts of him in every hero she created; there had to be, for her to consider the men heroes.

Until she resolved the issue of her new position in the

company, she wouldn't breathe a word about her need to create characters and romances.

"It's nothing that can't wait." Belatedly, she realized they were still standing just inside the door. She blushed again. "Come on in."

His hand lifted to trail along a looping pine garland, fastened in place around her doorframe with bright red and silver bows. He seemed intrigued by her Christmas decorations, examining the dancing Santa on the table where he'd placed her five-dollar tip, before gazing across the room to her collections of candles displayed on the fireplace mantel and the corner of the counter that separated her kitchen from her living space.

Every tabletop held some sort of Christmas paraphernalia, old and new. Eric was right that she loved the holidays and rejoiced in celebrating them.

Her small, freshly cut tree, heavily laden with ornaments and tinsel and lights, blinked brightly at the opposite side of the room. It fit perfectly in the small nook just in front of her desk and work space.

Eric nodded in satisfaction. "This is more like you."

She raised a brow, questioning.

"The holiday spirit," he explained, but his voice trailed off as his gaze lit on her laptop computer and the piles of paper littering her scarred antique oak desk.

Good grief, she'd all but forgotten about her newest chapters sitting out! From this distance, there was no way Eric could tell what it was, but that didn't reassure her overly. Trying to look nonchalant, Maggie crossed the room and closed her laptop quickly, then stacked the papers and shoved them in a drawer.

Eric watched her so closely, she flinched. "Bringing work home?" he asked.

As he spoke, he pulled off his shearling jacket and hung

it on her coat tree beside her wool cape. And just that, the sight of the two garments hanging side by side, made her wistful. It would be so nice if he hung his coat there every night.

"Uh, nothing important." She preferred working on the computer at her office during her lunch breaks, since the monitor was much bigger and easier to see than the laptop. But she also worked at home whenever she could. Finishing up a book on deadline while working a fifty-hour-a-week job was grueling. Once she finished this book, she planned to buy a new computer for her home. But the idea of getting things set up and functioning at this particular moment, with the rush of the holidays, the pressure of a deadline, and her escalating sexual frustration, was more than she could bear. The past six months had been adjustment enough. She didn't need the aggravation of breaking in a new computer.

Eric started toward her with a slow, deliberate stride.

She cleared her throat, gave one last glance at her desk to make sure nothing obvious was still out, then said, "Why don't I get us something to drink?"

She hoped to escape to the kitchen, thinking to divert Eric from his path. Though everything was now put away, she'd feel better if he kept plenty of distance between himself and the desk.

Before she could take two steps, Eric stopped her with a large hand on her elbow. Her living room was small and cozy, but how he'd moved across it so quickly, she couldn't imagine.

"Your place is nice. I haven't seen it before."

Until her father's death, she'd lived in their family home with him. Eric had been to that house many times. But since then, he'd been avoiding her for the most part, despite her efforts to get closer to him.

"After Daddy died," she whispered, "I couldn't quite take living in the house. It seemed too big, too cold, and I missed him too much. So I moved here." Her home was now a moderately sized condominium that suited her perfectly. She had her own small yard, complete with patio and privacy fence, a fireplace, and a balcony off her bedroom.

The space where her desk and various office equipment sat had been intended as a breakfast nook, but she'd commandeered the space for her office.

Her bedroom, a spare room, and the bath were all upstairs. Eric was looking at the heavy desk and she said quickly, "I kept Daddy's desk from home, and some of his furniture."

Maggie watched as Eric made note of the two straight-backed armchairs flanking the fireplace. They were antique also, repadded with a soft velvety material that complemented the subtle striping in her own overstuffed beige, rose, and burgundy sofa. Marble-topped tables that had been in her family for over fifty years were situated at either end of the sofa and each held an array of framed photos and Christmas bric-a-brac. On the matching coffee table was a large glass dish filled with candies, and two more fat candles. Over the warmly glowing parquet floor was a large thick area rug that had once decorated her father's library.

Nodding, his hand still cupped securely around her arm, Eric said, "You and your father were very close, weren't you?"

The warmth of his hand made casual conversation difficult. "I think more so than most daughters and fathers, because my mother had passed away when I was so young." She shrugged, but the sadness never failed to touch her when she thought of her father. "It was always just Dad and me, and he was the best father in the world."

Eric tugged her closer and stood looking down into her face. Memories flitted through her mind, the way he'd held her on his lap and let her cry the day her father had passed away. Eric had been the only other person she'd wanted to grieve with. When she'd come to him, he hadn't questioned her, hadn't hesitated. He'd held her, and she'd been comforted.

Eric lifted his free hand and smoothed her cheek. The touch was intimate and exciting. "I'm sorry you've caught me looking so wretched," she blurted.

He smiled and his hand slipped around her neck, his rough fingertips teasing her skin even as he bent his head. "You look adorable."

Maggie barely absorbed the absurd compliment before the feel of his mouth on hers scattered her wits. But this kiss was gentle and fleeting, his warm mouth there and then gone, leaving her lips tingling, her breath catching. Making her want so much more. She leaned toward him, hoping he'd take the hint—and her doorbell rang.

"You go get dried off," he whispered as he teased the corner of her mouth with his thumb, "and I'll get the pizza."

Flustered, she stepped back and retightened her belt. "It'll just take me a few minutes to change and get my hair combed out."

Eric straightened her chenille lapels, letting the backs of his hands glide over her upper chest, then lower. His knuckles barely fell short of actually coming into contact with her nipples. She gasped, waiting, in an agony of anticipation.

He met her encouraging gaze and ordered in a low voice, "No, don't change. I like this. It's sexy."

"It is?" She looked down at the faded peach robe,

threadbare in some spots where the chenille had fallen out from too many washings. Bemusement shook her out of her stupor. "*This* is sexy?"

"Are you naked beneath it?"

She gulped. "Yes."

His hazel eyes glowed with heat. "Damn right it's sexy."

She turned on her heel and stumbled out of the room. Eric appeared to be here for a reason, and her heart was racing so fast she could barely breathe. "I'll be right back," she called over her shoulder.

"Take your time," he answered on his way to her front door, but within five minutes she had her hair combed out and nearly dry, a touch of subtle makeup on, and her best perfume dabbed into the most secret places.

Eric didn't stand a chance.

Eric had set the pizza in the kitchen and was studying Maggie's colorful tree when he felt her presence behind him. He turned slowly and was met with the sight of her bright, expectant gaze. She watched him so closely, he felt singed. Anticipation rode him hard.

Maggie might enjoy writing hot love scenes, but he intended to see that she enjoyed experiencing them even more.

The idea of getting Maggie Carmichael hot made blood surge to his groin, swelling his sex painfully and making his heart race. He wanted everything from her, but he'd take what he could get.

"Come here," he whispered.

Lips parted, her pulse visibly racing, Maggie padded toward him on bare feet. She moved slowly, as if uncertain of his intent. Good. She had teased him at work, tempting him with that killer kiss beneath the mistletoe and then darting away. Did she sense her teasing had come to an end?

When she got close enough, Eric casually looped his arms around her waist. His hands rested on the very top of her sweetly rounded behind. Though his fingers twitched with the need to cuddle her bottom, to see if it was as soft and resilient as he'd always imagined, he didn't give in to the urge. That would be too easy, for both of them.

Nuzzling her cheek, he asked, "Do you know why I'm here, sweetheart?"

Her small palms opened on his chest and she nodded. "I think so."

He lightly bit her neck, making her gasp, then laved the small spot with his tongue. Fresh from her bath, her skin tasted warm and soft and was scented by something other, than Maggie herself. That disappointed him. Why did women always try to conceal their own delicious smell with artificial scents?

"You're wearing perfume," he noted out loud.

"I . . . yes."

"Where all did you put it, Maggie?"

Maggie's breath deepened, came faster. She shook her head, as if she didn't understand.

"When I'm this close to you," he said softly, "I want to smell *you*."

Eric let his hand glide up her waist to the outer curves of her breast. "When I kiss you here," he said, holding her gaze as his thumb brushed inward, just touching the edge of a tightly beaded nipple, "I don't want to be distracted with the smell of perfume. Do you understand?"

Her whole body trembled with her repressed excitement. "Yes."

"And," he added, trailing his fingers slowly downward,

watching her, judging her response, "when I kiss you . . . here—"

"Oh, God." Her eyes drifted shut and she shivered.

"I want to know your scent." His fingers brushed, so very gently, between her thighs. Her lips parted, her head tilted back. The robe was thick enough that his touch would only be teasing, but still she jerked.

Eric took the offering of her throat and drew her tender flesh against his teeth, deliberately giving her a hickey. He wanted to mark her as his own—all over. She moaned and snuggled closer to him.

"Damn, you taste good." He waited a heartbeat, letting that sink in, then added in a whisper, "I can't wait to taste you everywhere." His fingers were still between her thighs, cupping her mound, and he pressed warmly against her to let her know exactly what he meant.

Her hands curled into fists, knotting in his shirt. He waited for her to get a visual image of that, already planning his next move while he had her off balance.

Her eyes opened, hotly intent. "I'd like to taste you, too," she answered, and Eric barely bit back his groan.

"Damn." If she got him visualizing things like her mouth on him, he'd never last! He gave a half laugh at her daring, which earned him a startled expression. Maggie never failed to amaze him. "I want this to last, you little tease. Don't push me."

She didn't deny the teasing part, and simply asked, "This?"

"Mmmm." He slipped his hand under her collar and rubbed her nape, feeling the cool slide of her damp, heavy hair over the back of his hand. "I want you so much I'm about to go crazy with it."

"Eric." She breathed his name, attempting to wiggle closer to him.

He held her off. "No, not yet. I need you to want me as much, Maggie."

With her hands clenched in his shirt, she attempted to shake him. He didn't budge, and her brown eyes grew huge and uncertain. "But I do!"

"Shhh." He pressed his thumb over her lips, silencing her. "Not yet. But you will. Soon."

Wind whistled outside the French doors behind her desk, blowing powdery snowflakes against the glass. The twinkle lights on her tree gave a magical glow to the room. Eric stepped away from her, amazed at how difficult it was to do. "You need to eat your pizza before it gets cold."

Maggie's breathing was audible in the otherwise silent room. With a quick glance, Eric saw that her hands were folded over her middle, as if to hold in the sweet ache of desire, and her nipples were thrusting points against the softness of her robe. His testicles tightened, his cock throbbing at this evidence of her arousal, but he refused to make this so easy. He'd been suffering for a hell of a long time, wanting her, yet not wanting to make her unhappy. Now he knew that she was as physically attracted as he. But if that was all they could have, he wanted it to be the best it could be. And that meant being patient.

"Forget the pizza," she said. "I'm . . . I'm not hungry anymore."

Eric noted her stiff posture, the color in her cheeks. "Is that right?"

She lifted her chin in that familiar way that made his heart swell. "I'm hungry for *you*. So stop teasing me."

Against his will, Eric felt his mouth curling in a pleased smile. Maggie liked giving orders, further evidence that she fit the role of "boss" to perfection. He nodded slowly, keeping his gaze locked to her own, and said, "All right, sweetheart."

She accepted his hand when he reached out to her, her slender chilled fingers nestling into his warm palm. Eric turned them toward the sitting area and led Maggie to a single straight-backed chair. The Christmas tree with its soft glow was behind her, lending the only illumination other than the faint light from the kitchen.

Maggie looked at the chair, then at the very soft, long couch, but he could tell she wasn't brazen enough to insist they sit side by side, which he'd been counting on. If they settled together on the couch, she'd end up beneath him in no time and all his seduction would be over before it had really started.

That wouldn't do.

With a soft grumble, more to herself, though he heard her plain enough, Maggie slid into the chair and then fussed with her robe, making certain it folded modestly over her legs. A futile effort on her part, but for the moment he let it go.

Hiding his grin, Eric walked behind Maggie. She stiffened, alert to his every move. Eric touched her hair.

"Do you have any idea how much I loved your hair long?"

Tipping her head back, she looked at him upside down. "No."

Eric smoothed his hands over her throat, and when her lips parted, he leaned down and kissed her lightly. "I used to imagine your hair all spread out on the pillow, *my* pillow."

"But . . ." She started to twist around to face him more surely, and he held her shoulders to still her movements.

"I used to think about the fact that your hair was long enough and thick enough to hide your breasts. You could have stood topless in front of me, and I wouldn't have been able to see a thing. But now"—he slid his hands over her

shoulders and cupped her small firm breasts completely—
"there's no way you can hide from me. Can you, sweetheart?"

Her back flattened hard against the chair and she held
herself rigid, not in fear or rejection, but in surprise. The
erratic drumming of her heart teased his palm. God, she
felt good. Soft, round. Moving lazily, he chafed her nipples with his open hands until she gripped the arms of the
chair in a death hold and her every breath sounded like a
stifled moan.

Impatient, Eric loosened the top of her robe and parted
it enough to see her pale breasts and her taut pink nipples.
He caught his breath.

Just that quickly she jerked away and turned to face
him, yanking her robe closed in the process. There was so
much vulnerability in her face, he felt his heart softening
even as his erection pushed painfully against his slacks.

Her bottom lip quivered and she stilled it by holding it
in her teeth. Both hands secured her robe, layering it over
her throat so that not a single patch of her soft flesh showed.

Eric slowly circled the chair, never releasing her from
his gaze. When he was directly in front of her, her face, as
well as her fascinated and wary gaze, on a level with his
lap, he laid one large hand on top of her head. Her hair was
cool in contrast to the heat he saw in her cheeks. "What
is it, babe?"

She squeezed her eyes closed.

"Maggie?" Using one finger, he tipped up her chin. Was
he moving too fast, despite her bravado of wanting him to
get on with it? He frowned slightly with the thought. "I am
going to look at you, you know."

She winced. "It's just that . . . I'm actually sort of . . .
small."

Ah. Biting back his smile, Eric knelt in front of her and covered her hands with his own. Carefully wresting them away from their secure hold on fabric and modesty, he said, "You're actually sort of perfect."

She trembled, but met his gaze. "You like big-breasted women."

He remembered the woman in her story, with her full-blown, overripe figure. Was this why she'd put that particular female with his fictional counterpart? He ran this thumb over her knuckles, soothing her, then loosely clasped the lapels of her robe. "What makes you think so?"

She held herself in uncertain anxiety. Did she expect him to rip the robe away despite her wishes? Never would he deliberately push her or make her uneasy. He cared far too much about her for that. No, his plans were for sensual suspense, not embarrassment.

A small sound of frustration, or maybe more like resignation, escaped her. "*All* men like big breasts."

Perched on the edge of her seat, she looked ready to take flight regardless of the fact that Eric was on his knees in front of her, blocking her in. To prevent her from trying to do just that, he leaned forward until her legs parted and he was able to settle himself between them. Her eyes widened and her hands automatically clasped his shoulders for balance.

He released her robe to wrap his long fingers around her hips, then snugged her that small distance closer until their bodies met, heat on heat. He pushed his hips against her.

In a low growl that was beyond his control, Eric asked, "I've had a hard-on since I walked in the door. Does that feel like disinterest to you?"

Mute, she shook her head while staring into his eyes.

He cupped her breasts again, still outside the robe, and closed his eyes at the exquisite feel of her. "Beautiful. And sexy."

"But . . ."

"I want to see your pretty little breasts, Maggie. I want to see all of you. Will you trust me?"

She stared at his mouth. "Will you kiss me again first?"

He liked it that she wanted his mouth.

Leaning forward, he said, "I'll kiss you everywhere. In time." Her lips parted on a deep sigh as their breaths mingled and he took her mouth. So soft, he thought, amazed that a kiss could feel so incredible, taste so good. He devoured her with that kiss and relished her accelerated breathing. His tongue sank inside and was stroked by hers, hot and damp and greedy. It went on and on and when she relaxed completely, when her open thighs gave up their resistance and she slowly sank back in the chair, half reclining with her legs opened around his hips in a carnal sprawl, he lifted his head.

Watching her, caught by the sight of her velvety dark gaze and swollen mouth, he touched her lapels again. She swallowed, but didn't stop him when he slowly parted the material. As his gaze dipped to look at her, his heartbeat punched heavily inside his chest.

He couldn't imagine a woman more perfectly made. Her rib cage was narrow, her skin silky and pale. Her soft little breasts shimmered with her panting, nervous breaths. Pale pink, tightly pinched nipples begged for his mouth as surely as she had. "Oh, Maggie."

Her hands fell from his arms and flattened on the seat beside her hips, as if she needed to steady herself.

She inhaled sharply, then held her breath as he moved forward to nuzzle against her. Her body, softened only moments before, quickly flexed with tightened muscles and churning need. Teasing, he circled one nipple with tiny kisses, driving himself insane as he resisted the urge to draw her into the damp heat of his mouth, to suck her hard, to sate himself on her.

"Eric . . ."

"Shhh." He flicked her with the very tip of his tongue. "We've got all night."

"I won't last all night."

He chuckled soothingly and switched to the other breast. Deliberately taking her by surprise, he closed his teeth around her tender flesh and carefully tugged. Her whole body jerked; her hands clasped his head, trying to urge him closer.

From one second to the next, his patience evaporated. Wrapping one forearm around her hips, he anchored her as close as he could get her, pelvis to pelvis, heat to heat, then suckled her into his mouth.

Her groan, long and intense and accompanied by the clench of her body, nearly pushed him over the edge. He drew on her, his head muzzy with the reality of what he was doing, of who he was with. The mere fantasy couldn't begin to compare.

Openmouthed, he kissed his way to her other nipple, greedy for her. She guided him, squirming and shifting, and sighed when he latched onto her breast again as if she needed it, needed him, with the same intensity he felt.

"Do you see," he muttered around her damp nipple, "just how perfect you are?"

She hitched one leg around his hips and hugged him closer. Instinctively, she moved against his rigid erection, seeking what he wouldn't yet give.

Eric slowly pulled away from her, determined on his course.

"Eric . . ." She started to sit up, reaching for him while her legs tightened.

Pushing the robe down to her elbows, trapping her arms; his position between her thighs, combined with her movements, had parted the material over her legs, which now left her virtually naked. The robe framed her body, with the silly belt still tied around her middle. Her belly was adorable, and he kissed it even as he remonstrated with her for her small lie.

"You're not naked, sweetheart." He touched the waistband of her white cotton bikini panties. "Not that I'm complaining, because this is very cute."

"Don't . . . don't make fun of me, Eric."

He managed a grin in spite of the hot throbbing of his body. "Why would I make fun of you? Because of your conservative underwear? I like it."

"Like you like small breasts?"

His gaze met hers. In the pose of a confirmed hedonist, she lounged back, face flushed, body open to the pleasure he'd give her. Her dark hair was mussed, her eyes soft, her lips swollen. He absorbed her near nudity, her innate sexuality, and said gently, "Like I like you."

Her eyes closed briefly, then opened when he dipped one rough fingertip beneath the waistband of her panties and teased her stomach, low enough to just brush her glossy dark curls, high enough to keep her on a keen edge of need.

Her breath came in hungry pants. "Are you going to make love to me, Eric?"

"Absolutely."

"When?"

Situated as he was between her thighs, he could smell her desire, the rich musk of arousal. His nostrils flared. It was a heady scent, mixing with the perfume she'd put on, making his cock surge in his pants, his muscles quiver. "When I think you're ready."

"I'm ready now."

"Let's see." Slowly, he lifted each of her legs and draped them over the arms of the chair. The position left her wide open in an erotic, carnal posture. Eric trailed his rough fingertips up the insides of her thighs, seeing her suck in her stomach, hearing her gasp. Her breasts heaved in excitement and anticipation.

She looked so damn enticing he couldn't resist her. Without warning, he kissed her through the soft damp cotton, his mouth open, his tongue pressing hard. He breathed deeply and felt himself filled with her. He could taste her—and quickly grabbed her hips to hold her steady when she would have lurched away from sheer reaction.

She said his name in a breathless plea.

Her response thrilled him, drove him. He wanted to pull her panties aside so his tongue could stroke her slick naked flesh, heated by her desire, silky wet in preparation for much more than his tongue.

He gave her his finger instead.

Leaning back to watch her, he wedged his large hand inside her panties, stroked her once, twice, then pressed deep. The instant, almost spastic thrust of her hips, her coarse groan, the spontaneous clasp of hidden muscles, told him she liked that very much.

"Jesus, you're tight," he ground out through clenched teeth, struggling to maintain control. "And wet."

"Eric . . ."

He stared at her through burning eyes. "Am I hurting you, babe?"

She groaned, whispered something unintelligible, and her sleek, hot flesh squeezed his finger almost painfully.

"That's it," he encouraged softly, feeling himself near

the edge. "Hold on to me." He stroked, slowly pulling his finger out, then thrusting it back in, deep, teasing acutely sensitive tissues, mesmerized by the sight of his darker hand caught between her white panties and pale belly, her glossy black curls damp with excitement.

Eyes closed, body arched, she gave herself up to him as he fingered her, stretching her a bit, playing with her a lot. He pressed his finger deeper, measuring her, then pulled out slowly to tease her taut clitoris, making her entire body shudder.

He wanted all of her at once; he wanted her to feel all the same desperate need he felt. And maybe, just maybe, if he did this well enough, if he made her feel half of what he felt . . . what? She'd give up the presidency of her father's company just to marry him?

Eric hated himself for letting the selfish thought intrude for even one split second. He didn't want her to give up anything. He didn't want her to be forced into choices.

He loved her. *Goddamn it.*

To banish those thoughts, he pulled his hand away and stripped her panties down her thighs. She blinked at him, grabbing the chair arms for balance as he readjusted her and then once again settled himself close. Those long luscious legs of hers looked especially sinful lying open, leaving her totally vulnerable to him, displaying her pink feminine flesh, swollen and slick. Her hips lifted, seeking his touch again. He had to taste her, and leaned forward for one leisurely, deep stroke of his tongue.

Maggie cried out, her entire body jerking in response. Eric was lost.

With a harsh groan he covered her with his body, kissing her mouth deeply, consuming her, taking what he could because he couldn't have it all. Her small body cradled his larger frame perfectly. "I want you so fucking much," he rasped.

"Yes!"

He cupped her breast with a roughness he couldn't control and rocked his hips hard against her, feeling her pulsing heat through his slacks. She was silky soft, warm and female everywhere, and he wanted to absorb every inch of her. With one hand he lifted her soft bottom, grinding himself against her.

"Eric!"

Stunned, he looked at her face and watched her climax, her teeth clenched, her throat arched, her breasts flushed. His heart seemed to slow to a near stop as love consumed him, choking out all other emotions.

She whimpered as he continued to move her against him, more slowly now, carefully dragging out her pleasure, his fingers sinking deep in her soft bottom, letting her ride it out to the last small spasm until finally she stilled and her muscles relaxed.

Limp, eyelashes damp on her flushed cheeks, her lips still parted, she was even more than he'd ever imagined. Eric gathered her close and rocked her gently, attempting to regain control of his own emotions—which were far beyond sexual.

As if each limb were made of lead, Maggie struggled to resettle her legs, locking them around his hips. So slowly he couldn't anticipate what she wanted, she got her arms around his neck, one hand tangled in his hair. Finally her sated, dazed eyes opened.

"Sorry," she muttered in such an endearingly drowsy and somewhat shy voice, he couldn't help but smile with a swell of satisfaction and tenderness.

His hand still held her small backside and he gave her

a gentle, cuddling squeeze. "For what, sweet-heart?" His tone was soft in deference to the moment.

She studied his face, her own pink, then managed a halfhearted shrug. "Okay. I'm not sorry." She yawned. "Now will you please make love to me?"

How humor could get him while he was so rock hard he could have driven in railroad spikes, he didn't know. But the chuckle bubbled up and he tucked his face into her breasts as he gave in to it.

"Are you laughing at me?"

She didn't sound particularly concerned over that possibility, which made the humor expand.

"Eric?"

Her hand tightened in his hair, causing him to wince. He lifted up, kissed the end of the nose, and grinned. "I'm just happy."

"Why?"

Tenderly, he smoothed a tendril of dark hair behind her ear. "Well, now, I just made Maggie Carmichael come. Why else?"

She snorted, but her face was so hot she looked sunburned. Her hand loosened its grip, her fingers threading through his hair, petting him. "I've wanted you so long, it wouldn't have taken much. Except you kept playing around. . . ."

"Look who's talking."

She raised a brow, but the effect was ruined by another yawn.

"Never mind, sleepyhead. Have I put you out for the night?"

"Absolutely not." She shifted subtly, then whispered, "I'm just dying to feel you inside me, Eric."

"Jesus." He didn't feel like laughing now. Though his legs were shaky, he managed to loosen her hold and stand.

He didn't want to make love to her in a damn chair. He wanted her in bed, under him, accepting him.

He reached a hand out to her and when she took it, he hauled her up—and then over his shoulder.

"Eric!"

Flipping the robe out of his way, he pressed his cheek to her hip and kissed her rounded behind. "The bedrooms are upstairs?"

She had both hands latched on to his belt in back, hanging on for dear life. "Yes, but don't you dare. . . . Eric, put me down!"

Instead, he stroked the backs of her thighs with his free hand as he started up the steps. Using just his fingertips, he teased her with light butterfly touches, getting her ready again, keeping her ready.

"Eric . . . *Eric*." She groaned as he explored her.

Four

"I'm done playing, Eric. Make love to me."

As if he hadn't heard her, Eric strolled into the bedroom and slowly brought her around in his arms. His strength amazed her, not that she was a heavyweight, but considering how boneless she felt right now . . . Of course, he hadn't climaxed.

And she wanted to remedy that as soon as possible.

The second her feet touched the floor, she reached for his belt. Thankfully, he didn't stop her. Instead he began emptying his pants pockets, putting his wallet, a condom, and the sprig of mistletoe he'd removed earlier from the office doorway, onto her nightstand. Seeing the condom and the mistletoe so close together, Maggie shivered.

As she hurriedly worked on his clothes, Eric calmly unknotted the fabric belt still caught around her waist. He finished first and tossed her robe aside. His hands, so incredibly large and warm, settled on her waist, holding her loosely, allowing her to slide his leather belt free and then waiting patiently while she unbuttoned and unzipped his slacks.

"Your hands are shaking," he noted.

She peeked up at him. "I'm excited. I've wanted you . . . well, longer than you can imagine."

"Try me."

To distract him from her words, she abandoned his slacks and quickly began unbuttoning his shirt. The promise of his nudity gave her incentive and her fingers literally flew until his shirt was hanging open.

With a type of reverent awe, she bared his chest. Fingers spread, she ran her hands over his upper torso, absorbing the feel of crisp dark hair, solid muscle, and manly warmth. "I've wanted you since the first time I saw you."

The breathless words took him by surprise, then skepticism narrowed his eyes. "You were barely seventeen, sweetheart. A child."

"Mmmm. And so creative." With the edge of her thumb, Maggie brushed his right nipple and heard his intake of breath. His knees locked. "I got so tongue-tied around you," she whispered, "because at night, alone in my bed, I imagined this very thing. Touching you, having you touch me."

She looked up, saw his flared nostrils, the dark aroused color high on his cheekbones, and she went on tiptoe to kiss his chin, now rough with beard stubble.

Eric caught her wrists as she began a downward descent to his slacks. "You're saying you fantasized about me?"

"From the very beginning." She pulled her hands free and sank to her knees in front of him. She felt like a sexual supplicant, kneeling before him, naked, hot. His erection was a thick ridge plainly visible through his slacks. She leaned forward and pressed her cheek to him, nuzzling.

"There's nothing I haven't done to you in my imagination."

"Maggie." One large hand cupped around her head, trembling.

"Lift your foot." He obliged and she tugged off first one shoe and sock, then started on the other. Her face close to his groin, deliberately tantalizing herself—and probably him, given how heavy his breathing had become—she knotted her hands in his slacks and pulled them down.

Eric didn't move as she reached for his snug cotton boxers. More slowly now, savoring the moment, she bared him.

Her breath caught. She'd never seen a fully grown man naked, up close, personal. She'd seen photos, which didn't do the male form justice.

Tentatively, she touched him with just her fingertips and then smiled as he jerked, his erect flesh pulsing, hot. A drop of fluid appeared on the broad head, and she used the tip of one finger to spread it around, testing the texture, exploring him.

Breath hissed out from between his teeth. "That's enough."

Maggie paid him no mind. In her novels, the men always pleasured the women with their mouths; the very idea of it excited her incredibly. But now she wondered why the reverse had never occurred to her. The idea of taking Eric into her mouth, licking him, tasting him, flooded her with heat and doubled her own desire.

"Tell me if I do this wrong," she whispered. And even as he cautioned her to stop, his voice a low, harsh growl, she wrapped one small hand around him to hold him steady. Amazingly, she could feel the beat of his heart in her palm, could feel him growing even more. Her tongue flattened on the underside of his hot, smooth flesh, slowly stroked up and over the tip—and Eric shattered.

She'd barely realized the taste of him, the velvety texture, before he went wild, shaking and gasping. He roughly pulled her to her feet and she found herself tossed on the bed. Before she'd finished bouncing, Eric had kicked his pants off and donned a rubber.

She opened her arms to him and he came down on top of her. Using his knee, he spread her legs wide, then wider still. "I wanted this to be slow," he said through his teeth, reaching down to open her with his fingers, "but I can't wait now."

She started to say she was glad, that she didn't want to wait, but then he thrust hard, entering her, filling her up, and she lost her breath in a rush.

It wasn't at all as she'd imagined, smooth and easy and romantic. Instead, Eric anchored a hand in her hair and held her face still for an all-consuming, wet kiss that made it impossible to breathe, impossible to think. He stroked into her fast and hard. *Deep.* And though she was aware of her own wetness, her own carnal need, the tight friction was incredible.

Her senses rioted over a mix of heated perceptions. There was discomfort, because she was small and inexperienced, but also building pleasure, too acute to bear, because this was Eric and she'd wanted him forever.

Not romantic, but so wonderful, so real and erotic and . . .

Her climax hit suddenly, making her clutch at him, her fingers digging deep into his shoulders, her heels pressing hard into the small of his back. Eric lifted his head, jaw locked tight, eyes squeezed shut, and gave a raw groan as he came.

Through the haze of her own completion, Maggie watched him. She loved him so much, and she wanted him, in every way, always. Seeing his every muscle taut and trembling, his temples damp with sweat, left her feeling curiously tender, softened by the love and the depletion of physical strength.

Eric slowly, very slowly, lowered himself back into her arms. His heart beat so hard against her breast, she felt it inside herself. Threading her fingers through his warm, silky hair, she said, "Eric?"

He gave a small grunt that she supposed might have been a response.

"Will you stay the night with me? Please?" If he refused, if he left now and this was all she'd ever have, her heart would simply crumble, leaving her empty.

But he didn't refuse her. Instead, his arms tightened and he rolled to his side, bringing her with him. Long seconds led into longer minutes before his breathing ultimately evened out. Idly, he stroked her, her shoulder, her hip, her back. "I'm not going anywhere," he finally said in a rough whisper.

She snuggled closer, letting out the breath she'd been holding.

Eric kissed her forehead and, with a sigh, moved to leave the bed. Enjoying the sight of his naked backside, Maggie watched him go into the bathroom, heard running water, the flush of the toilet, and then he came back. The condom was gone and Eric, in full frontal nudity, his sex now softly nestled in dark hair, was more appealing than she'd ever imagined a man could be. Amazingly, she wanted him again. She licked her lips.

Eric smiled at her as he climbed back into bed. "You little wanton, you," he whispered, and she heard the amusement in his tone. Tucking her into his side and covering them both, he affected a serious tone. "Maggie, this was your first—"

"Yes." She felt a little embarrassed over her inexperience. "I didn't want anyone but you. Not ever."

He absorbed that statement with a heavy silence, then kissed her temple with a gentleness that brought tears to her eyes. "I want you to tell me about this long-hidden admiration you have for me."

Maggie knew her time had come. It took her several seconds to screw up her courage before she could force herself to look up and face Eric. When she did, his hand cupped her cheek, and there was a softness in his expression she'd never seen before.

She swallowed hard. "Not an admiration, Eric. Love."

He remained quiet, waiting.

"I've loved you," she declared, "since the first time I saw you. My father knew it, and that's why he left me the company. He believed you wanted it, and he had hoped . . . that is, he thought that perhaps the company would be a lure, to get you to notice me."

Eric stared at her as if someone had just hit him in the stomach. She felt him tense and prayed he'd at least hear her out.

Rushing, hoping to get it all said before she chickened out, she explained, "I don't want the company, Eric. I never have. I wish I'd known what my father was going to do, because I would have stopped him. Not only did it not lure you in, you've been distant since I got the damn controlling stock."

Eric sat up, his expression dumbfounded. Feeling suddenly naked, Maggie clutched the sheet to her throat and came up to her knees. "Eric, I swear we didn't mean to manipulate you. That is, I didn't even know until it was too late—"

"Shh." Eric put a finger to her lips, silencing her. He looked thoughtful, with a frown that wasn't quite annoyance, but rather confusion. "You don't want to run the company?"

Since his finger was still pressed to her mouth, she didn't try to reply. Instead, she shook her head.

Eric left the bed to pace. That was enough of a distraction to make her regret the damn topic. She wanted him back in bed with her. She wanted to do more exploring.

"Now that we're involved," he said, and he looked at her, daring her to challenge his statement, "there's going to be some gossip."

Maggie scrambled off the bed and stood before him, the sheet held in front of her. "I won't let anyone insult you, Eric, I swear!"

A grin flickered over Eric's firm mouth. "Ready to defend me, huh?" He touched her chin. "I can handle gossip, sweetheart. I just don't want it to hurt you."

Heart pounding, she said, "I can handle it—as long as you can."

"Then we're agreed." He cupped her face and kissed the end of her nose. "Now, about the company . . ."

"You don't have to worry that I'll make you responsible. I'm going to sell my shares. I don't want to be tied to the business so much. I have . . . other interests right now. And Daddy was only trying to make me happy—"

"You're not selling the shares."

Her brows lifted. "I'm not?"

"No. I'll run things for you." His expression was so intent, she squirmed. "If . . ." he said, emphasizing that one word beyond what was necessary, "if you'll marry me."

Maggie caught her breath. Slowly, to make certain she understood, she asked, "You're willing to take the extra shares off my hands—"

"No. The company will remain yours."

"But . . ."

"I won't have people saying you were part of a bargain, Maggie, that I married you for the company. I want it clear that I want you for *you,* not for the added benefits."

"Do you . . . see the company as a benefit?"

He shrugged. "I always assumed I would one day be in charge."

"But you don't want that." Maggie felt swamped in sudden confusion.

"Not true. It's just that I wanted you more." His voice dropped, became seductive. "Much, much more than any damn company."

"Oh."

Eric sat on the bed and pulled her into his lap—after he tossed the concealing sheet aside. Cupping her breast and watching intently as he thumbed her nipple into readiness, he said, "Just as you say you used to daydream about me, I sure as hell dreamed about you. I planned to make my intentions known after you graduated, except so many things happened then. You lost Drake and inherited a company. Everything got confused. You were missing your father, and I assumed, judging by your competence, that you enjoyed running the company. I thought if I came after you then, you'd never be certain what it was I wanted."

Maggie searched his face, almost afraid to believe. "But you wanted . . . me?"

"God, Maggie." Eric squeezed her tight, and his voice sounded raw with emotion. "I wanted you to the point I about went crazy." He kissed her, then kissed her again.

Big tears gathered in her eyes and she blinked hard to fight them off. "I was so afraid you'd never ever notice me. I tried everything. I thought if I was more sophisticated,

if I showed you I wasn't a kid anymore, you'd stop ignoring me."

Eric riffled a hand through her hair. "I love you, Maggie.
Exactly as you are, any way you want to be."

Maggie wanted things clarified about the company, but
Eric returned to her mouth, and his hand on her breast was
lightly teasing, and she felt him hardening against her
bottom. She decided further discussion could wait.

Eric rolled over and reached for her, but she wasn't there.
A heady contentment had him smiling even before he was
completely awake. *Maggie was now his.* Once his eyes
were fully open, he saw that it was still night. Where had
Maggie gone?

He left the bed, shivering as the cool night air washed
over his naked body. Before leaving her bedroom, he
pulled on his slacks, but didn't bother buttoning or zipping
them.

Creeping silently down the steps and into the living
room, he found Maggie at her desk, writing on her laptop
by the lights of the Christmas tree. Her beautiful silky
hair tumbled around her face, and she'd donned the same
soft robe, though sloppily, so that one shoulder was mostly
exposed. The twinkling lights of the tree reflected in her
big dark eyes, while the eerie glow of moon-washed snow
outside the French doors framed her in an opalescent halo.

She was absorbed in her writing, oblivious to her surroundings, and didn't notice him. Eric lounged against the
wall watching her. So precious. A grin tugged at his mouth
as he wondered exactly what scene she was working on
now.

The sprig of mistletoe that he'd brought from the office
lay on the desk beside her.

"Getting the facts down while they're still fresh in your mind?"

With a yelp, she jerked her head up to stare at him. "Eric! What are you doing down here?"

He strolled toward her, still smiling, filled with contentment and masculine satisfaction. "I was going to ask you the same thing."

She pushed her chair back and stood, then glanced at her laptop. Nervously, she began to tidy her desk. She picked up the mistletoe. "I was just . . . too excited to sleep. I figured I might as well get some stuff done."

"Mm-hmm." Eric closed in on her and she turned her back to the desk, her hands clasped at her waist. The mistletoe crushed against her belly. "Ah, now, there's an idea," he said.

Maggie blinked. "What?"

He traced her stomach with one finger, edging underneath her robe. "I read part of your book at the office."

Her mouth fell open, then snapped shut and she scowled.

"You're incredibly talented."

The scowl disappeared. "I am?"

He nodded. "I can't wait to read the rest of it." Eric met her eyes and asked, "Have you been using me for research?"

"Oh, for crying out loud," she blustered, "I don't—"

"Because I wouldn't mind. At all." He kissed her lips, her throat. Pressing his palm against her beneath the mistletoe, he said, "I kind of like the idea."

A tad breathless, she said, "If you read the book, then you know we haven't done all the things that the characters did."

"But I'd sure like to." His fingers searched her through the chenille. "And the guy in your book reminded me a lot of me."

"Yes." She closed her eyes and sighed. "I've sold three

books, Eric. This one will be my fourth. I've written about a doctor, a Navy SEAL, a car salesman, and now a businessman."

Eric froze. "So who were the other guys?"

He watched her lips twitch into a smile. "They're all you, at least in part." Her beautiful brown eyes opened and she stared up at him. "They may not all look like you, but the qualities they have that make them interesting, that make them heroes women want to read about—those I get from you. Those are the things that are most important."

Her words touched his heart. "I do love you, Maggie."

With a crooked smile, she said, "And you like the way I write?"

"I think you're incredible." Slowly, deliberately teasing her, he dropped to his knees. "Will you let me read the rest?"

It took her a breathless moment to say, "When . . . when I'm finished with it."

Eric parted the robe and pressed a kiss to her naked belly, just beneath the mistletoe now crushed in her hands. "And you'll let me run the company for you?"

She dropped the mistletoe. It landed beside Eric's knee. Bracing her hands on the edge of her desk at either side of her hips, she said, "Yes, thank you."

Eric grinned. He used his thumbs to gently part her so he could kiss her where she'd feel it most. "And will you," he asked against her hot flesh, "marry me, sweetheart?"

Her groan was long and loud and unselfconscious. *"Yes."*

"I've got to hand it to you, Maggie," he said, feeling her legs tense. "This is the best Christmas bonus I've ever gotten."

Epilogue

Eric stood beside Maggie at the Christmas party as she called for everyone's attention. He had no idea what she might do, but he intended to be beside her regardless.

She positively glowed, he thought, watching her dark eyes as she laughed and held up a hand—a hand that sported an engagement ring she'd picked out yesterday. Her hair was pulled back by a red and green headband and she had tiny Christmas bows as earrings. Over her left breast, a miniature Santa head with a blinking red nose drew his attention. He loved it that she'd quickly given up her frumpy suits, and that she was every bit as energetic and enthusiastic as he remembered.

She was especially enthusiastic in bed. Eric had to chase those thoughts away, or be damned with a hard-on for the entire staff to see. He cleared his throat and concentrated on what Maggie was saying.

"This year," she called out, "besides getting the Christmas bonus bucks and a ham, I'm giving everyone a share of company stock."

Eyebrows lifted in surprise and a buzz of hushed conversation filled the hall. Eric stared at Maggie, floored by her declaration.

"It's not much," she explained, "but I didn't want controlling shares, and Eric refused to take them off my hands. So now, he and I are equal partners in the company, and all of you have a stake in it as well. I know my father would have approved."

Heads turned; everyone now staring at Eric. He chuckled, amused at Maggie's way of settling any thoughts of gossip.

"And just for fun, I wanted you all to know"—she flashed the ring, her smile wide—"we're getting married!"

A roar of applause took Eric by surprise. No one seemed the least surprised by her declaration, or suspicious of his motives. Maggie snuggled up against his side and he automatically slipped his arm around her.

Someone, he thought it might have been his secretary Janine, called out, "It's about time," and everyone laughed as if they all agreed.

Maggie put her hands on her hips and pretended to scowl. "How come none of you are surprised?" she asked, laughing.

Janine, accepting the role of leader, stepped forward at the encouragement of her fellow employees. "We've been taking bets," she explained with a smile, "on when the engagement would take place. Everyone could see you were both in love."

"You asked me out," Eric accused her.

"We all did." Janine shrugged, unrepentant. "We thought it might get Maggie moving. And that's why the guys asked Maggie out—"

Eric narrowed his eyes. "Yeah, who did that?" He scanned the crowd, but the men all started whistling and shuffling their feet, trying in vain to hide their humor. Maggie lightly punched Eric in the arm while laughing out loud.

The sound of her laughter never failed to turn him on. He wanted to get the party over with so he could take her home. "We're officially engaged," Eric stated, holding Maggie close, "so you can all keep your distance from her now. Understood?"

The men bobbed their heads, still grinning, while the women smiled indulgently.

Janine made a fist and waved it in the air. "A Christmas engagement. I win!"

Eric shook his head, then tipped up Maggie's chin. "No, I win." He didn't need mistletoe to prompt him. Right there, in front of everyone, he kissed Maggie until her knees went weak—and no one had a single doubt that love had brought them together.

Naughty Under
the Mistletoe

Carly Phillips

To Mom and Dad
who made me believe I could do anything.
To Phil
who loves and supports me through everything. And
to Jackie and Jennifer
who make it all worthwhile.

One

Antonia Larson fastened the white fur anklet adorned by three silver bells and a green velvet bow, closing the accessory around her leg with a single snap. From the radio on the edge of her desk, a traditional Christmas carol ended and the Bruce Springsteen version of "Santa Claus Is Coming to Town" now reverberated through her small office. Pulling her hat over her head and securing it with bobby pins, she hummed her own off-key rendition of her favorite Christmas tune. She twirled once, pleased with the jingling accompaniment to the gruff voice of The Boss.

If Santa was coming to town, he wasn't going to find Toni being a good girl. Not this year. Not this night. Tonight she was a woman on a mission. A mission to seduce the man she'd been attracted to for too long. She planned to act on what was a physical attraction and indulge in a safe interlude she could easily walk awa from when their time together was through. Something Stephan, the firm's confirmed self-proclaimed bachelor, would appreciate and understand.

Because they'd been working closely as colleagues, acting on her desire had been impossible until now—but today had been her last day of work before the long holiday vacation. When she returned after the New Year, she'd be in the new suburban offices of Corbin and Sons. Work and office protocol no longer stood between them. Nothing did except her courage and the nice-girl role she'd played all her life. A role she could afford to let go of, at least this once.

After yet another night of tossing and turning for hours in her lonely double bed, she'd pulled out the December issue of the women's magazine she'd subscribed to on a whim. What other reason could there be since she had no time in her busy lawyer's life to read tips on how to attract men and what turned them on?

But as she'd read the steamy article on naughty versus nice, Toni realized she'd spent the better part of her life as a nice girl, following the rules to get ahead and working overtime to make a good impression. Her two thousand-plus billables over the last few years had put her in a prime position for a promotion. The ailing Mr. Corbin had been thrilled when he'd named her the senior associate to work with the as-of-yet unnamed partner who'd run the new office. She'd never have come this far without performing to perfection. Being naughty had had no place on the ladder to success. Neither had coming on to a man she worked alongside.

But having earned her position, she felt free to act on other, impulsive desires. Then with the onset of the new year, Toni would put Stephan behind her and step back into the stable, secure, independent life she'd created for herself.

If the article were to be trusted, the clichéd adage was

true and nice girls finished last. So Toni would just have to be bad. She smoothed her skirt and straightened her hat, giving one last jingle of her bells for good luck. In matters of the hormones and the heart Toni intended to come in first.

No matter how naughty she had to be to accomplish her goal, Toni intended to get her man.

They called this a party? Maxwell Corbin glanced at the dark suits milling about the large conference room. Muffled laughs, discreet corner discussions, and a handshake every now and then to clinch a deal. Not an ounce of fun in sight, he thought and immediately remembered why he'd traded in his SoHo apartment and his family's downtown New York City law firm for a place in the suburbs and his PI office on the Hudson River. An office he'd return to. No matter how happy it would make his father if Max decided to return to the fold, he had to live his own life, his own way. Three years at the family firm had taught him practicing law wasn't it.

As he made for the eggnog across the room, his sneakered foot crushed a stray pretzel, marring the otherwise pristine carpet. Beside him, someone made a toast to an upcoming merger, increased income, and the guaranteed all-nighters to come. Max shook his head in disgust. The only thing worth staying up all night for was sex—something he hadn't had in too damn long, mostly because no woman had interested him enough. But lately he'd begun to wonder what being discriminating and picky had gotten him besides a cold bed at night.

He lifted the ladle to pour himself a drink when the faint ringing of bells caught his attention. He turned toward the sound and the expensively decorated Christmas tree, a pine, lavishly trimmed with white and gold, with dozens of boxes beneath the branches to increase holiday spirit. He stepped to the left so he could see around the tree and caught sight of a dainty elf kneeling over a bulging bag of toys. As she reached inside the large bag, the hem on her miniskirt hiked up higher, revealing black lace beneath white fur trim.

Max swallowed hard. So much for disinterest, he thought wryly. A longer glance as she dug through her huge bag and he discovered the lace ended at mid-thigh. He wondered what she wore beneath that green suit, if the hands-on exploration would be as satisfying as his imagination.

He tried to swallow but his mouth had gone dry. If he had to spend time in the hallowed halls of Corbin and Sons— make that Corbin and Compliant Son, he thought, thinking of his twin—then maybe the pixie in the corner would make his time here worthwhile. He dodged his way around the business suits and headed for the tinsel-laden elf.

On his way, he realized that not only, was she the sole focus of his attention, but he was the center of hers. She'd straightened from her chore and looked at him dead-on, heat and something more in her smoky gaze. Drink forgotten, he walked the rest of the way to where she stood. Despite the drone of preoccupied, chattering attorneys, Max felt as if he were approaching her in silken silence.

As he closed in, he raised his gaze from the white fur anklet to her belted, trim waist to her green-eyed stare. Sea-green scrutiny made more vibrant by the interested flush in her cheeks. After promising his father he'd show up at this gig, he'd mentally called the day a bust, but when she pulled him behind the tree, rose onto her booted tiptoes, and touched her mouth to his, he reassessed his opinion.

He'd been kissed before—but he'd never *been* kissed. Not with such intensity and single-minded purpose. She tasted sweet and smelled sensual and fragrant, making both his mind and his body come alive. Her hands gripped his shoulders in a death-lock as her champagne-flavored tongue darted past his willing lips.

She had a potent effect, yet despite it all her touch was endearingly hesitant, turning him on while arousing a fierce protectiveness within him at the same time. He gripped her waist to anchor himself, something she obviously took as a sign of acceptance, because a soft but satisfied sigh escaped and he caught the erotic sound with his mouth, deep in his throat. Though he hadn't a clue what he'd done to become the lucky recipient of her attention, he wasn't about to question good fortune. He'd rather make more of his own.

He began an arousing exploration, mating his tongue with hers in a prelude she couldn't misinterpret or mistake. And obviously she didn't. Her head tipped backward and she welcomed the onslaught of his roving tongue and hands. His fingers locked onto her petite waist and he pulled her forward, her breasts flush with his chest, her hips brushing his.

Such close contact with his elf had him aching for more and he sucked in a startled breath, inhaling deeply. The scent of pine assaulted his senses and reminded him of their surroundings and the possibility that despite the barrier of the Christmas tree, they might have an audience of attorneys taking copious notes. With regret he raised his head and took a safe step back from temptation. Emerald eyes glazed with desire stared back, an engaging smile on her well-kissed lips.

"Mistletoe," she said in a husky voice, pointing upward.

He glanced at the bare ceiling. So she had passion as

well as a desperate need for an excuse. A grin tipped the edges of his mouth as he wondered what other surprises this mystery lady had in store. "Whatever you say."

She touched her lips with shaking fingertips. "I say you're not *him*. You're nothing like Stephan."

Kind of her to point out something he'd been told hundreds of times before. But she'd spoken low, more to herself than to him, and not with the well-aimed need to hurt, the way the information had been used against him in the past.

Her gaze darted from his worn basketball sneakers, up the length of his dark denim jeans, and focused on his face. "In the dim lighting and from a distance you kind of looked like him." He saw as well as heard her searching for answers. "The same dark hair and piercing blue eyes, though yours are somewhat warmer." A glimmer of passion infused her voice. "Similar dimple but yours is deeper." She reached out with the same hesitant determination he'd sensed behind the kiss.

Her touch burned him straight to his soul.

"And when he works weekends, he . . . dresses . . . like . . . you." She jerked her hand away from the same fire consuming him.

Max was surprised to learn Stephan ever veered away from conservative suits and ties. Maybe he and his twin had come from the same egg after all. Maybe they had more in common than either of them let on. And maybe they *could* be friends as well as brothers. The thought arose, not for the first time in ages, but it was the first time he considered acting on the impulse.

He had his elf to thank for revealing the surprising similarities and possibilities. *His* elf. Funny how proprietary he'd become in such a short span of time. But it wouldn't be funny if she had any kind of relationship with his twin, and based on that hell of a kiss, the odds tipped against Max.

"Since it's not the weekend, I should have known," she murmured. Scrutiny complete, she settled her stare on his New York Rangers jersey, an obvious attempt to avoid his gaze. Then she folded her arms across her lush chest, chewing on her bottom lip as the enormity of her mistake obviously set in.

He remembered the feel of those curves pressed intimately against him, recalled the sweetness of her mouth, and he struggled not to groan aloud. "Something against the Rangers?" he asked, seeking the more mundane.

She shook her head, her button nose crinkling in answer. "I don't have time for basketball."

"Hockey."

"Whatever. But baseball's another story. How 'bout those Mets?" A twinkle sparkled in her glorious eyes.

Apparentl she'd been giving him a hard time and was probably as big a sports fanatic as he, something he'd never expected to find in a woman.

"Hard to believe a Corbin would wear a jersey to an office party, though." Her brows rose in surprise.

On an other woman, the gesture would remind him of his judgmental federal court judge mother. But on *her*, the otherwise critical display indicated curiosity and interest, not disdain. "You've got that right. But I'm not a typical Corbin." He felt the welcome tug of a smile.

She inclined her head, her silky black hair brushing her shoulders much the way he'd like it caressing his skin. "Tell me something I don't know."

Once again, her trembling fingers touched her mouth, this time tracing the outline of her reddened lips before she caught herself and stepped around the tree, reaching for the first gift-wrapped package she could find. He allowed her escape for the moment, watching the sex sway of her hips in retreat. And in that instant, her words immediately after that mind-blowing kiss came back to him. *You're not him. You're nothing like Stephan.*

She'd kissed him and known instantly. And she wasn't all that upset and she definitely wasn't unaffected. The thought pleased him. Though Max could never compete with his twin as a Corbin son, he'd obviously made headway with . . . his brother's woman? His gut clenched at the thought.

"Hello, Max." Stephan walked up beside him.

"Hey, little brother." Catching the scowl on his twin's face, Max grinned, feeling on safe, sibling-sparring ground. " 'Little brother' is a figure of speech. You know that. But you also know I got sprung first."

"Three minutes isn't enough to hold it over me our entire lives," Stephan said with characteristic grumbling. "But I'm glad you made it." He surprised Max by slapping him on the back. Obviously his brother wasn't threatened by his father's summons of his wayward, prodigal son. Another reason for Max to suddenly hold out hope he'd leave this party with more than he'd walked in with.

At the very least, a renewed connection to his twin and at best a new woman in his life? Possible, Max thought, unless—he glanced at his brother. "Who's the elf?"

Stephan folded his arms across his chest and glanced around the tree to where the woman who'd kissed Max senseless now tried to feign interest in her bag of toys and not the Corbin brothers. Max stifled a smile.

"Who, Toni?" Stephan asked.

"Toni." Max tested the name on his tongue, liking the sound as well as the incongruity of a man's name on such a feminine creature.

"She's an associate—something you'd know if you didn't make yourself so scarce."

His brother was right. Other than the obligatory holidays at home, Max avoided family situations—especially family business functions like this one—if only because they were always fraught with tension between himself and his parents.

"Any interest?" Max asked, ignoring his brother's jibe but still needing to lay other cards on the table.

Stephan shook his head. "Maybe when she first started working here, but that was a while ago. And once we became colleagues and friends . . ." He waved his hand in dismissal. "No interest."

It was obvious to Max that she didn't feel the same—at least she hadn't before kissing the wrong twin, but no point in informing his brother now. "You sure?"

"No interest. Not that way." Stephan glanced at him, surprised but obviously certain. "Field's clear."

And so were his brother's words. Nothing stood between Max and his elf.

He turned, determined to stake his claim, but she was talking with a female colleague, and then without warning the conference room was overrun with scampering, chattering children. "What's this?" Max asked over the din.

Stephan laughed. "*This* is Toni's contribution to the annual firm Christmas part. We always made a cash donation to a charity, but she insisted we do something more personal, too. Now we buy gifts for the kids at one of the local women's shelters and Santa hands them out—with her help."

"Santa?"

"Dad. But not this year. He'll be here but, the doctor's

banned him from anything too stressful like picking up the kids and putting them on his lap. At least until next year."

A twisting pain lanced through Max. "You sure?"

"That he'll be around till next year?" Stephan asked, finishing Max's unspoken question in a was only a twin could. "I'm sure. Spend some more time with him and you will be, too."

Max had seen the older man in the hospital and again when he'd been released, but they'd never been alone long enough to get into serious conversation. Yet apparently the stroke had prompted a renewal in the older man's determination to get Max back into the family firm, because he'd been summoned here by his father, who claimed he had an offer Max couldn't refuse.

"He's determined enough for four men," Stephan said.

"Swell." Determined to stick around and determined to get his way with his one ornery son. Well, one out of two wouldn't be bad. Max glanced at his twin, knowing he had to be honest about not wanting to take over in the office, or in his brother's hard-worked-for domain. "Hey bro, you should know I have no intention of coming back—"

Stephan cut him off with a slug to the shoulder. "*I* know. The only one you have to convince is Dad."

Max nodded. His brother was obviously secure in his place and position within the firm and the family. One potential problem taken care of.

He looked over. His elf—Toni—was kneeling down with kids beside her, tickling one, laughing with another. Not only did she have an altruistic streak but from the looks of things she was a natural-born nurturer, too. Add that to her sexy-as-hell appearance and her knock-out kiss and Max knew he'd found a gem. Getting to know her would be a real pleasure.

"Who's replacing Dad as Santa this year?" Max asked.

"Even cash couldn't sway any of these uptight jokers to do the job and I wasn't sure I'd make it on time, so Toni's handing out the gifts herself," Stephan said.

"Really."

His brother chuckled aloud. "You sound awfully pleased. Aren't you too old to be telling Santa what you want for Christmas?"

Max grinned. "Hell, no. Especially not if it'll let me get close to his sexy emissary." And as soon as the children were finished, he planned to tell Santa's helper exactly what he wanted for Christmas.

Two

Toni was one part mortified and two parts completely turned on. She was in a sweat that owed nothing to the crowded, overheated room and everything to the man watching her out of the corner of his eye. With hindsight and the rush of adrenaline to act on impulse gone, she saw the differences in the brothers more clearly. This man had slightly longer though equally black hair, and razor stubble gave him a more rugged, less clean-cut appearance. He exuded a raw masculinity that appealed to her on a deeper, more carnal level. One she hadn't known existed inside her until that kiss.

That kiss. Toni hugged her arms around her chest, as if she could hold tight to the feelings he inspired. As always, she forced herself to take an honest look at herself, her actions, and the situation. She couldn't deny the truth. At a crossroads, about to embark on a new professional life, she couldn't afford more than a one-night stand, no matter how out of character it was. She'd thought Stephan Corbin was the perfect man on whom to test her feminine wiles, but she'd been wrong. Whatever attraction she'd felt for Stephan paled in comparison to what she'd experienced under the nonexistent mistletoe with his twin. And darned if she didn't want an instant replay.

But with the onslaught of children from the shelter, she had no choice but to wait. In the meantime, she continued the cat-and-mouse game of eye contact he'd begun earlier. Her heart beat frantically in her chest and anticipation flowed through her veins.

"Only two more kids, Toni," Annie, her secretary, whispered in her ear.

"I don't know whether to say thank goodness because I'm beat or thank goodness because even one child here is one too many." She ought to know, having spent more than one night in a shelter as a child.

"How about thank goodness so you can go play get-to-know-you with the Corbin twin?"

Toni felt the heat rise to her cheeks. Had Annie seen that consuming kiss behind the tree?

"He hasn't taken his eyes off you since you sat down in this chair."

Toni shifted in her seat to accommodate the next little girl. "Did you know Stephan had a brother?" she asked Annie.

"No, but I wish I had, at least before you nailed him for yourself. I've got to run. I have a date. Have fun tonight," she whispered on a laugh and walked away before Toni could respond.

The last two children and their requests for Santa went quickly. Toni kept her mental list of extra things to send over to the shelter from Santa and soon the kids, their chaperones, and the gifts were bundled up and on their way. She started to rise, knowing she still had an office to pack before the night was through.

"Not so fast."

She recognized the seductive voice that rumbled from behind.

She curled her hands around the arm of the office chair she'd appropriated, steadying herself with a firm grip. "Something I can do for you?"

"Since you have a special relationship with the big man in the red suit I was hoping you could relay a wish." His strong fingertips brushed her hair back from her face and around her ear, strumming across her skin with perfect precision.

Her stomach fluttered with longing and she forced an easy laugh. "Aren't you too old to believe in Santa?"

"Aren't you too young not to?"

"I'm dressed like one of his elves. Doesn't that tell you something about who and what I believe in?" And right now she believed in this man—and anything he said or did.

She tipped her head to the side and found herself sharing breathing space, close enough to kiss him if she desired. And she did, badly. She'd never experienced anything as strong as her immediate attraction to this stranger.

"It tells me some. But I know too little about you and I intend to change that." He walked around and eased himself onto the arm of her chair, not on her lap but close enough to increase her growing awareness.

His hip brushed her arm and her body heat shot up another ten degrees. She glanced around at the thinning group of people. Though she and her companion didn't seem to be garnering added attention, Toni was still aware of this being a place of business.

Even if she had temporarily forgotten once she'd gotten him behind the tree, they were in full view of the masses now. "I'm not Santa Claus so there's no lap-sitting involved," she warned him.

He bent closer. "I'll accept those barriers . . . for now."

She inhaled a shaky breath. His masculine scent, a heady mix of warm spice and pure man tempted her to throw caution aside. Before she could lose common sense she grasped onto the one thread of the conversation she could remember. "So what can I tell Santa you desire . . . I mean want. What can I tell Santa you want?"

She'd caught her phrasing, an obvious extension of her thoughts and needs, and attempted a too-late retraction. But the word "desire," once spoken, hovered in the air, teasing, arousing, and building upon the electricity arcing between them.

"I know what you meant." He laughed and the deep sound both eased and aroused her in ways she didn't understand. "I also know what you want and it's the same thing I do."

A tremor shook her hard. "And what would that be?"

"To finish what we started under the so-called mistletoe."

A rousing round of applause erupted around them, interrupting their banter and his huskily spoken words. Despite the beat of desire thrumming inside her, she forced herself to look for the cause of the stir. She glanced up and saw Mr. Corbin, the firm's senior partner—Stephan and his twin's father—standing in the doorway. *His twin.* But beyond the obvious resemblance Toni drew a sudden blank.

Oh, Lord. For as quickly as they'd connected, she didn't even know his name.

He brushed his knuckles across her cheek in a gesture more tender and caring than overtly sexual. She could have melted at his feet. And then there was the heat rushing

through her body. She felt on edge, the desire inside her
out of control.

He rose to his feet. "I've got to go greet the old man
but no way are we finished."

She bit the inside of her cheek. When she'd decided to
go after Stephan, the firm's bachelor, she'd known nothing long-term could come of it. She'd just wanted to enter
the new year feeling good and knowing she could get the
man she thought she desired, if just for a brief time. But
she'd kissed the wrong brother—or the right brother depending on her perspective—and knowing nothing about
him, all bets were off.

So she could continue her bold act and see where things
led or she could run, something she'd seen her mother do
too many times. Toni Larson didn't run.

"Oh, we're finished all right." She licked at her dry lips.
"At least until you tell me your name."

"It's Max." Amusement mingled with desire in his blue-
eyed gaze.

She grinned. "'Bye, Max."

He shook his head. "Only until later, Toni." His words
held certainty, his voice the promise of sharing more than
just an introduction. With a last glance, he reluctantly
turned and walked away.

She watched as he approached the older man and witnessed what was so obviously a reunion between a father
and a son he loved deeply. A lump rose to her throat. Looking at Max, Toni saw concern and love cross his handsome
features, no hint of the playful man in sight. Apparently this
reunion was emotional for both men.

But as Max broke from his father's arms, he said something light enough to make Stephan laugh. Then he turned
and, from across the room, his compelling gaze met hers

and he treated her to a sexy wink. One that assured her he hadn't forgotten her or his promise of seeing her later.

Her stomach curled in anticipation and searing heat assaulted her senses. She shook her head, amazed. Not only had she been naughty, she'd most certainly gotten her man. Just not the man she'd expected. Fate and irony were at work, tonight. She touched her fingers to her lips and imagined the feel of his mouth working magic over hers, his warm breath and his masculine scent wrapping her in seductive heat.

She let out a breathless sigh, knowing the night she'd desired was about to get much, much hotter.

Max hadn't wanted to leave Toni's side, not for an instant, which he supposed told him something about the strength of his attraction to a woman he barely knew. An attraction he wanted to explore further.

After spending time and discussing everything *but* business with Max, the older man, had grown tired and said he'd see Max at home, tomorrow. He just hoped the truce they'd begun to forge today lasted once Max told his father that no offer, no matter how supposedly enticing, could coax him back into the family firm. The most the older Corbin could expect from Max was a loving son who'd always be there for him. Max hoped it would be enough.

But before he had to deal with tomorrow, he had tonight ahead of him and he looked forward to every last minute. He walked down the darkened hallway, lit onl b lights from some occupied offices, and stopped by the door his brother had told him belonged to Toni.

Light shone from beneath the partially closed door and

the low strains of music sounded from inside. Anticipation and arousal beat heavy inside him as he let himself in. Toni was emptying her office, packing boxes and singing while she worked.

The woman couldn't carry a tune to save her life. Max folded his arms across his chest and grinned. "You can serenade me anytime."

She yelped and jumped. "You shouldn't sneak up on me like that."

He stepped forward, moving closer. With each step he took toward her, she inched back until she hit the wall, looking up at him with wide eyes. "What are you doing?"

"What you asked. Making my presence known."

"As if I could miss it," she said wryly.

"But you're afraid of me."

She shook her head in denial but he backed off anyway. He wanted this woman in many and varied ways but frightened wasn't one of them:

"You don't scare me . . . Max." His name fluttered off her lips. Then as if to prove her point, she held her hand out for him to shake. "And it's nice to officially meet you."

"Likewise." He eased his hand inside hers. Warm and soft, her skin caressed his coarser flesh.

"You just surprised me," she said in a husky voice.

"A good surprise, I hope."

"Definitely that. So why are you here?"

"I was hoping to talk you into going for dinner."

She bit down on her lower lip. "What if I have plans?"

He propped a shoulder against the wall beside her. "Break them," he said with more confidence than he felt. His biggest fear was that she'd blow him off before they had a chance to explore what was between them.

"Convince me." Her teasing smile invited him to do just that.

He curled his fingers around her hand and pulled her toward him, wrapping one arm around her waist and holding her other hand out in front of them. "Let's dance."

Her eyes opened wide. "You're kidding?"

"Do you see me laughing?" He pulled her flush against him and swept her around the small office in time to the beat of the music. He had no idea what had come over him except he had no intention of losing her now.

She anchored her hand around his back for support, molded her body to his and let go. He felt it in the swa of her hips and saw it in the sassy tilt of her head. She was enjoying herself and he was glad.

His body couldn't ignore her lush curves and his groin hardened, unsatisfied with a single dance. But Max wasn't in this for a one-night stand. He was a man who'd spent his life trusting his own instincts and he wasn't about to question his gut now. He wanted much more than sex with this woman and for Max that was a first.

She tilted her head back. "You've got good moves."

"I give my partner all the credit."

Her smile was nothing short of incredible. "Is that what I am?"

"You tell me." He turned her once and stilled. They were so close, their warm breath mingled. So aware of one another he thought, as he stared into her expectant eyes.

Toni's legs shook beneath her and she tightened her grip on the only available means of support—Max's waist and hand. Then she waited as he lowered his mouth to hers, slowly, surely, his blue-eyed stare never wavering until his lips touched hers.

Their first kiss had been spontaneous, unplanned, and yes, she admitted to herself, a bit desperate. But this was so much more. He took his time, his tongue delving and discovering the deep recesses of her mouth, learning *her*, not once rushing the moment.

Her stomach curled in response to the drugging kiss, much the way her fingers curled into his skin.

His lips slid gently over hers, making the most of the moisture they generated together. Strong yet gentle, he took control, mastering the moves that made her sigh into him and spin dizzily out of control. Toni needed to participate on equal footing and she traced the outline of his strong lips with her tongue and reveled in his uninhibited verbal response. He was a man who not only expressed his physical desire but was bold enough not to hide his emotional reaction. The masculine groan found an answering pull deep inside Toni, in a place she'd kept hidden, uncharted until now.

Without warning, he pulled back, leaning his forehead against hers, his breathing rough in her ear. But the intimacy of continued body contact felt both good and right. Teetering on an emotional precipice, Toni shook deep inside.

"Have I convinced you yet?" he asked.

"Convinced me of what?" She was out of breath, stunned by the intensity of the short but extremely emotional encounter. She couldn't call it just a kiss, not when he'd engaged her heart and soul in every move he'd made. Did he really expect her to think clearly now?

"I am so glad to see I can make you forget ever thing but me." He laughed, a husky, tender sound that sent ribbons of warmth curling through her. "I asked you to break dinner plans to go out with me. You said I should convince you, remember?"

He reached out and traced the outline of her moist lips with his fingertip, reminding her of the kiss and all that had passed between them. "So did I convince you?"

Her tongue darted out, coming into contact with his salty skin.

He sucked in a startled breath and he met her gaze. "I'm going to take that as yes," he warned.

He could take her anywhere, anytime, but she wasn't about to tell him that. Instead she cleared her throat and straightened her shoulders. "Dinner sounds great. But I can guarantee ou that without a reservation there's not a place around that doesn't have at least an hour or more wait."

Dinner, reservations, Toni hoped everyday conversation would center her somehow, but after this interlude, she doubted her feet would touch the floor again tonight.

"Then it's a good thing I have an in at someplace special. You ready?"

"Dressed like this?" She glanced down at her green tights and fur-lined skirt and wished she hadn't come to work dressed as an elf but had changed at the office instead.

He took in her outfit, one she hadn't thought of as sexy until she saw herself in his glazed eyes. "The place I have in mind doesn't have a dress code."

"How about a people code?" She pulled at her hat until the pins gave way and she tossed it aside.

He slid his fingers over a long strand of her hair. "Everyone's allowed, bar none, including elves." His eyes twinkled with mischief. "Just leave the reindeer outside."

"Cute."

"No, I'm serious. The place is called Bar None and you're more than welcome. My old college roommate owns the joint. So will you come with me?"

In his eyes, she saw the same hope and anticipation alive inside her and grabbed for her courage. "Okay, Max. Lead the way."

* * *

Max had a hard time concentrating on driving with Toni beside him. She shifted in her seat and he felt the heat of her stare.

"While you were twirling me around my office . . ." she began.

"And kissing you senseless . . ." He couldn't help but remind her of what he'd never forget.

Toni shot Max a wry glare. "You didn't mention this place was in the boonies."

"That's because you didn't ask."

She held her hands out in front of the heater, but he doubted she needed the warmth. He pulled his truck past the train station, lit by traditional colored Christmas lights that gave the place a festive look, much like the rest of the small town. Another half-mile down, Max turned into a private street and pulled the car into a gravel parking lot. The Bar None, an old-fashioned pub and restaurant, was in the same upstate town, where he lived and worked, a good forty-minute car ride from New York City.

"Forget me asking. I think you were more afraid I'd say no."

He grinned. "That, too." After their second kiss, the one where they'd connected on too many levels to count, Max hadn't been about to lose her by mentioning a little detail like distance. "I gave you the chance to turn around, didn't I?"

She laughed. "While you were doing fifty-five, yeah, you did."

He'd then proceeded to find out as much about his elf as possible, discovering she was at a turning point in her life. Feeling overburdened and overworked, she had the new year pegged as a fresh start. She hadn't elaborated and he'd given her the freedom to reveal as much or as little as she desired.

Though he didn't want to spook her by getting too serious too fast, Max knew he had every intention of being part of her new beginning. He shifted to park.

"So your friend owns this place?" she asked, glancing around her.

He nodded.

"Gorgeous decorations."

Max took in the icicle lights dripping from the shingles and overhang along with the colored lights circling the surrounding shrubbery, seeing the setting he viewed daily from her new, awed perspective. "They are incredible." And so was she.

"How do you plan on explaining me? My outfit, I mean." She laughed, a lilting but embarrassed sound that reminded him of her jingling bells. Those she'd removed somewhere during their ride up the West Side Highway, and they lay in the center console.

"I'll just tell him you're Santa's helper." He turned in his seat and reached for her hand.

She tipped her head to one side, a wry smile curving her lips. "And you think he'll buy that?"

He shook his head. "Doesn't matter to me what Jake believes. But it matters to me what you believe." He'd only known her a few hours but the connection he felt with her was real.

Her lashes fluttered upward as she met his gaze. Deep and compelling, her eyes settled on him. Did she know? Understand? Feel the same overwhelming attraction and need as he felt pulsing through his body at this very moment?

Max wondered. He'd never fallen hard and fast for a woman he barely knew, but he had now. Feeling vulnerable wasn't something he was used to and he suddenly needed proof she felt the same. "Tell me something. Since you brought it up, what was behind the elf outfit?" He'd heard his brother's version. He wanted to hear hers.

She glanced away. "I was just spreading some holiday cheer."

"Maybe that's part of the reason, but I doubt it covers everything. And before we go into that crowded bar, I want to know more about you." Something that would show him she trusted him. Something to prove to him that this . . . thing . . . between them wasn't all one-sided.

She bit down on her lower lip. "What did Stephan tell you about me? And don't tell me you didn't ask."

He laughed, admiring both her intuition and nerve. "That you organized the children's visit to Santa and the gifts. That's all."

She inclined her head. "And you want to know why."

He shook his head. "I want to know *you*."

Looking into his eyes, Toni believed him. Though nothing had been said aloud, somewhere between kissing him and . . . well . . . kissing him, a sense of caring had developed, too. They didn't know nearly enough about one another but he was giving her the opportunity to change that.

She'd never admitted her past to a man before, never felt close enough—yet she felt that closeness now. The vulnerability she normally associated with opening up to a man was nowhere to be found. Considering she wasn't planning anything more than the here and now, the notion rattled her. Badly.

His hand brushed her cheek and remained there. "You can trust me, sweetheart."

As she turned her head so his palm cupped her face, a renewed sense of rightness swept through her. "I spent my childhood in and out of a women's shelter," she admitted. "Whenever my mother got up the courage to leave, we'd find one my father didn't know about. Then when things got rough, she'd go back to him and it would start all over again."

He let out a low growl. "That shouldn't happen to any child."

"Exactly." She shrugged self-consciously. "Which explains the Christmas party and my elf outfit."

"Which explains my attraction to you," he murmured.

"You have a thing for little women dressed in green?"

"You make ourself sound like a Martian." He burst out laughing but sobered fast. Nothing about what she'd revealed was funny. "Actually, I have a thing for a certain raven-haired beauty with a big heart."

She shook her head, flushed. "Don't give me that much credit. Really. It's all very self-serving. When I got out of high school, I swore I'd finish my education somehow. No matter how many student loans I had to take, I promised myself I'd find a way to be self-supporting so I'd never run out of options like my mother had."

"And you've accomplished that."

"With a little unexpected help," she said, gratitude evident in her tone. "I found out when my mother passed away she'd taken out an insurance policy. Enough money to cover my education—after the fact. So my loans are paid off, but I spent years working like a demon for that sense of security."

"But you've got that now."

"Most definitely." She turned away, reaching for the door handle. "I'm starving," she said, changing the subject.

Obviously she didn't want to take things too quickly, but Max made a mental note to find out more. "Toni, wait."

She glanced over her shoulder.

"One more question."

"Yes?"

"You thought you were kissing my brother."

Even in the darkened car he could see the heat of a blush rise to her cheeks. "Mistaken impulse," she said.

"Any feelings behind it?"

"Just one."

He waited a beat before she finally finished.

"Regret."

Max felt as if he'd been kicked in the gut. Until she turned completely and scooted over in the seat, so close he could smell her perfume. "I regret that you obviously think there was something going on between me and Stephan. Or that I have feelings for your brother other than friendship."

"Don't you? You initiated that kiss. I have a hard time believing it was born of feelings of friendship." Despite the fact that she'd let him into her heart and the painful parts of her past, she'd yet to openly admit her interest in him.

"This is so humiliating and I'm going to sound so desperate." She laughed and shook her head. "I thought I was interested in your brother and I acted on the opportunity." She shrugged. "Turns out I was wrong." Those velvet green eyes met his. "I thought I wanted Stephan—until the second I kissed you."

Max had his answer and let out a ragged breath of air. She wanted him, too. So, he thought, let the night begin.

Three

"Hey, Detective, how's it going?"

"Just fine, Milt."

Detective? Max had grabbed Toni's hand and she followed him through the crowd at the bar to the back of the paneled pub, decorated with silver and green tinsel along the top of dark wood. There was no way he could hear her above the din so she waited until they'd reached their destination before yanking on his hand and capturing his attention. "You're a detective?"

"Private investigator. Why?"

"No special reason. I just had no idea what you did for a living."

"And now you do." He turned toward the bar. "Hey, Jake, give me a round of . . ."

Max turned toward Toni and she shrugged. "Whatever you're having is fine."

"Two Coronas."

The man he'd called Jake, a light-haired man about the same age and height as Max, nodded in return. "Hey, Brownie," Jake called to someone across the room. "Get your ass up and give the detective his table."

Max laughed. "I have a standing seat in the corner." He gestured toward a high table with two barstools where an older man was clearing out.

"He doesn't have to give up his seat for us," Toni said.

"He damn well does. If we don't boot him out of here, he drinks too much. He's too lazy to stand on his feet all night. This way he'll go home and sleep it off." Max caressed her face with his knuckles. "Trust me. I've been through this routine before."

"You've booted him out for his own good? Or booted him out to make room for you and another woman?" She bit the inside of her cheek, hating herself for asking but needing the answer just the same.

"There are no *other* women."

Toni liked the answer, but couldn't help wondering if he was telling her what he thought she wanted to hear. Seconds later, he dispelled her concerns by cupping her cheeks in his palms and lowering his lips for a seductive, heated kiss. One that left her gasping for air, unable to think, and the subject of intense speculation, she realized, as he lifted his head.

The stares of onlookers turned into a slow round of applause and more than one whistle of approval. "Way to go, Detective."

Embarrassed, she lowered herself onto the nearest barstool with shaking knees, just as Jake arrived with their drinks.

"You sure do know how to make an entrance, Corbin. Now are ou going to introduce me to your lady?"

"*His* lady?"

Jake laughed. "I've owned this place nearly ten years and he's never brought a woman here before. If you can think of another label, just let me know."

Max joined his friend's amused chuckling. "See? Proof to back up my claim. Jake Bishop meet Toni . . ."

"Larson," she said, extending her hand before his friend realized how little they knew about each other.

"Nice to meet you, Toni." Jake swung a towel over his arm. "Can I get you two something to eat? My burgers are the best." Without waiting for an answer, he disappeared into the kitchen.

"Modest guy."

Max dragged the empty stool close to hers and swung himself into it. "He can afford to be full of himself. Look at this place. It's a gold mine. Of course it is the only bar for miles."

She nodded. "And one where you've got your own table and every one seems to know you. Do you call this place home?" Toni liked the rustic, comfortable decor. The place emitted warmth and a down-home atmosphere that welcomed its customers and she could see Max spending his free time here.

"As a matter of fact I do." He gestured upward. "I rent the place upstairs."

"Really." She leaned forward and rested her chin on her hands. "And here your friend said you don't make it a habit of luring unsuspecting women to your lair."

He shook his head, his gaze never leaving hers. "I haven't lured you anywhere you didn't want to go. And if you want me to drive you back to the city after dinner, I will."

Her heart beat out a rapid crescendo in her chest. She didn't want to go anywhere without him. They'd just met tonight but she'd never felt so much so fast. "And if I don't?" she asked softly.

Max leaned closer. "If you don't want to go back, then you stay with me."

His warm breath tickled her cheek and she realized she could easily fall hard for this man. All six feet of him put her at a petite disadvantage, yet for a woman who prided herself on her independence, she had to admit she liked his overpowering air and the heady way he made her feel.

Enough to consider spending the night?

"Burgers, folks." Jake arrived, interrupting the electric current of awareness running between them. After serving them their meals, Jake grabbed a chair and dragged it over.

Max eyed his friend warily. Jake never knew when to butt out. Max ought to resent Jake's intrusion, but hell, the man was a bartender. Being nosy was his business, and besides, Max needed a break or else he'd grab Toni's hand and drag her upstairs to his bed—the one thing he wanted and the last thing he ought to do. He needed to build on the tentative start they'd made, not rush into a one-night stand. Which wasn't to say he wouldn't follow her lead, Max thought.

"So where'd you two meet, a costume party?" Jake asked, then gestured to the food in front of them. "Go 'head and eat."

Max rolled his eyes. "We met in the city."

"I work with his brother," Toni explained.

"She's a lawyer?"

"Not a typical one," Max said, knowing Jake was already questioning why he'd fall for one of what Max had always labeled a stuffy breed.

"This true?" Jake asked.

"I guess." Toni shrugged. "At least no more than he's a typical Corbin."

"You two seem to have a handle on each other."

Not nearly well enough, Max thought. Not yet.

Jake leaned forward in his seat, ready for more conversation. "Sounds like a match made in heaven to me."

"You realize the place is emptying out while you're hanging out here?" Max asked.

"Are you looking to get rid of me?"

"Could I if I tried?"

Toni laughed. "You two sound like brothers."

Max shrugged. "Live with a guy for four years and you get the urge to kill him every once in a while."

"The man speaks the truth." Jake leaned back and took in the emptying bar. "Less money, more family time. I don't know whether I love or hate the holidays."

"He closes early during the week before Christmas," Max explained.

"That's nice."

Max wondered if he mistook the wistful look in Toni's eyes when Jake mentioned family time and holidays in the same breath. Recalling her childhood, he doubted he was off base and he wanted the opportunity to replace older, sadder memories with newer, happier ones.

"Well, you two be good." Jake turned to Toni and winked. "I'm going to start wrapping things up for the night."

For the next hour, while Jake cleared out the remaining customers and then locked the door behind Max and Toni, promising to return early for a real cleanup, Max ate and watched Toni do the same. He wasn't a man prone to talking about himself but she had him explaining the types of cases he handled and describing the thrill of working in the field as opposed to behind a desk or in a courtroom. To his surprise, she didn't turn her nose up or question his choices. If anything, she not only approved but seemed to envy his ability to walk away from the pressure and grind to do what he enjoyed.

Max studied her. Now that she'd paid off her student loans, she could afford to start making choices out of enjoyment and not necessity. He wondered if she even realized she had that option, but before he could delve deeper into her life, the conversation detoured yet again.

But no matter what they discussed Max found himself drawn to her. Not just because they shared a passion for take-out Mexican food and Rollerblading in fresh air, but because she was unique: She was a woman who made him want to open up, a woman who interested him so much he wanted to know more about her life, and a woman who accepted the choices he made. A woman he desired not just in his bed, though that was a given, but in his life, to see where things led.

And if her footwork was any indication, she wanted the same thing. She'd obviously let her elf boots fall to the floor and she'd brushed her foot against his leg once too many times for comfort or accident. The light flush in her cheeks and her inability to look him head-on told him she didn't find her overt moves easy. But he was grateful for her interest and he intended to keep things light and fun—to give her space to decide how far she wanted to take things, knowing he wouldn't accept just tonight. It would be *her* decision to stay or go, no matter how much his body throbbed with growing need.

Conversation became more difficult as she intentionally massaged his calf with the arch of her foot, inching upward beneath the table.

He leaned closer. "You're a naughty girl, Toni." He captured her foot between his legs, stilling her arousing movements.

It was either stop her or let her continue her upward

climb, in which case their evening would end before it ever began. And with the bar empty and Jake gone, Max would much rather start their time together fresh and new.

"Being naughty's the whole point, Max."

"You sound like a woman with a plan." He paused, thinking of their unusual meeting. "And it started with that kiss."

"You're astute. No wonder they call you detective." Her lips lifted in a smile. "I already told you I acted on opportunity."

"In a way that was out of character." Max was as certain Toni wanted him as he was that she had a bad case of nerves.

"And you know this how?" She drummed her fingertips on the table, trying hard to maintain her nonchalant façade.

Max grinned. "Gut instinct."

Toni inclined her head. Not only did he understand her well, but he seemed to see inside her, too. Her aggressive act was just that, but in no way did that minimize how badly she wanted this night.

He stopped her nervous tapping and threaded his fingers through hers. "Relax, sweetheart."

The softly spoken endearment wrapped around her heart and her adrenaline picked up speed. "You really think that's possible?"

He shrugged. "I know so. We're going to get to know each other better. We'll have fun. And nothing will happen that you don't want to happen. So relax and come with me."

She'd follow him anywhere, Toni thought. And despite the fact that she'd never done anything that resembled a one-night stand before, she wanted *everything* to happen. She just needed to gather her nerve. Her hand entwined with his, she let him lead her around the bar and into a back room she hadn't seen earlier because of the crowds.

In the corner, beside the rack holding the pool cues, a Christmas tree took up a lot of space in the small room. The tree beckoned to her, with its worn ornaments, aged by time and handling, hanging from its branches. Though it wasn't professionally decorated with pricey ornaments like the one in the office, this Christmas display showed thoughtfulness, warmth, and caring.

She reached out and lightly fingered a cut-out teddy bear hanging from a crudely bent pipe cleaner. "This is so sweet."

Max came up behind her. His body heat and masculine scent put her nerve endings on high alert.

"Jake's daughter made it her first year in kindergarten," he said.

"And this one?" With a trembling hand, she pointed to a clay angel, made with obvious talent and love.

"A customer." Max's warm breath fanned her ear. "Jake could tell you who gave him each one."

Toni nodded, impressed. "And what was your contribution?"

"What makes you so sure I made one?"

"Intuition." The man would put his mark on everything in his life, she thought. Including herself.

"Smart woman. I supply the tree each year."

Toni turned to find him very close and what little composure remained nearly shattered beneath his steamy gaze.

"Ever play pool?" he asked, changing the subject.

Toni's shoulders lowered and she smiled, feeling on safer ground. "Too many times to count."

"Then we don't need lessons." He grabbed her hand and strode the few steps to the pool table. Wrapping his hands around her waist, he lifted her onto the lacquered edge.

She licked her lips, wondering why she'd deluded herself into an illusion of safety. Around Max, she was constantly off balance, desire never far away. "No lessons," she agreed, wondering what would come next.

"Then how about we play each other? For intriguing stakes." His deep eyes bored into hers.

"What do you have in mind?"

"It's called getting to know you. For every ball I miss, I admit something about myself. Something deep and personal or . . . something I desire." His voice deepened to a husky drawl.

She tried to swallow but her mouth had grown dry. "And if you get the ball into the pocket?"

She watched the pulse beat in his neck, and acting on impulse, she pressed a light kiss against his skin. He let out a low growl. "If I make my shot, you remove an article of clothing. Same rules apply for you. What do you say?"

Arousal beat a heav rhythm in her veins. Naughty or nice, Toni thought. Did she have the nerve to participate in his game? To take their night to its ultimate conclusion?

Under ordinary circumstances, probably not. But nothing about Max or her growing feelings for him was typical—or easy. However, her pool game had never been a problem—not since she'd waitressed in college and learned from the best. "I say why not?"

He handed her a cue, then proceeded to set up the table. "Do you want to break or should I?"

"I'll do it." Toni figured it was a win-win situation. Either she revealed something about herself or he revealed a bare body part—either way *she* wouldn't be the one overexposed.

Max stepped back, leaning on his cue as Toni lined up her shot. The one thing he'd forgotten when suggesting this game was her skimpy outfit—and if the thought of their rules had him hot and bothered, the reality of watching her bent over the table inspired erotic images to rival his steamiest daydream.

"You do realize the lighter the stick, the farther the follow-through," she said.

"It's also been said a heavier stick gives you more power," Max replied but he wasn't concentrating.

The white fur trim of her skirt had lifted a notch, revealing thigh-high stockings and an enticing glimpse of the pale skin peeking above the elastic lace trim. The sudden rise in heat owed nothing to room temperature and everything to his sexy elf. His fingers itched to cup her soft flesh and his body begged to be cradled in her feminine heat.

The sudden crack of the stick hitting the cue ball broke his train of thought and echoed in the otherwise silent room. Still in a sweat, Max forced himself to focus on the game in time to see a flash of color and a ball ease into the corner pocket. "I'm impressed."

She straightened and grinned, looking pleased with herself. "One lesson I learned earl in life was to never agree to a game I couldn't win."

"I'll keep that in mind." He reached for the bottom of his shirt and yanked it over his head, grateful for her decent shot and the opportunity to cool off.

Her lashes fluttered quickly and her eyes opened wide as she stared at his bare chest.

"What's wrong? Did you forget the rules?" he asked.

She shook her head. "Of course not." Appearing more flustered than before, she settled in for the next round of play. But this time her hands shook and Max knew for sure his lack of clothing had rattled her. At least now they were on equal footing, he thought, taking in the seductive wiggle of her behind as she lined up her shot.

Sure enough, the next ball went shimmying toward the back wall, missing the pocket. "Sorry, sweetheart. Confession time."

She turned toward him, eyes big and imploring, a pout on her lips.

He shook his head. "No poor-me look is going to sway me, now spill." He paused, thinking of her alternatives. "Or you could always opt to speed the game along and remove an item of clothing."

"My sweet sixteen was my worst birthday," she said quickly, obviously making her choice.

He suppressed a laugh. "What happened?" He stepped closer, wishing she'd taken him up on his alternative offer.

"My dog ran away."

"I'm not buying that." He folded his arms across his chest, gratified when her eyes followed the movement. "But I am listening."

Her arm brushed his and she didn't break contact as she said, "My father died suddenly, the day before I turned sixteen."

Max breathed in deeply. A punch in the gut would have been more gentle, but it was his own fault. He'd suggested they reveal something deep and personal, and she had. She trusted him, showing it far more than if she'd removed her clothes.

"What happened?" he asked softly. Though she couldn't have any fond memories of the man, losing a parent couldn't be easy. "Heart attack?"

She nodded. "And instead of grief, I felt nothing but relief." The strain in her face and the guilt in her eyes were obvious. "And here I thought my shooting first would leave *you* more exposed." She shook her head and treated him to a brief smile. "Your turn." She gestured to the cue.

Max swallowed hard. Had he really thought this would be light and easy?

"Okay." Still shaken, he bent over the table and took in his options before lining up his shot, missing the pocket by too much.

He felt her light touch as she tapped him on the shoulder. He turned to find her in his personal space, within kissing distance. He reached for her shoulders and held on.

"You didn't have to do that," she whispered, calling him on his deliberately missed shot. An easier play had sat by the corner pocket but he'd chosen to forfeit instead.

"No, I didn't. But I wanted to." He'd had two choices. Open a vein and exchange information or watch her peel off the clingy green suit.

No matter how much he'd rather see her undress, he owed her and had to reveal a personal secret. She'd opened up to him tonight. Twice. If his goal was getting closer, he had to return the favor. Besides, he wanted to let her in. For the first time, he wanted to connect with a woman in more places than in bed. He'd proven himself adept at making selfish choices in life, Max thought, but not when it came to Toni. She was too special.

Gratitude flickered in her eyes and she waited in silence for him to pay up. He wasn't comfortable and hated like hell for having put himself in this position, but he supposed that spoke of Toni's effect on him. "My father resents me for leaving the business and I've never measured up to Stephan as Dad's favorite son." He tensed, having admitted his deepest vulnerability and laid it out there for her to see.

Her gaze softened. "Your father's a fool, and if you repeat a word of that to my boss, you'll pay in spades," she said, then wrapped her arms around his neck and pulled him closer.

Her lips lingered over his and as his chest rasped against

her fur-lined V-neck, he needed more than a simple kiss. He fumbled for her zipper, the one that would allow him to peel off the outfit and bare her for him to see. But she pulled back before he could get a decent grasp and he groaned.

"Your last miss didn't count," she said in a husky voice. "Now play pool."

He wagged a finger in the air. "Like I said, naughty girl."

"What fun is it if you don't have to work for it?"

"Trust me, sweetheart, it'd be plenty fun. But if you insist, I'll take another turn." Having laid his soul bare, he knew it was time to turn up the heat. "But before I make this next shot . . ."

"You're too confident about your gaming abilities," she said, interrupting him.

"Aren't you the one who said never play a game you can't win? But if at any point you change your mind . . ."

She shook her head. "I wouldn't have let you drive all the way out here if I wasn't sure."

He let out a slow breath of air that did little to help his rapidly beating heart. "Just remember, it's your choice."

She looked at him in a way no one—no woman—had ever looked at him before, with just the right mixture of trust, reverence, and desire to make a man fall to his knees.

"You're a nice guy, Max."

He'd never been called nice before and he knew his actions tonight were as unique as she was. "You're pretty damn special yourself." He leaned over the table and easily made his next shot, then walked a few steps to line up the next. "But something tells me you won't be thinking such great thoughts about me after this," he said, sinking another ball as he spoke, then his third before shifting her way.

He focused on her and his breath caught in his throat. She'd left her shoes under the table in the other room and Max hadn't realized how little remained—the shirt, skirt, and belt, all three items she'd discarded while he was upping the ante and making his shots.

She faced him now, his most erotic dream come to life. Her clothes lay in a pile beside her. Her black hair, tousled and full, caressed her shoulders. The body he'd glimpsed through the barrier of clothing and imagined in his mind had nothing on reality. A black lace bra cut in a deep V contrasted with and revealed creamy white mounds of flesh, while a whisper-light-looking bikini barely covered her feminine secrets.

She met his gaze and shrugged, a deep blush staining her cheeks and an embarrassed fidget to her stance. "I forgot to mention that when I lose—no matter how unlikely—I always pay up."

He edged his finger beneath one delicate bra strap, savoring the feel of her soft flesh beneath his roughened fingertips. "If you consider this a loss, then we have nothing further to—"

"Shh." She placed one finger over his lips. "That was a figure of speech."

His tongue darted out and he tasted her, a combination of salty skin and female softness. She sucked in a startled breath but she didn't remove her hand. Instead she traced the outline of his mouth with her fingertip, leaving him incredibly aroused by her touch.

"The game's over, Max, and I'd call it even."

He grinned. "Win-win."

"Mmm-hmm."

Taking that as his cue, Max did what he'd been dying to do since he'd laid eyes on her standing beside the Christmas tree—he spanned her bare waist with his hands, curling his fingers around her back and kneading his palms into her skin.

She let out a low, throaty moan. Need, want, and desire collided as her back arched and her breasts reached toward him, almost as if in supplication. Max didn't want to deny her.

And he could no longer deny himself.

Four

One night. Toni told herself she'd earned one night with this very special man. Then she could hang on to the memories and get on with her busy life. She refused to let herself dwell on what kind of emptiness that life would hold now that she'd known Max.

He'd settled her on the table and the lacquer felt cool against her hot, fevered skin, making her more aware of her surroundings and what was to come. She spread her thighs and he stepped inside, then bent his head and captured her nipple in his mouth, suckling her through the filmy black lace. His teeth grazed her flesh, then his tongue soothed and white-hot darts of need pulsed inside her. Her reaction was immediate, the pull starting at point of contact and causing intense contractions deep in her belly and down lower.

"You like that?"

Her answer came out a low, husky growl.

"Is that a yes?" He cradled her tender flesh in one hand and treated her other breast to the same lavish attention as the first.

She squirmed against the hard surface and slick moisture trickled between her legs as warmth and desire exploded inside her. "That's a yes."

He lifted his head and met her gaze. "You like to play."

"When it goes both ways." She raised her hands, placing both palms not just on his bare chest, but against his nipples.

Slowly, she raked her nails downward, watching, gratified, as his eyes glazed with heated emotion.

He groaned aloud. "You have no idea what you do to me."

"Oh, I think I can guess." Because she knew what *he* did to her. Every nerve ending came to life, raw and exposed, sizzling with live currents of desire.

"No need to guess when I can show you," he said, bringing his mouth down hard on hers. Frenzied, his kiss expressed an immediate need to be as close as possible.

His tongue swept inside the deep recesses of her mouth, mimicking the ultimate act. It wasn't a joining of bodies in the biblical sense, but another, just as intimate means of climbing toward satisfaction. His strong hands slid from her waist to her thighs and he grazed the tops of her stockings with his thumbs while his fingertips teased the outer edges of her panties. With his whisper-soft and erotically arousing movements, he let her know what he had in store.

And Toni wanted, more. She arched her back and her hips jerked forward, reflexively, searching for his harder, deeper touch. He didn't deny her. He broke the kiss and concentrated on her need, cupping her feminine mound in his palm. The heat and weight of his hand against her barely covered flesh stirred long-dormant sensations and when he pushed aside the thin lace and dipped his fingers inside her moist, waiting heat, she thought she'd died and gone to heaven.

She was hot and aroused, on the brink of falling over a precipice, a tumble she had no desire to take alone. She leaned back to catch her breath, intending to make her desire known and she caught a glimpse of their position. She was barely dressed, her legs spread wide, with Max's lean body settled between them. She was open and vulnerable, physically as well as emotionally. The intimacy they were sharing struck her as strongly as her rampaging emotions. And when he leaned over, covering her body with his so he could rest his cheek against hers, he found a way closer to her heart.

She shut her eyes against the wave of emotion she wasn't ready to deal with and instead wrapped her legs around his waist in a provocative suggestion. "Make love to me, Max."

His deep blue eyes met hers. "Be sure, Toni." His breathing was as ragged as her emotions. "Because if we go any further there's no way I can stop."

She'd come into this night with seduction in mind and though everything had changed, including the man, there was no way she could walk away from him now. Still, he had to understand her behavior wasn't normally so wanton. She didn't know why it mattered so much, but it did.

She caressed his face with one hand. "I wouldn't have asked you if I wasn't sure, but . . ."

He grabbed for her hand. "But what?"

"No matter how bold I've been tonight, I want you to know I don't usually sleep with a man I just met."

"I know."

"You do?"

He nodded. "Because I feel like I've known you all my life."

She felt the same but couldn't bring herself to admit the truth out loud. She licked her already moist lips. "There's something else you need to know." She couldn't think beyond now. Not that he'd asked, but the emotional pull between them was too strong to ignore.

He shook his head. "Enough talking, don't you think?" To make his point, he slipped one finger back into her panties, parting her sensitive folds and moving his fingertip deeply inside her.

She closed her eyes and exhaled a soft moan as he encountered the desire he'd created inside her.

"So wet, so ready for me."

The man did have a point. "Talking can wait." She forced her heavy eyelids open. "So what did you have in mind?"

"I'm going to do, what you asked, sweetheart. I'm going to make love to you. But I want you to do something for me first." He reached into his front pocket and pulled out the anklet she'd had on earlier in the evening.

She eyed the object with surprise.

"I took it from the car." He answered her unspoken question and shook the accessory in the air. The light chime of bells echoed in the silent bar. "Wear these for me."

Her heart beat out a rapid pulse and excitement tingled inside her. "Mind if I ask why?" she asked, curiously aroused by the suggestion.

"I want to hear bells when I come inside you," he said and his blue eyes flared with heat. "And ever time you hear the ringing of chimes, I want you to think of me."

She never broke eye contact as she raised her leg and

perched it on the edge of the table. With a nod of approval, he turned to his task, taking his time, rolling the stocking down her leg, inch by tantalizing inch. When he finished one, she propped her other leg so he could peel off another of her few remaining layers.

Then he snapped the anklet closed. "Perfect," he said, taking in her wanton pose.

With her legs spread wide, Toni ought to be embarrassed, but all she felt was a keen sense of carnal anticipation. "Well, you've got me where you want me."

She shifted her leg, shaking her foot so he could hear the light tinkling of bells. To her surprise, the sound turned from light and playful to highly erotic, charging the already electric atmosphere even further. "So what do you plan to do with me?"

With her help, he eased the last remaining undergarment off her legs, letting her panties fall to the floor. "I already told you. I'm going to make love to you." Then he knelt down, dipped his head, and proceeded to do just that, in a way she hadn't expected or anticipated. In a way much more intimate than she'd imagined.

His hot breath covered her feminine mound and his tongue delved deep into her core. Resting back on her elbows, she gave herself up to sensation, to the masterful strokes and fiery darting motions that had her hips gyrating and her body arching, beseeching him for more. He complied, bringing her higher, nearly to the brink of orgasm.

"Max!" She writhed beneath him, unable to express her desire further, not with her body tense and her climax so close. But she knew she didn't want her first time to be alone. Wonderful yet unfulfilling at the same time. He seemed to understand because his nuzzling caresses slowed and the waves subsided, leaving her empty.

Next thing she knew, she was being lifted and carried in his arms. "We're going where?" she wondered aloud, her body protesting the very cessation of pleasure she'd asked for.

"Upstairs." Max made his way to the back door and up a dimly lit staircase. "Somehow, thoughts of our first, time on a pool table don't work for me."

Not that he'd had the presence of mind to realize that before she'd called out his name, he thought. Prior to that moment, he'd have taken her on the hard surface without thought or reason, he'd been so far gone. Lost in her dewy essence.

"See? I told you you were a nice guy." Her arms snaked around his neck, her bare body crushed against his chest. "Now hurry."

He managed a laugh, barely able to make his way up the stairs, open his door, and hit the bedroom before lowering her to the bed and sealing his mouth to hers. But kissing wasn't enough for either of them and her hands fumbled with the snap on his jeans. Frustrated with the barrier between them, he rose to shuck his pants and briefs, and to dig protection from the back of his nightstand drawer, not an easy task in the dim room, lit only by the glow of light from the street lamp outside.

As he knelt over her, a wash of emotion swept through him, strong and tender, something he knew damn well he'd never felt before. He cupped her thighs, widening her legs, then slid his fingers over her damp flesh. He met her velvet gaze, watched as her eyes glazed at the same moment her hips rose in response to the slick strokes of his hand.

A soft purr escaped her throat, a sound of frustrated need.

"Just making sure you're ready for me, sweetheart."

"I am." She took him by surprise, managing to flip him

to his side, switching their positions, her ending up on top. "I realize you're trying to be a gentleman our first time." Toni swung her leg over his until she straddled his thighs. "But there's no reason to wait."

"I like the way you think." And he more than liked her.

After making use of the condom he'd found earlier, he grasped her hips, fully participating as she lowered herself onto his hard erection. He gritted his teeth as heaven surrounded him and he entered her tight, moist heat.

She let out a shuddering sigh. "It's . . ." She bit down on her lower lip. "It's never been like this before." Awe and something more infused her voice, letting him know she felt not just the physical, but the emotional connection, as well.

Needing to touch her in other ways, he lifted his upper body to meet her lips in a too brief kiss before leaning back against the pillows. She shifted slightly and his bod shook with the restraint of holding back, of letting her mentally adjust to a connection he'd already recognized and accepted.

He reached up to unhook the clasp of her bra and she let the flimsy garment fall to the side, revealing twin mounds of rounded flesh. Her black hair fell over her shoulders, in stark contrast to her pale skin. He'd never seen a more incredible sight. His body swelled and hardened further while her muscles contracted to accommodate him, arousing him even more.

Max had said he felt as if he'd known her forever, and cocooned inside her, he knew he was right. His heart pounded as hard and fast as the adrenaline flowing through him. And then she began to move, beginning a rhythm he picked up immediately. Each circular motion built upon the alread growing waves rocking his body. Every clench of her thighs ground their bodies more intimately and drove him that much deeper inside her. Fire licked at his skin and waves of desire pushed him higher, and from the soft cries escaping her lips, he knew she felt it, too.

Carnal sensation mixed with a basic awareness. He'd had sex before, but Toni was right. They were making love.

He glided inside, her tight, slick passage accepting him, taking, him with her just as her frenzied movements carried her up and over the edge.

"Max." She cried out his, name, her body pulsing around his, beckoning him to follow. And as his climax hit, engulfing him in sensation, Max heard the ringing of bells.

Toni curled her legs beneath her and poked around in the candy dish he'd brought from his small kitchen. She clenched her thighs together and the waves of awareness hit her once more. How could she still be so sensitive and aroused?

She glanced over at Max through hooded eyes. He watched her intentl , not saying a word. What was there to say? What they'd just shared defied description. Though she knew she'd clammed up on him afterward, her thoughts were in turmoil. She'd planned a seduction she could walk away from, not a relationship that would be hard to let go of. But no matter how she tried to tell herself she barely knew him, he'd not only touched her body, he'd touched her heart.

"Do you always work up such an appetite?" He rested his arm across the pillows, skimming his fingertips along her shoulders.

"I already told you I don't do this often, so how do you expect me to answer that?" She knew she'd snapped and held up her hands in apology. "I don't know what's wrong with me."

"I do."

He gently took the bowl out of her hands and placed it on the nightstand. "It was intense and it scared you."

She narrowed her gaze, not sure if she liked how well he read her. "If that's the case then how come you're so calm and composed?"

He took her hand, his thumb tracing slow circles into her palm and her stomach curled with warmth. "I'm a jaded guy who's been around?" he said lightly.

Toni sensed more beneath his words but she couldn't tell if she was projecting her hopes and dreams into his unspoken words.

"And if I'm not thrown, I think the more important question is how come you *are?*" he asked.

She bit down on her lower lip. She couldn't very well tell him she'd slept with him wanting only one night. For one thing it was callous, and regardless of what he wanted from her, she had no desire to hurt him. And for another, what she'd wanted going into this night was no longer what she desired now.

Now she wanted a chance to see where things with Max could lead, but the thought frightened her be ond reason. After all, what did she know of long-term, stable relationships? Of depending on another person when she only knew how to depend on herself? Most of all, she feared losing her independence to a man and what it could cost her.

But she wanted to learn about sharing and caring, and she wanted to see that being in a relationship didn't mean losing the autonomy she cherished. She wanted to learn all those things.

With Max.

"Let's say you're right." She forced herself to meet his compassionate and oh-so-sex gaze. "And let's say what's between us is passionate and . . ."

"Intense." He treated her to his most charming grin.

Then again, an grin she'd seen from him was appealing and her heart twisted with emotion. "Okay, intense. It's been one night. What exactl are you proposing we do about it?" she asked and her heart clenched with possibilities.

In response, he pulled her into his arms and toppled her to the mattress, sandwiching her body between his and the bed. "I suggest we go with the flow and see where things lead."

And if his hard erection against her stomach was any indication, she knew exactly where the were headed. At least for now. "You do know how to tempt me." And going with the flow wasn't a high-pressure situation.

In fact, it was one she couldn't wait to handle. She reached down and grasped his hard erection in her hands. He exhaled and a masculine groan reverberated from his body through hers.

He somehow managed a harsh laugh. "Tempting you is a pleasure." He brushed a sweet kiss across her lips. "Then I have one da at a time to show ou we can be as good out of bed as in."

His hips jerked forward, brushing against her thigh. Heat rocked her and arousal began a steady pulsing rhythm.

Toni closed her eyes. Easier to concentrate on the physical than on the emotional, she thought, letting sensation take over. He had only to let his desire be known and her body came alive.

"Look at me."

She opened her eyes but she wasn't able to meet his gaze.

"I'm not going to let you hide from me." He cupped her cheek in his hand but didn't turn her head for her.

The tender gesture brought an unnerving lump to her

throat. Not only did he understand her so well but he cared, too. What they'd found in one night was rare and special and she sensed he felt it, too.

She fought the inclination to flee and met his patient gaze. "I don't want to hide from you." Her words came out a whisper and she realized she meant it. Reservations be damned.

"Then don't." Max pulled the covers back, revealing their bare bodies to the cooler air, then reached over and turned on a bedside lamp. He wanted her trust, wanted no secrets, no clothing, not even darkness between them. Physical intimacy was the only way he knew how to start.

The rest would have to come. They'd already made love once, and when they did again, there'd be no hiding.

For either of them.

He caressed her body with his gaze, following the slender lines and full curves, appreciation and more settling inside him. Then he watched as she did the same. She took in his body, her eyes widening as they traveled from his face, down to the erection he couldn't hide.

"What do you want from me?" she asked softly, but he had a hunch she already knew because as she spoke, she slid backward, settling into the pillows behind her.

Her black hair fanned across the ivory sheets. *His* sheets. A primitive urge to possess her, to make her his again—this time forever—took hold. "I want ever thing, sweetheart. But I'll take as much as you're willing to give."

He inched forward, making his way toward her. Her eyes lit with excitement and desire, diluted by an apprehension only his time and trust could overcome.

She surprised him by extending her arms. "I want to make love to you, Max. Lights on, nothing hidden."

Her vulnerability hit him hard where it counted most—his heart.

* * *

Toni awoke feeling decadent and relaxed after falling asleep without trouble for the first time in ages. Of course her late-night activity could have had something to do with that. So could her . . . lover.

Lover. She tested the word on her tongue, realizing it was too generic, too detached and indifferent, to describe their encounter. Whatever sexual relationships she'd had in the past, no one had made it past the walls she'd built up since she'd been a child. How could any man have gotten inside her when she'd feared emotional closeness would result in unhealthy dependence? But Max had not only found her heart, she'd willingly let him in.

"Max?" She sat up in bed, realizing she was alone.

Noise from the shower in the bathroom alerted her to his location. She was in Max's bedroom while he showered for the day. Soon he'd come out—would he wrap a towel around his neck? His waist? Neither? Curling her legs beneath her, she forced deep breaths into her lungs. Whatever sharing a morning together entailed, it couldn't be any more intimate than the night they'd just spent.

And it wasn't reason for panic, she told herself, until the waves of anxiety began to ease. The man wasn't asking her for anything more than she was willing to give, and a nurturing, caring relationship would be a wonderful start to both the holiday season and a brand-new year.

The ringing of the telephone startled her and the answering machine picked up soon after. "Hi, Max." Toni recognized Stephan's voice. "Dad tells me you'll be running the new office. Since Santa's helper will be your assistant, it won't be too much of a strain," he said, a wry sound to his voice. "You owe me one. Later, big brother."

No sooner had Stephan's, voice clicked off than Toni

tossed the covers off, adrenaline flowing fast in her veins. Or maybe she was feeling a full-blown anxiety attack coming on. Was this fate's version of a joke? Or was she being punished for her descent into the world of the less repressed?

Where were her clothes? She glanced around the room, desperate to find something to put on. She'd finally found a man she could relate to, a man she desired, a man she trusted enough to let down her guard with.

And he'd be her new boss. A man she'd slept with the first night they'd met. A man who was now in control of her job—the symbol of the very independence she cherished. One-night stand or full-blown affair, it didn't matter. Because office romances never worked out, and when they fell apart, who was the one gone? Not the boss, but the coworker. Office-wrecker.

She'd be out on her ear, no job, no references, no money—her blessed independence shot to hell, all because she'd fallen for the wrong man. "Where are my clothes?" she wailed aloud.

Downstairs. Scattered around the poolroom. She rolled her eyes, realizing her life had taken on surreal proportions. Her gaze fell to a pile of clothes on the chair which obviously substituted for a laundry hamper or a closet. She grabbed a sweatshirt and then turned to the desk and pilfered a sheet of paper.

"Dear Max," she wrote, feeling as if it were like "Dear John" and hating herself for it. She finished her letter, hoping what she said would be enough to save, if not her job, then at least a letter of recommendation for a position at a new firm. Starting over, Toni thought. Like her mother had each time she'd tried to make a stand and failed.

Her stomach clenching, she bolted for the door without looking back.

Five

Max looped a towel around his neck and headed out of the bathroom. He had to be at his parents' house early but damned if he'd miss one minute of time he could spend with Toni—who, he realized, was nowhere to be found.

Max glanced around but all he saw was a rumpled bed. "Son of a bitch." He muttered more under his breath.

He didn't need to look around his small apartment. Every instinct he had and prided himself on told him she was gone. What he didn't know was why.

He ran a frustrated hand through his hair. Yes he did. He knew exactly why she'd bolted. Fear, pure and simple. Because Max Corbin, ace detective, had made a major miscalculation when dealing with a vulnerable, skittish woman. Despite her calculated seduction, he didn't kid himself that Toni was anything less than vulnerable. That innocence was what held him in thrall. Her beauty would never fade but her looks weren't what had caused him to fall so damn hard. It was the whole package.

And Max had blown it. He'd tread lightly when he should have hit harder. He'd kept his feelings to himself, afraid of frightening her after one night. Maybe if he'd let her know he was certain they had long-term written all over them, she'd still be in his bed and not on her way back to New York City.

"Damn." Curses and regrets were the only things he could manage about now. He walked to the bed the 'd shared and lowered himself onto the mattress. The sheets had cooled but his body hadn't. Not even a cold shower could dull the aching need she inspired.

He glanced at the clock but a folded note blocked his view of the numbers and his stomach plummeted as he read her hastily scrawled words. "Dear Max, Please remember I don't normally sleep with men I don't know. And don't hold last night against me. Toni."

Confusion mingled with a deep pain in his gut as he realized what she must have felt on waking up alone. Another reason to kick himself in the ass, Max thought. He should have let his family wait, and would have if not for his father's frail health.

Another choice curse rose to his throat but he stifled it, knowing it would do no good. He just needed to find Toni. He crumpled the note and tossed it to the nightstand, noticing his blinking answering machine for the first time. He wondered who'd called so early and hit play.

Listening to his brother's message provided not only insight into Toni's run but another reason to kick himself hard. Only Max would understand the sarcasm in the message and the fact that his brother was giving him a headsup before his meeting with the old man. Only Max and Stephan realized he had no intention of returning to

Corbin and Sons. But Toni, to whom he'd admitted his biggest failing and disappointment, might well believe he'd want to make his sick father happy.

She obviously thought she'd slept with her boss. For a woman who needed security as much as other people needed air to breathe, that had to have been one hell of a slap in the face.

Max pulled on his jeans and made his way down to the empt bar. The pool table was just as they'd left it last night, but Toni had retrieved her clothing. Not a trace of her remained except in Max's heart.

Max entered his brother's luxury condo, an apartment opposite in furnishing and feel from Max's own casual over-the-bar rental.

"So what brings you to my neck of the woods?" Stephan asked, gesturing to a chair in the kitchen.

Max shook his head. He didn't have time to sit. Still, his brother had asked a fair question since Max couldn't remember the last time he'd shown up here unannounced. But today was different, just as his relationship with his twin had undergone a subtle shift since last night. Many things had changed since last night, he thought wryly.

Including his priorities. Max had driven into the city, postponing his meeting with his father in favor of finding Toni. Unfortunately, he had no idea where to begin, so he'd landed on his brother's doorstep first. Swallowing both his pride and his rule against talking about the women he slept with, Max unloaded on his brother. It was the first time in too damn long he'd had a heart-to-heart with his twin. Realizing how much he missed it and seeing the same in Stephan's face, Max knew the distance had closed.

Distance Max had placed there for no good reason. Just

as Toni's insecurities drove her to succeed and to bolt this morning, Max now knew his own insecurities had driven him from his family. He planned to rectify both his and Toni's misperceptions—immediately.

Max finished relating last night's history to his brother.

Stephan nodded, while shaking his head at the same time. "I'm glad to see you screw up every once in a while. Makes the rest of us feel like you're human, too."

"Come again?" Max raised an eyebrow. "I screw up more than once in a while. Isn't that what Dad always says?"

"Dad says it to instill guilt and you buy into it every time. But you alwa s hold your ground and live your life. To me that's not screwing up, that's playing it smart. A part of me has always envied that."

Shock rendered Max mute. For twins, he and his brother had been operating on opposite wavelengths for too long. "You don't want to be a lawyer?" Max asked.

"I never gave it a thought. It was expected and I followed through. Now it's all I know and I can't imagine doing anything else. But sometimes I wonder 'what if.'" He shrugged. "Then I take a look at how following a different road has kept you far from the family and I figure I'll accept my life as it is. But in case you're wondering, distancing yourself is the only screwup I think you've made." His brother let out a wry laugh. "Until now."

"Now meaning Toni." Just saying her name caused the, twisting in Max's gut to return. He had the rest of his life to process his brother's admission and make things right. He had too little time to catch Toni and explain before she withdrew for good. "I need her address."

"There's no point." Stephan pushed off the wall and headed for the mugs in the cabinet. "Coffee?"

"No, thanks, and why the hell not?"

"She's not at home. I stopped by the office to pick up a file and she was there sorting through boxes." Stephan laughed. "Damn but you need to calm down."

"After I talk to her."

His brother eyed him in surprise. "This is a hell of a lot more than a one-night stand, isn't it?"

Max clenched and unclenched his fists. "It'd better be or I'm looking at a lousy Christmas and a miserable New Year."

"Well, I'll be damned. I wonder what I missed in her."

"Too late for you to find out now," Max said in warning, turned and started for the door before spinning back to face his brother. "Hey, Stephan, I owe you one for the heads-up on what the old man wanted."

His twin shrugged. "I figured since you showed up last night, it was the least I could do."

Max laughed. Showing up had brought Toni into his life. "Then it looks like I owe you double. See ya later." Max opened the door and stepped into the hall.

"Don't think for one minute that I won't cash in," Stephan called as Max slammed the door shut behind him.

Toni needed to keep busy or else she'd think and she could not afford to think. Not about last night and how much she'd enjoyed herself, not about Max and how much she'd grown to like and care for him, and certainly not about the fact that she'd slept with her new boss. What irony. After years of avoiding the situation with Stephan, she'd stepped right into it with his twin.

She let out a slow breath of air. Okay, apparently she couldn't avoid thinking but maybe she could drown out the sound of her own thoughts. She flipped on the radio in her near empty office. As expected, Christmas music filled the air. She tried humming and when that didn't work she sealed the last box, while singing out loud, but no way could she escape the fact that she'd fallen in love with Max Corbin.

Fallen in love. She shook her head, unable to believe the truth. She was a woman who hadn't grown up watching a loving relationship and who'd never once deluded herself that happily ever after was in her future. Yet in one meeting, over the course of one night—one glorious night—she'd fallen in love. And all the security she'd worked for, all the independence she'd strived for, now hung in the balance.

Her heart beat out a rapid cadence, panic and other undefinable emotions parading inside her while the music mocked her thoughts. No merry Christmas, no happy new year for her this year. She closed her eyes, singing the final verse along with the song. "We wish you a merry Christmas, we wish you a merry Christmas, we wish you a merr Christmas . . . and you're out on our ear." Toni added her own ending to the well-known tune.

"Is that really what you think of me?"

Startled, Toni whirled around to find herself face-to-face with Max. Leaning against her doorframe, he was the epitome of her fantasy come to life. And to think, she hadn't known she had any. "Hello, Max."

He inclined his head. "Toni."

She attempted to swallow but her mouth was too dry. "What are you doing here?"

"I wanted to get a few things straight." He walked into her office, making the small area even smaller by virtue of his overwhelming presence.

She grasped the cardboard edges of the box. "I can tender my resignation if it would make things easier." She spoke without meeting his gaze.

She heard him exhale hard. "Again, is that what you think of me? Do you really believe I'd have taken you home and made love to ou, knowing I was your boss, and then demanded your job the next day?"

Toni wondered if she imagined the hurt in his voice. She shook her head. "Truthfully, I haven't thought things through."

"No, you're just feeling, aren't you?" His voice softened. "Acting on instinct and fear."

"What do you expect, Max? I woke up to find out I had slept with my soon-to-be-boss. Whose job is on the line now? Yours or mine?"

"No one's, I hope." He eased himself onto the edge of her desk, too close for her peace of mind.

So close she could inhale his masculine scent and arousal hit her all over again, but he wasn't asking permission and she wasn't in a position to argue. "So you're suggesting we put last night behind us and work together?" She tried to laugh but the sound was harsh and she didn't mean it anyway.

If he could work side by side with her, after what they'd shared, she'd misjudged him. Yet even before she met his serious and compelling gaze, she knew better. How could she not? She'd accepted him into her body, felt him hard and hot inside her, giving as much as he got in return.

Then there were the emotional revelations, Toni thought. Men didn't open up and share unless they cared. But she was still at a loss.

"I'm not suggesting we work together, either. I told you last night I do my own thing. And yes, my father's disappointed, and no, he's not finished trying to convince me to return. But he's been unsuccessful in the past and he'll continue to be unsuccessful in the future. Law isn't what I want. I am *not* going to be your boss."

She glanced down and saw her hands were shaking. "But Stephan said . . ."

"Stephan was giving me advance warning about what to expect at my meeting with Dad. You heard what Dad wants, not what will be." He touched her cheek, his hand strong and gentle. "But that's not the real issue, is it?"

She forced herself to meet his gaze. "If you know so much, then tell me what is."

"I'm not your boss. I'm just a man who's desperately in love with you. So the issue is, are you going to run from your feelings because of your past? Or are you going to stay and face them . . . and give us a chance?"

In that instant, Toni's past and present flashed in front of her eyes, a kaleidoscope of memories, some good, some bad, some satisfying, but way too many lonely ones. Lonely by choice not necessity, she thought. Last night she'd chosen Max and last night she hadn't felt alone or isolated.

She was a woman who'd always prided herself on her ability to stand on her own two feet, yet she wanted nothing more than to throw herself into his arms.

"So what are you waiting for?" he asked.

She blinked, refocusing on her surroundings. On Max. "Did I speak out loud?"

He watched her intently. "No, I'm just a mind reader."

Her mind was jumbled, her heart racing, and his earlier words came back to her. "What did you say?"

"I'm just a mind reader."

"Before that."

"I'm not your boss," he said.

"In between those two things."

"I'm a man desperately in love with you?" He grinned.

His devastating smile nearly knocked her off her feet and a sparkle twinkled in his blue eyes. A weight she hadn't been aware of carrying her whole life eased and lifted inside her.

She could run and hide or give the future a chance. No contest, Toni thought, a smile pulling at her lips.

"I asked what you're waiting for?" His voice was gruff with emotion, his once-certain smile faltered as his insecurity became obvious.

More than anything else, his ability to own up to his feelings and emotions touched her heart. She could free hers and learn from him. Be independent and still be in love.

If she dared.

His gaze locked with hers. He lifted his hand, revealing a green sprig of mistletoe and holding it up high. "I thought we could try it again." He extended his free hand, holding it out to her. "Get it right this time."

Toni rushed into his arms and Max lowered his head for a kiss that felt too long in coming. He'd never admit it out loud but she'd had him sweating there for a minute. But now she was his.

Her lips were soft and willing, welcoming him. His hands slipped around her waist, beneath the band of her sweatshirt until he encountered soft skin. She let out a faint sigh and leaned back against the desk, letting his body mesh with hers. Her thighs spread and his groin settled hard against her stomach.

But warning bells went off in his head. "Not again, sweetheart. Not until we've got a few things settled."

"Mmm." She purred in his ear and her hand slipped to the bulge in his jeans.

Max nearly caved right then, but knowing his future was on the line, he forced himself to pull back. He'd messed up once and she'd run at the first opportunity. He wasn't about to screw up again. "I love you" was saying a hell of a lot for a man who'd always lived alone—but it wasn't a declaration of future intent. And a woman like Toni both deserved and needed one.

And for the first time, Max realized, so did he. "Toni."

She met his gaze.

"I don't usually sleep with women I just met."

She grinned. "That's good because I feel as if I've known you all my life."

"Then prove it. I'm a slob. I don't put my clean clothes away, I wear them straight from a pile on the chair. I squeeze the toothpaste from the middle, I drink milk out of the carton, and those are the positives." He paused, deadly serious. "But I still think we have a chance."

Her eyes were misty and damp but her smile never dimmed. "I've been known to hang stockings from door-knobs and eat Chinese food out of the carton. For breakfast." She smoothed one hand down his thigh, the other hand never leaving its strategic position on his groin.

His body protested his prolonged wait in making her his but his mind and heart knew he was doing it right this time. "I go to sleep too late and wake up too early. But I promise to give you the best that I've got to make us work. You can trust me and you never have to fear me—" Max never got to finish.

She covered his mouth with hers in the sweetest, hot-test, most honest kiss he'd ever known. He paused only to slam her door closed and undress her, dropping his jeans as quickly as possible. He entered her quickly, this time on the desk she'd be leaving behind. When the aftershocks subsided, his body was still deep inside hers.

"This was naughty," she murmured.

"I thought that was your plan."

She laughed. "Only with you, Max. You bring out my decadent side."

"My pleasure, sweetheart. It's something I plan on doing again." His groin began to harden once more, and Max proceeded to seal their bodies, just as they'd sealed their future. Being naughty under the mistletoe.

Some Kind of Wonderful

Beth Ciotta

One

Nothing says holidays like a fruitcake cupcake! ~Daisy Monroe

"Talk about your winter wonderland. Is this place for real? Are you sure we didn't drive through some sort of wormhole that redirected us to the North Pole?"

Nerves brittle from navigating a snowstorm in a cheap-a-zoid rental car, Maya Templeton glanced at her friend and business partner, Giselle (just Giselle), as they breached the limits of Maya's hometown. "Is that your way of saying Sugar Creek looks like Santa's Village?"

Tricked out in festive decorations, the two-story brick-faced mom-and-pop boutiques featured regional novelties, season's tidings, and bountiful holiday specials and sales. Even the most down-and-out shopper would be able to find a meaningful gift within their restricted budget.

"I'm surprised you ever moved away," Giselle said. "This place has you written all over it."

"Except it doesn't look magical year-round," Maya said while focusing on the icy road. "Just around Christmas."

And especially in the midst of a snowstorm.

Peering through the frosty windshield was like looking into a snow globe, the old-fashioned scenery reminiscent of a Norman Rockwell painting. Enchanting innocence with a dash of whimsy.

Considering the location and purpose of Maya's self-started business, you'd think she'd be numb to magic. Cupcakes & Dreamscapes operated out of Orlando, Florida—a city that boasted multiple theme parks. A city that perpetuated whimsy. Then again there was all kinds of magic. Whereas Orlando had death-defying amusement rides and dazzling production shows . . . Sugar Creek had heart.

"Quaint, but small," Giselle said as they crawled down Main Street. "And from what you told me most everything closes by six. No dance clubs or martini bars. No concert halls or theme parks. I'm pretty sure I'd die of boredom."

"You'd absolutely die of boredom." Maya noted her dark and sultry business partner, wishing she possessed half her charisma. And, okay, maybe Maya was a smidgeon envious of Giselle's exotic and curvaceous blessings. When she walked into a room all heads turned—male *and* female. Although Maya wouldn't give up brains for beauty. Not that Giselle was dense, just . . . reckless. A bona fide adrenaline junkie, Giselle got her kicks on roller coasters and the stage (or any venue that provided her with an audience). A professional actress, she operated the "Dreamscape" portion of their co-owned company, appearing as select "characters" and performing interactive games and adventures with the party guests—most usually children. Maya handled the custom-made "Cupcakes" and bookkeeping. Their personalities were vastly different, yet they clicked to the tune of a healthy friendship and lucrative business.

Giselle fidgeted in her seat, then rooted in her purse. "I can't believe how nervous I am about meeting Zach. My freaking palms are sweating."

Zach.

Heart thumping, Maya flexed her hands on the wheel as she made a left onto Maple Avenue, her mind awash with childhood memories. Zachery Cole was also a native of Sugar Creek. He was Maya's oldest friend and at one time he'd been her closest. Sadly, they'd grown apart after she'd gone off to a top-notch pastry school and he'd joined . . . *The Few. The Proud. The Marines.*

She remembered the first time she'd seen a televised recruitment advertisement—long before that famous slogan had been introduced. She'd been ten and she'd been with Zach. She'd seen his eyes light up and his shoulders roll back. He'd only been eleven at the time, but she'd known then and there he was serious about serving—like his father and his grandfather before him. He'd enlisted in the Marine Corps straight out of high school. Then there'd been 9/11—that awful attack on home soil—and Zach hadn't been able to blast through training fast enough. He'd aimed high. Just like Maya. Only his goals involved vanquishing evil with specialized skills and rifles. Maya championed good via cupcakes and fairy tales.

Like Maya and Giselle, Maya and Zach were opposites. The diplomat and dreamer versus the rebel and realist. Yet he'd been her best friend. Someone who held a special place in her heart.

And she'd set him up with her beautiful and charismatic business partner.

"I've read those letters and e-mails you composed for me a million times," said Giselle.

"A million?"

"Okay, maybe a dozen. The point is I've read them a

lot. I'm not keen on going blank if Zach asks me to expand on something *I* supposedly wrote."

Maya wasn't keen on that happening either. She still couldn't believe she'd pulled a Cyrano de Bergerac.

Thirteen months ago, while feeling lonely and nostalgic, Maya had been going through her scrapbooks, reliving some of the best times of her life through a collection of photographs. Snapshots of Maya and her best friend, Zach—from ages eight to eighteen. Then there were random photos Zach had occasionally sent of himself over the last several years. They hadn't stayed in constant touch, but they did send cards and notes on holidays and other special occasions. Giselle had walked in while Maya had been admiring a photo of Zach decked out in his dress blues. It had been lust at first sight for Giselle, and Maya had been certain Zach would drool over a picture of G as well. That's when Maya had had the bright idea of setting her friends up as pen pals. What deployed soldier wouldn't want to correspond with a superhot woman like Giselle? G, who didn't have a shy bone in her curvaceous body, had jumped at the chance to hook up as Zach's "pen pal." Sending sexy pictures of herself? No problem. But composing something more than a 140-character tweet?

Why Maya had ever agreed to help Giselle write several letters and answer the occasional e-mail from Zach was a mystery. A lapse in judgment. A moment of insanity. But Giselle, whose many talents did not extend to creating intelligent, engaging prose, had begged Maya's help. And Maya, who'd wanted to provide Zach with a mindless, playful fantasy during his dreary and dangerous time on foreign soil, had complied. She'd been so focused on providing Zach with an element of sexy escapism and so entranced with his sexy responses, she'd lost herself in the fantasy, giving little thought to Zach and Giselle meeting in person. Especially since he'd cooled on the epistolary liaison a few months back. Whether out of boredom or due to his combat situation Maya didn't know.

She hadn't anticipated his sudden and surprising leap from Gunnery Sergeant to civilian. She hadn't anticipated her own parents, who'd moved to the Sunshine State five years prior, booking a Christmas cruise, leaving Maya to fend for herself over her favorite holiday. She hadn't anticipated the invitation to join the Coles for Christmas in Sugar Creek or Giselle's insistence to tag along.

The thing that worried Maya most was that the invitation hadn't come from Zach himself. This was a surprise visit arranged by his great-aunt, Helen Cole. Helen was a senior member of the local charitable club, the Cupcake Lovers, a club Maya had admired since she'd been old enough to appreciate their noble mission as well as their unique recipes. If Maya still lived in Sugar Creek, she'd be a member of that club. But she'd had big dreams and those dreams had led her to Orlando. She'd been happy there (although not so much recently), but she'd been happy in Sugar Creek, too. Thanks to Zach, who'd rescued her from a schoolyard skirmish in the second grade and who somehow ended up being her closest friend up until and throughout high school. Theirs had been a unique and cherished bond.

When Helen had called to say her great-nephew had returned unexpectedly to Sugar Creek and that she thought he'd benefit from a surprise visit from his oldest friend, Maya hadn't thought twice. Not to mention, she was curious as to why Zach hadn't informed her he was leaving the military. She never thought she'd see the day, and now that it was here Maya felt unsettled on several counts.

"How much farther to Mrs. Cole's house?" Giselle asked while flipping down the visor mirror and reapplying her already perfectly applied lipstick.

"About five minutes unless I spin out and wreck this miserable excuse of a car. I don't think this thing has front-wheel drive, let alone four-wheel drive. Who loans out a death trap like this knowing Vermont's harsh winters?"

"You've driven two and a half hours in blinding snow and haven't spun out yet. You slid that one time, but for what? A millisecond? I haven't feared for my life even once. Obsess much?"

"Connect with reality much?" Maya breathed deep and tempered her caustic tone. "Sorry. I know you don't know the area. Here's the thing: Normally the drive from Burlington to Sugar Creek takes a little over an hour."

"I may be a southern girl," Giselle said, "but even I know a snowstorm puts a kink in travel time. That said, we're not that much off the mark. If this Cupcake Lover Christmas bash were an evening party instead of an afternoon mixer, we'd be ahead of the game. As it is, we'll only be an hour late." She glanced at her watch. "Scratch that, forty-five minutes late. Not all that late. Fashionably late. All the better to surprise Zach." She squealed as she spritzed perfume. "What fun!"

"We'll see." Maya couldn't shake the feeling that something was wrong. Because of his elite position as a Marine sniper scout, Zach had never shared much about his exact location or assignments. Mostly because of security issues. Not that Maya had ever pressed for details. She knew the gist of Zach's job, and though she knew his motivation and purpose were noble, it wasn't something she felt comfortable dwelling on. Their typical exchanges focused on waxing nostalgic, touching base regarding their families, and providing random updates on Maya's adventures in party planning—hence the natural introduction of Giselle. By keeping their personal correspondence light and mostly rooted in the past, Maya had kept Zach forever young and safe in her heart and mind. She'd kept their relationship chaste and on familiar ground.

It wasn't until she'd stepped out of her safety zone and shared a more sensual part of herself under the guise of Giselle that Maya had connected with Zach on a different level, a level beyond platonic. Even so, he hadn't intimated he'd be leaving the military anytime soon—even to "Giselle." So why now and why had he kept it secret? What's more, why had Helen skirted the subject when Maya had asked the woman outright?

An image flashed in Maya's mind as Helen Cole's house came into view and her meeting with Zach became more imminent. A picture of Zach in his cammies and protective gear, a picture he'd sent to Giselle six months back. He looked handsome and fierce and, as G had pointed out, drool worthy. Maya had always appreciated Zach's good looks, but she'd never lusted after him. Not until she'd read some of the frank and sexy letters he'd written in response to *Giselle's* notes. Not until she'd laid eyes on that photo. Although, unlike G, Maya wasn't dazzled by the sharpshooter rifle clutched in his right hand. She was enamored by the way he hugged the dog on his left. A scraggly mutt he'd rescued from a "precarious situation." Whereas Giselle was attracted to the warrior, Maya was attracted to the savior. The man just inside the house Maya was parking in front of. The same house where, as kids, they'd played hide-and-seek, then, years later, crammed for Algebra exams.

Pulse racing, Maya cut the engine and wrangled her emotions.

Giselle fluffed her luxuriant sable locks. "As you know,

Zach and I were pretty intimate in our correspondence," she said, looking uncharacteristically anxious.

"As close to a threesome as I'll ever get," Maya said, remembering one particularly graphic exchange.

"When we meet I'm wondering if I should shake his hand, hug him, or kiss him."

Maya stared up at the illuminated reindeer and sleigh sitting atop the Coles' roof, remembering the winter she'd braved her fear of heights to help Zach reanchor that same decoration after a powerful windstorm had blown it off. She thought about the, "intimate correspondences" she'd been party to this past year. "Funny," she said, trying to reconcile the Zach of her youth to the Zach who'd recently stirred her soul. "I was wondering the same thing."

Two

Since they were in the business of planning, coordinating, and throwing special events, Maya wasn't the least bit uncomfortable joining a party in progress. Especially since she was acquainted with most everyone in attendance.

Giselle was the ultimate party girl whether she knew anyone or not. She didn't even blink when, after she was greeted at the door by Helen, Daisy Monroe (another senior member of the Cupcake Lovers) whisked her away to pick her brain about the costumed characters at Disney Resorts. Apparently Daisy was now the sometimes mascot of her recently co-purchased café—Moose-a-lotta. Maya didn't get the full story, but she was certain Giselle would fill her in later.

Meanwhile, Maya hung up their coats, then enjoyed a second extended hug from a teary-eyed Helen. "So glad you're here," the older woman said.

"Me, too." Maya's own eyes stung as childhood memories welled. Stepping into Helen and Daniel Cole's house was like stepping into the past. Since Zach's mom (once a widow and now deceased herself) had waitressed the evening shift in a local tavern, Zach had spent his after-school hours here under the watchful eye of his aunt Helen and uncle Dan. Maya had been a frequent guest.

Looking over Helen's shoulder into the bustling living room, Maya recognized older members of the Cupcake Lovers and their spouses, and she thought she recognized Rocky Monroe, Daisy's granddaughter, but she definitely did not see Zach. The scene, however, the furnishings and décor, the scents of homemade cooking and cinnamon potpourri, was so familiar, Maya's heart fairly burst with nostalgic joy.

Some things never change.

Like the various sized, colorfully painted nutcrackers Helen hauled out and arranged atop the fireplace every December and the humongous spruce Daniel always managed to squeeze into the northeast corner of the room. As always, the star topper grazed the eight-foot ceiling and the branches sagged under the weight of numerous Victorian ornaments, metallic garland, and strings and strings of colorful twinkling lights.

The hand-knit stockings pinned to the fireplace mantle. The holly garland wrapped around the staircase banister. The four-foot singing Santa positioned alongside the antique umbrella stand. All familiar. All comforting.

Merry thoughts danced through Maya's travel-fogged brain until Helen grasped her hand and pulled her in the opposite direction of the party, into Daniel's den. "There's something I have to tell you," the woman said in a hushed voice while closing the door behind them. "Don't panic," she said, "but something happened to Zach."

Maya felt nauseous.

"He's okay. Or he will be okay, but he'll never be one hundred percent the way he was."

"Are you saying Zach was injured?" The question scraped Maya's throat like a razor blade, and it was all she could do not to fall back in a chair. Her legs felt *that* shaky. "What happened?"

"I don't know precisely. He won't talk about it." Helen, who now looked twenty years older than her seventy-five, wrung her age-spotted hands. "I didn't mention this to you on the phone, Maya, because I didn't want you to worry the whole way here. He's been stateside now for three months, recovering and undergoing physical therapy. Something to do with his legs. It must have been bad, because he won't be returning to active duty. I don't think they'll let him, even if he eventually conquers that limp. He says he's fine and he looks fine," Helen said. "But his spirit is somber. I keep thinking about the way you two used to laugh. I thought . . ." She broke off and looked over her shoulder. "I should get back to my guests. I just . . . I wanted to break the news to you before you saw him."

Maya palmed her brow, willing her head not to explode. "I don't understand. We traded e-mails over Thanksgiving. He didn't say a word about being injured, let alone being back in the states."

"Don't take it personally, dear. Zach didn't tell anyone."

"Not even you and Daniel?"

She shook her head. "We didn't have a clue until he showed up on our doorstep two weeks ago."

Maya felt her dismay morphing into anger. Why in the world would Zach keep something like this to himself? Why would he pretend . . . "Where is he?"

"In the kitchen having a beer with Sam McCloud. I'm not sure if you'd remember Sam. He's probably ten years older than you. Former military. Widowed father of two and a doozy of a baker. The only male member of the Cupcake Lovers."

The information barely registered in Maya's buzzing ears. "What are they, trading war stories?"

"I don't know about that. As I said, Zach's tightlipped about whatever happened in Afghanistan. If that's even where he was when it happened," Helen said. "Daniel has his doubts."

The more Helen shared, the more Maya's blood burned. "But he's okay, physically, aside from the limp, as far as you know."

Helen nodded, then narrowed her eyes. "Are you upset or angry? I can't tell."

"A little of both."

"I should have broken it to you differently."

"You shouldn't have had to tell me at all, Helen." Maya hugged the woman, then stalked toward the door. "It should have come from Zach."

She couldn't remember the last time she'd been this angry. She couldn't remember anything before five minutes ago when Helen had said, *Something happened to Zach.*

Maya made a beeline for the kitchen by utilizing the back hall. She knew this house well—every room, every closet and hidey-hole. She knew how to get to Zach without having to pass within sight of the living room and partygoers. A blessing considering she would have blown off anyone who tried to say hello. Maya had tunnel vision. One thought, one goal. To get to Zach. To see for herself he was okay. She couldn't think beyond that. Her brain had all but shut down.

Something happened to Zach.

Maya pushed through a side door and into the kitchen. Zach was leaning against the counter, swigging beer alongside another man. Sam, she guessed. Maya only had eyes for Zach, and at first glance, a swift glance, he did indeed look *fine*. He looked whole and healthy, and incredibly handsome in casual trousers, a suit jacket, and an open-necked oxford, his short blond hair sticking out every which way.

Seeing her, Zach set aside his longneck. "Maya?"

Her hearing buzzed. Her vision blurred. A million memories swirled, sucking her back to a time when they'd been as close as pine needles on a twig. Heart pounding, she ran across the room and threw herself into Zach's arms. He felt warm and solid, and when he hugged her tighter she realized she was trembling. She clung, trying to find her voice, her wits. Her eyes burned. "Are you okay?" she croaked.

"Yes."

"Truly?"

He gave her a reassuring squeeze, his own voice tight. "Absolutely."

Blinking back tears, Maya pushed out of Zach's arms, and as she focused on his fit form and the familiar surroundings the world righted. In that instant she regressed twenty years, vibrating with the same rage she'd felt when Zach had taken a spill off his skateboard and instead of bouncing back up had teased her by playing dead. Fuming, Maya punched him in the shoulder. "Bastard."

"I think that's my cue to leave," another voice said.

Maya had forgotten about Sam. Normally she would have been embarrassed by her emotional display. But there was nothing normal about this moment. Her best friend had been severely injured, so much so, he'd spent months recuperating and he hadn't reached out, hadn't confided in family. In her.

Still, she'd been raised to be polite. Glaring at Zach, she

jabbed a hand in greeting at Sam. "I've heard of you, but I don't think we've met. Maya Templeton."

"Sam McCloud." He squeezed her hand in a brief, warm shake. "You live in Florida now, right?"

"Did your parents fly up, too?" Zach asked, holding her gaze but looking puzzled.

"No," she said, crossing her arms over her chest. "My parents took a holiday cruise. Giselle came with me."

Zach just stared.

Sam cleared his throat. "*The* Giselle?"

Maya flicked her gaze to the dark, rugged man, then back to Zach. "You told him about G?" She assumed by Sam's tone that he knew about the sexy letters. Letters she'd had a part in writing. Which made Sam, a man she didn't even know, privy to Maya's sensual side. She wanted to die. She wanted to punch Zach's other shoulder.

Zach shifted his weight, shrugged. "Giselle was a bright spot in a rough year."

Maya's cheeks burned and a weird feeling swirled in her gut. Something dangerously close to jealousy. "Well, your bright spot is only a few steps away, partying in the living room with the Cupcake Lovers. Feel free to bask in her effervescence."

"Definitely my cue." Sam stepped away and dropped his bottle in a recycle bin, "Nice meeting you, Maya," He nodded. "Zach." And then he was gone.

"We need to talk," Zach said to Maya.

"You got that right."

"Not here. Someplace private."

"The pantry." The place where they used to hide and sneak snacks, particularly filched cupcakes. No one would walk in on them there.

"Fine." He reached over and nabbed a dark-colored stick that she hadn't noticed before. A stick with a handle.

A walking aid.

Chest tight, Maya watched as the boy who'd raced her to the ice-cream stand, the man who'd provided reconnaissance and surveillance to an infantry battalion in a harsh, rugged land, hobbled toward the food pantry of his aunt and uncle's home sweet home.

Three

Zach had never been fond of surprises. Especially those laced with danger. In the field, he responded on instinct. On training and experience. He relied on quick thinking and cool confidence, and he almost always mastered the moment.

Almost.

Three months and two weeks ago he'd been coldcocked by a sneak attack that had left him bloody and broken and his spotter (and close buddy) dead.

This day, Zach had been shocked by Maya, who'd breathed life into his comatose heart.

Dodging into the pantry appealed on multiple levels. It harked of simpler times, happier times with the girl who'd been his confidante and friend. A girl who, through e-mails and letters, had recently introduced him to her business partner, whose sexy photos and flirtatious notes had brightened several long and lonely nights. It also afforded him a chance to get his act together in private before rejoining the party. His reaction to seeing Maya, to holding her in his arms, had been unsettling. Even more so than the prospect of meeting Giselle in person.

After flicking on a dim light and shutting the door behind them, Zach followed Maya deeper into the expansive walk-in pantry. Nabbing a step stool and an oversized caramel-popcorn tin, they squeezed past crammed shelves of canned and baking goods and hunkered behind the ceiling-to-floor spice rack. Zach's leg twinged with the effort, but he ignored the pain. Part of him felt ten years old again, without a care more serious than how he was going to earn enough money to buy that superrad mountain bike he'd seen at J. T. Monroe's Department Store. Except the woman sitting across from him barely resembled the gangly-legged, freckle-faced kid he'd given rides to on the handlebars. She didn't even remind him of the high-school junior who'd tutored him on those damned math exams. Or the young woman he'd grilled hamburgers with six years back, during a week when they'd both been back in Sugar Creek visiting family.

Maya's hair was longer and blonder, her skin kissed by the Florida sun. She brushed aside her bangs as she huffed in frustration, and he noticed a slight crinkle in her forehead. A mark of someone who spent a lot of time in deep thought or fierce concentration. A year younger than Zach, Maya was twenty-nine. She'd matured physically in ways that appealed to him as a man. He was especially attracted to her lush mouth. He'd never noticed her lips in a sexual way. He was damn well noticing now. There was also a new edge, a harder edge, to her personality that intrigued and worried him at the same time.

"You called me a bastard," he blurted.

"You're scrutinizing my language?"

"I've never heard you swear."

"I've never been so angry. Criminy, Zach. Why didn't you tell me you were in the hospital? I would have visited."

"That's why I didn't tell you."

"You didn't want me to visit?" Her sweet face screwed up with confusion and hurt. "Why?"

"Remember that time we visited your grandpa at the hospital? How upset you were? How you puked after coming out of his room?"

"I was eleven, for goodness' sake. And he was hooked up to all those tubes and machines. It was scary."

"What about the time we were building that tree fort and Davey Wilcox fell out of the maple and busted his leg? You puked then, too."

"The bone was sticking out of his skin. Jeez, Zach."

"What about the time—"

"Point made. I get queasy when I see people in pain. I can't help that. I feel bad."

Zach reached over and tucked a hank of hair behind her ear. "I didn't want to put you through that. And before you protest, saying you would have managed, which I know, I didn't want to put *myself* through that. I had enough on my plate without seeing the worry in your eyes or anyone one else's. I didn't want your pity or Uncle Dan's tough love. I can't explain exactly, and I don't want to talk about it. Any of it. I just want to move on."

"You're not going to tell me what happened?"

"No."

"Ever?"

"Why are you in Sugar Creek, Maya?"

"Your aunt thought you could use some cheering up."

"Is that why you brought Giselle?"

"She sort of insisted. She's smitten with you."

"She's hot for a soldier."

"She's hot for the man," Maya snapped, getting fired up again. "What? You think she'll be turned off because of your injury? Because of the cane? I'm not."

Zach shifted his weight, rattled once again by a new twist in his relationship with Maya. Something that hadn't been there before. Sexual awareness. He'd felt it in the kitchen when they'd hugged. He felt it now. It was stimulating . . . and unwelcome. With that carnal appeal came a sense of deep caring. This was Maya after all. Zach wasn't ready to care for anyone like that. Not now. Maybe not ever. "We should join the party before someone comes looking. You want Aunt Helen to know about our secret snack hidey?"

"Like we're going to sneak snacks at our age."

Zach cocked his head and forced a playful smile. "You never know."

"You're not going to tell me how you got hurt, are you?"

He shook his head.

"Because you think I can't take it?"

Images flashed in his brain. Memories. Feelings. "No one should have to take it." Zach gripped the handle of his walking stick and pushed to his feet. *Never saw it coming,* Ben had said.

Zach felt the same way about Maya.

He held her green gaze a charged second before holding out his hand and then pulling her to her feet. "How about you introduce me to Giselle?"

Four

Maya had been to some parties from hell in her eight years as a party facilitator, but this one took the cupcake. Instead of enjoying the opportunity to catch up on everyone's lives, she'd smiled and nodded, remembering to respond occasionally, wishing she were anywhere but there. Anyplace where she wouldn't have to watch Zach and Giselle getting to know each other. He was sinfully handsome. She was knockout gorgeous. Physically they made a stunning pair. More than one person had commented to Maya on *that* fact.

How wonderful that your friends became pen pals.
You were sweet to fix them up.
How thoughtful to bring her along.
Now there's a girl to put a hitch in Zach's hitched step.
And from Daisy Monroe: *Those two would make beautiful babies.*

It's not that Maya didn't want Zach to be happy. It's not

that she doubted Giselle deserved someone as wonderful as Zach. It's that Maya felt robbed.

Yes, it had been Giselle's picture he'd drooled over. What man wouldn't admire G's exotic beauty and voluptuous curves? But the letters . . . those letters had been infused with Maya's heart, wit, and affection and, at Giselle's prodding, a couple of Maya's sexual fantasies. If Zach was truly enamored with his "pen pal," then Maya was at least half the reason.

"Your friend is as loveable as you are," Helen said to Maya as Zach ushered the dark-haired bombshell out the front door. "I'm so glad you brought her along. She's good for Zach." The older woman squeezed Maya's waist. "As are you. Why did you beg off when they invited you to join them for a drink?"

"Not keen on being a third wheel."

"You could never be a third wheel with Zach."

If Helen only knew about the "threesome" letters. "Are you sure about Giselle and me staying here?" Maya asked as a way of diverting the conversation. "I did book us a room at the Pine and Periwinkle."

"We have plenty of space," Helen said. "Even with Zach here. Don't insult me, Maya."

"Not in a million years. Of course we'll stay. Thank you, Helen." Maya hoped her smile looked sincere, because she was seriously faking it. She'd never been so confused in her life. Her insides had gone all squishy the moment she'd seen Zach. When he'd hugged her, she'd ached with ravenous desire. When they'd hidden in the pantry, even though she'd been angry with him she'd had some wicked inappropriate impulses. Inappropriate because she and Zach were friends. Longtime friends. Platonic friends. And because he and Giselle—who was also Maya's friend—had a mutual thing for each other. Oh yeah. Maya was the third wheel big-time. Zach and Giselle were headed for the Sugar Shack, Sugar Creek's most popular bar and restaurant. They'd slam back a few drinks, play a game of darts or pool. Zach could play parlor games with a bum leg, right? *Right*. As for Giselle . . . she'd be all over that. Liquor and competition. Bring on the adrenaline. Zach would respond to her charisma and beauty, her unabashed sexuality. They'd hook up in the bathroom or his rented car or, criminy, maybe back in his room. *Or not.* Maybe Maya's imagination was running amok. But they were smoldering and inevitable and Maya wanted to stab a fork in her eye.

Okay. Maybe not anything that extreme, but Maya was definitely on edge. Nerves stretched. Festive spirits challenged. Desperate for distraction, she'd helped Helen clean up after the party. Then she'd sat in front of the cozy fireplace with Helen and Daniel, listening to Christmas carols while catching up on Sugar Creek gossip, then sharing her own latest adventures via Cupcakes & Dreamscapes. At long last they broached the topic uppermost in their minds.

Zach.

"All we know for certain," Daniel said, "is that he's been retired from the military for medical reasons."

"And that he's considering staying on here in Sugar Creek," Helen said, "although I'm not sure what he'd do."

"I think he should look into a position with the SCPD," said Daniel. "He's more than qualified to be a law official."

"Won't there be physical requirements?" Maya asked. "What about his limp?"

"He says he's going to conquer it," Helen said. "I'm more worried about his state of mind. He tries to hide it, but he's broody."

"Zach's wrestling with something," Daniel said. "That's for sure."

"Maybe if we contacted his spotter." Ben and Zach had worked as a team for the last three years. Maya didn't know Ben and had never corresponded with him, but she knew the two men were tight. "I'll look into it," she said, not wanting to put any more pressure on Helen and Daniel, especially since tomorrow was Christmas Eve.

Later that night, dressed down in loungewear and hunkered on her bed with her laptop, Maya was sick-to-her-stomach sorry she'd pried.

Zach returned to his aunt and uncle's house just before eleven. The house was dark except for the Christmas tree lights that were set to go off at midnight via a timer. Helen and Dan usually crashed around ten, so Zach wasn't surprised by their absence.

He was, however, shocked to find Maya in the downstairs bathroom hugging the porcelain throne. Concerned, he barged in even though she told him to *go away*. "What's wrong?"

"Sick."

"I can see that." He shut the door behind him and ambled to the sink.

"Hello? Privacy?"

Her raspy voice echoed in the bowl and tugged at Zach's heart. He soaked a washrag with cold water, wrung it out, then swept aside her hair and pressed the cool compress to the back of her neck. She retched once again and he smoothed a hand down her arched back. He'd seen her like this before and he had to wonder. "What upset you?"

"Food."

"Something you ate?"

She nodded, flushed the toilet, then reached around and nabbed the rag, wiping it across her mouth. "This," she croaked as she slumped back against him, "is mortifying."

"I've seen you puke before."

"Thanks for the reminder."

Zach held her steady while she caught her breath. Yeah. He'd seen her like this on various occasions, but almost all of those instances had been triggered by an emotional response to an ugly situation, not bad food. "Did you eat too much or was something tainted?"

"What is this? The Inquisition?"

"Not nearly as gruesome."

She pushed away from him, then pushed to her feet. She swung to the sink and washed her face, brushed her teeth. She opened the medicine cabinet.

"What are you looking for?"

"Pepto? TUMS?"

Zach dipped into his jacket pocket and passed her a half-used roll of antacids. His own stomach had been giving him fits for weeks. "Want some ginger ale?" he asked as she popped two tabs of the chalky white stuff.

She shrugged. "Okay."

"Meet me in the living room."

Zach's mind raced as he leaned on his walking stick and hurried (as much as he could) into the kitchen. There was nothing sexy about a woman hurling in the toilet. Yet he'd been more attracted to Maya in the last five minutes than he'd been to Giselle in the last five hours.

Giselle—exotic perfection.

Maya—a sweet mess.

As if life weren't complicated enough, Zach was confused by his reaction to both women. He'd spent months lusting after Giselle, albeit long-distance. In person, there'd been no spark at all. Yet he was suddenly and intensely hot for Maya, his longtime platonic friend.

Zach filled two tumblers with ginger ale, then eyed the walking stick he'd propped against the counter, gauging his ability to carry two glasses one-handed. "Screw it."

Leaving the stick behind, he made his way to the living room. He wouldn't win any trophies for a sexy swagger, but he didn't falter or spill their drinks. *Oorah,* he thought. Which made him think of the Marines. Which made him think of Ben.

Damn.

Maya had been pissed when Zach had refused to let her in on why he was no longer military. Had she investigated on her own? Snooped around online?

Hell.

"Here you go."

Maya, who'd curled into the corner of the sofa, reached out and took her glass. "Thank you."

"Sure." He knew she'd watched him limp into the living room. It was hell on his pride, but he'd just seen her hugging the toilet. Maybe that made them even. Funny that it made him smile. He hitched back his jacket and sank next to Maya. Ignoring the pain in his leg, he focused on the twinkling lights adorning the massive tree. "Every year Uncle Dan buys the biggest spruce he can find and Aunt Helen still has two to three boxes of untapped decorations."

"I think it's sweet that she's collected so many ornaments over the years. And there's a story behind each one. I was telling G . . ." Maya's gaze flicked toward the garland-laced stairway. "Where is she anyway?"

Zach tensed. "Giselle's still at the Shack."

Enjoying the lively atmosphere and the attentive company of the popular pub. *Without him.*

"You abandoned her?"

"You know me better than that." He always left with the girl he came with. When he was a young boy, Zach's mom had drilled a lot of things into his head. Good manners and being respectful of women topped the list.

Maya sighed. "I know G, too. I'm guessing she wanted to party after hours and you didn't. I'm guessing she made fast friends with a few people and told you not to worry, she'd find a ride home or call a cab."

"Adam Brody offered to see her home. He's a good guy." Adam was also tight with Nash Bentley, a local pilot and a trusted acquaintance of Zach's. Nash, who'd been drinking beer on the next bar stool over, had heard Giselle giving Zach a kind but definite brush-off. After, Nash had nudged Zach, assuring him that the woman was safe with Adam. "I'm not worried," Zach said honestly. Otherwise, he would have hung out even though he'd been jilted. "Giselle said she'd text you."

"She probably did. My phone's upstairs." Maya shifted, looking increasingly uncomfortable as she sipped her soda. "I can't believe G blew you off."

"She wasn't rude about it and I don't blame her." After two games of pool he'd grown tired of the jovial company. Even after three beers, he'd still felt wound tight. Everyone else, including Giselle, had grown more animated and talkative as the liquor flowed and the night stretched on.

Not Zach.

He'd been withdrawn whereas Giselle was all about cutting loose.

"We're in two different places," he said.

"Did you click at all?" Maya asked without meeting his gaze.

"Not like I thought we would." They'd spent the first hour talking about Maya. How they'd both met her and how their friendships had evolved. At one point Giselle had mentioned how Maya had seemed distracted and even a little melancholy this past year, which Zach couldn't imagine because Maya was the most focused and intense optimist he'd ever known.

He'd been shocked to learn Maya rarely dated although she'd had an on-again, off again relationship with a real-estate agent who was crazy about her. Some even-keeled, benevolent dude named Charlie. Successful and nice, according to Giselle, but boring. Which meant the man was grounded and played life safe, which meant he was perfect for Maya. So why hadn't they hooked up on a more permanent basis? She was definitely the marrying kind. The happily ever after, white picket fence, and kids kind. Was Charlie waffling on committing? Was Maya hung up on him? Hence their on/off history? If that was the case then Charlie was an imbecile. Every man should be lucky enough to have a girl like Maya Templeton.

They may have only corresponded sporadically over the last several years, but Zach had known Maya his entire lifetime. She was sunshine and rainbows, everything bright and hopeful, everything good, which was maybe why he'd never gone out of his way to visit with her, even when he was furloughed. She'd said he was always welcome, but stepping into her cheery, dewy-eyed world took him out of his comfort zone. Her name alone had reminded him of things he'd missed, things he'd chosen not to pursue, a home he'd left. She represented the innocent time in his life, something quickly gone once he'd shipped out. He'd chosen that solitary path, and as long as he'd known he was protecting people back home, good people like Maya, it was all worth it.

Except now he was back and Maya was in his face. In his blood. One hug, one punch in the shoulder, and she'd sparked a sexual yearning that raged stronger by the hour.

Zach had felt uncomfortable prying Giselle for deeper details regarding Maya's feelings for that real-estate agent, so instead he'd subtly pumped Giselle for updates on Maya's life in general, although maybe he hadn't been subtle at all. Giselle's attention had started to drift to the plasma screens and pool table, and Zach had scrambled to turn his focus back on her.

Too little, too late, and a definite disconnect. The conversation with Giselle quickly tanked. Zach's attempts to introduce pieces of their long-distance correspondence had bombed. Giselle shouldn't have felt like a stranger, but she did. The fire that had burned between them via the written word was ash. He assumed Giselle's lack of interest was due to his lack of uniform and his damned bum leg. He'd expected disinterest on her side. But not on his. She was Playboy-bunny hot and he hadn't felt even a twinge of lust.

On the other hand, Zach had it bad for the woman sitting next to him, a woman dressed in soft pink fleece bottoms and an oversized sweatshirt featuring Sleeping Beauty. Or maybe it was Snow White. Unlike Maya, Zach had never been able to keep those Disney heroines straight. Unlike Maya, he'd never been a fan of fairy tales or a hard-core dreamer.

Zach had always been a realist. Now he was a realist and a cynic.

Early on, Zach had been inspired to serve in the military. In school he'd sucked in science, but he'd excelled in history. He knew the politics, the necessities and atrocities of war. He understood the need to protect and preserve. To fight for the persecuted. To combat evil. He'd joined the Marine Corps to honor his dad and grandfather, both Devil Dogs. He'd entered the sniper program because his uncle had taught him to hunt and he'd always been a crack shot. He'd been the best of the best, and it hadn't been enough.

"Whatever happened over there," Maya said as if reading his mind, "maybe you'd feel better if you talked about it. Letting it fester can't be good."

"You sound like a shrink, and I've already been down that road."

"I just want you to know . . . I'm here. If you ever want to talk about what happened."

Zach was pretty sure she already knew at least part of what had happened. He'd bet his last dime she'd learned about Ben's death and the partial circumstances. Then, being an imaginative person, she'd spun all sorts of ugly scenarios, filling in her own grisly details until she'd made herself sick.

Zach's chest grew tight, as he knew she was willing to endure his personal nightmare in hopes of making him feel better. Knowing the truth of it, even if he skated over graphic descriptions, would make her ill. Maya wasn't cut out for the ugliness in the world. He'd always been simultaneously charmed and frustrated by that.

Right now, he wanted to make sure she didn't go to bed harboring whatever scenarios she'd cooked up. He wanted to replace fear and death with cheer and hope. Zach set aside his soda and shrugged out of his suit coat. "I'm too wired to sleep. How'd you feel about a movie?"

She drew her knees up to her chest. "What kind of movie?"

"A Christmas movie."

"You hate Christmas movies."

"Only the sappy ones."

Her lip twitched, drawing his attention to her mouth. "They're all sappy," she said with a half grin.

He wanted to kiss her.

A wisp of panic, something he rarely experienced, heightened his senses. Would she stop him? Encourage him? Would it taint their friendship? Spark something deeper? That thought alone scared the devil out of him.

Tempering his runaway thoughts, Zach nabbed the remote and flipped through channels. He stopped on one of the many versions of *Scrooge* or *A Christmas Carol*. Whatever it was called. The one starring those dopey-faced Muppets. It was as close as he could find to Disney. The frog was mid-song, a chipper melody that made Zach swallow a groan. They'd missed the beginning, but Zach didn't figure Maya cared. She'd probably seen this movie a million times. "How about this one?"

"Not *too* sappy," she said with a smile that tripped his pulse. "Perfect."

Battening down his lustful impulses, Zach opened his arm and motioned her closer. She snuggled against him and his heart hammered like a mother. *Yup. Perfect. Perfectly screwed up.* And for tonight, perfectly welcome.

Five

"Deck the halls with boughs of holly—"

"I'm going to deck you with this pillow if you don't shut up." Giselle rolled onto her stomach with a groan and buried her face in the potential fluffy weapon.

"Not my fault you have a hangover, Miss Grumpy Pants." Maya donned one of her favorite holiday cardigans (the one featuring each of Santa's reindeer, including Rudolph and his glowing nose), squelching the urge to break into even louder song. That would be cruel. Not that Giselle didn't deserve some grief. "What time did you roll in anyway?" Physically and emotionally exhausted, Maya had been asleep.

Giselle mumbled into the pillow.

"Seriously? Four a.m.?" Maya pulled on the insulated boots she kept specifically for winter visits to Vermont. "What were you and Adam doing until . . . Scratch that. I don't want to know."

"Good. Going back to sleep now."

"But it's Christmas Eve morning."

"Bah humbug."

"You don't mean that." Maya's cheeks warmed as she remembered the way she'd cuddled on the couch with Zach while Michael Caine as Ebenezer Scrooge endured the antics of Victorian-clothed Muppets, not to mention visits from three ghosts, four if you counted his business partner. She still couldn't believe Zach had sat through the entire musical adaptation without making fun of it even once. He didn't even roll his eyes during Tiny Tim's famous *God bless us, everyone.*

Maya had looked.

Instead, Zach had smiled and winked down at her, and her stomach had flipped. In a good way. Not in a nauseous way. She didn't even want to think about what had ravaged her stomach last night. She'd lied to Zach saying food was the culprit because she didn't want him to think she couldn't bear the truth of his situation. It didn't matter that she didn't know details. Just imagining what Zach had seen and endured twisted her every which way and inside out.

Instead, she preferred to dwell on his kindness and the way her pulse had skipped when he'd held her close and kissed the top of her head. He'd done that before. Strictly platonic. But last night it had felt different.

At least for Maya.

For the first time in days, her mind flew to Charlie, her sometimes boyfriend. Right now they were in the friend phase, only he wanted much more. The problem was, so did Maya. Charlie was everything she hoped for in a life partner—kind, hardworking, reliable, fun, and optimistic. He was successful, too. But he'd never made her pulse skip or her heart flutter. The missing chip. A chip she'd found with her best friend, of all people. A man who lived life on the dark and dangerous side. Not Maya's cup of tea, but a wonderful blend of person all the same. Any woman would be lucky to have Zachery Cole.

Tying off her laces, she rose and clomped over to the other twin bed. The one occupied by her partner, her friend, and, at this particular moment, a Scrooge. "How could you dump Zach like that?"

Giselle growled into the pillow, then showed at least half of her mascara-smudged face. "I didn't dump him. I gave him an out. Zach was miserable. He didn't want to be at the Shack with me. He wanted to be here with you."

"Get . . . out."

"Would you? Please?"

"He said he wanted to be with me?"

"He didn't have to. He talked about you incessantly. How you met. What great *pals* you were. He must've told me a dozen different stories about one of the two of you bailing the other out of some or another jam. *Blah, blah, blah.* Then he asked me about our relationship—yours and mine. Our business and whatnot. When talk turned to me specifically . . ." She grunted. "Let's just say, our time together roared downhill faster than a high-speed roller coaster."

Maya frowned, going on sudden and unexpected defense for Giselle. "What? He didn't think you were interesting? You're one of the most fascinating people I know!"

"*Shh.* Not so loud." Giselle covered her eyes with her arm. "Thank you for that, by the way. But we never really got to talking about the real me."

"What do you mean?"

"He kept referring to the letters, Maya. The e-mails. Mostly your thoughts. Or my thoughts but written in your words. I didn't realize I'd feel so bad about duping him. I felt awkward and pretty much fumbled the conversation. That's when I pushed to play a game of pool. I thought if we met some other people I'd feel more comfortable and then Zach would get a chance to know the real me. Only that didn't work out either. The more I loosened up the more he shut down: Not for anything, but that man is broody with a capital *B*."

The same word Helen had used to describe Zach. *Huh*. Zach hadn't struck Maya as broody. Then again, he'd been working hard to lighten Maya's own mood. Just now she was fixated on something else Giselle had said. " 'Dupe' is a strong word, don't you think?"

"Pretty sure it's the correct word for what we did."

"You didn't tell him, right?"

"And make him feel like a fool? The man's suffering from a war wound. I don't intend to add insult to injury."

Maya's stomach clenched as she picked at the hem of her cheery sweater. "Did he tell you how he got hurt?"

"No. You?"

"No."

Maya's mind twisted with several thoughts. Her own unexpected attraction to Zach aside, had she unwittingly ruined a potentially wonderful thing between her old best friend and her new best friend. As most of the Cupcake Lovers had pointed out, Zach and Giselle were indeed a physically striking couple. If Zach had truly wanted to be with Maya last night, in a sexual way, as G had intimated, wouldn't he have made some sort of move? Kissing her head didn't count, did it?

All sorts of confused, Maya rocked back on her Trekkers. All she wanted for anyone ever, and especially for friends and family, was a charmed life and a happily ever after.

"Are you sure you won't join us for breakfast?" Maya asked.

"Are you still here?"

"The Coles always start holiday mornings with a scrumptious breakfast. Apple Cinnamon Pancakes with real butter and tons of pure Vermont maple syrup. Piles of crispy bacon—"

"Do you *want* me to hurl?"

"And then they do this old-fashioned sleigh ride which I think you'd really like—"

"Don't take this wrong, Maya, but get lost."

Maya knew Giselle well enough not to take the dismissal personally. Still, Maya felt awkward about the whole triangle thing and would feel better if G provided Zach with another chance to know her for real. Maya just wanted Zach to be happy. He deserved to be happy. And maybe reckless, carefree, absurdly beautiful Giselle (just Giselle) was the ticket. There had to be some sort of cosmic revelation, a Christmas miracle even, in the works. Everything was just too weird otherwise.

"I'll ask Helen to save you some pancakes. You can nuke them. It won't be the same, but—"

"Maya."

"What?"

"Zach was especially keen on your marmalade fantasy."

Six

Zach had gone to sleep dreaming about Maya and Muppets and a Scrooge getting a new lease on life. He'd woken up thinking about Ben, whose life had been snuffed in an ambush. Ben wouldn't be getting a second chance at anything ever again. That thought filled Zach with grief and anger and, dammit, guilt, because he *had* been given a second chance. He just didn't know what to do with it. Once a Marine, always a Marine. Only he wasn't. Not in an active capacity. Not doing what he did best.

While Ben's parents spent Christmas mourning their son's death . . . While several of Zach's buddies still risked their lives rooting out evil . . . Zach was here. In Sugar Creek. Eating decadent flapjacks soaked with syrup. Listening to his aunt and uncle arguing about post-Christmas sales—"Swear to gosh, Helen, if you buy one more ornament this house will explode!"—and watching a sun-bronzed blonde in a ridiculous reindeer sweater, chowing down on crispy bacon and a puffy pastry.

So wrong yet it felt so right, which only made Zach feel worse.

The guilt piled on and featherlight pancakes settled in Zach's stomach like the craggy stones of insurgent-infested mountains.

"About the sleigh ride," Zach started, only the phone rang.

"Hold that thought, sweetie," Helen said as she headed for the landline.

"I could use more coffee," Dan said as he stood. "What about you kids?"

"Sure," Zach and Maya answered as one, just like twenty years ago when offered seconds on ice cream. Zach's heart squeezed much like it had last night when Maya had snuggled next to him for the movie. There hadn't been one sexy thing about that sappy musical and Maya hadn't come on to him in any way, but he'd gone to bed randy. Desire pulsed even now. Even with his aunt and uncle in the room. Affection and desire—a powerful combination. Zach didn't scare easily and he rarely second-guessed his gut feelings, but right now he felt close to clueless and paralyzed.

As soon as Dan moved to the counter, Maya leaned in. "Don't you dare bail on the sleigh ride, Zachery Cole," she ordered in a stern whisper.

"Who said—"

"It's written all over your face. You look miserable."

"I'm not—"

"Liar."

Helen shuffled back to the table sporting a huge frown.

"Who was it? What did they want?" Dan asked while refreshing everyone's mug.

"It was Ethel. Her nephew, John, came down with a virus. He won't be able to deliver our care package to Roscoe Marx."

"I wouldn't worry about it," Dan said. "It's not like Marx appreciates the Cupcake Lovers' efforts. Has he ever said thank you? Has he ever even been cordial?"

"Who's Roscoe Marx?" Zach asked.

"The grumpiest cuss in Franklin County," Dan said.

"A war veteran," Helen said. "And a recluse." She turned to Maya. "As you know, the CL club was founded in the early forties by women whose husbands and sons were away fighting in WWII."

"Once a week they gathered at one of the members' houses to enjoy the host's featured cupcake," Maya joined in. "They swapped recipes and shared news regarding loved ones. It was all about companionship and compassion." She smiled. "I've always loved this story."

"It's more than a story," Helen said. "It's fact."

Zach sipped coffee, absorbing his aunt's and Maya's enthusiasm. Dan looked bored. Zach got that. They'd both heard this saga a million times, but for some reason this version felt different to Zach. Maybe it was the passionate twinkle in Maya's eyes.

"Soon after inception," Helen said, "the Cupcake Lovers decided to spread some joy. Up until then they'd felt useless, helpless. So they sent care packages overseas. What soldier wouldn't love a home-baked cupcake? That part's tradition now. Decades ago we branched out, by participating in fund-raising events to help various causes. Then, five years ago, we started a new tradition. Christmas care packages for any veteran within Franklin County. We always gift the food baskets on Christmas Eve. We divvy up the deliveries and usually enlist volunteers to help. Ethel said she tried to find a replacement for John but couldn't. I suppose—"

"I'm already carting you to three different homes this afternoon, Helen," Dan cut in. "I'm not driving all the way up Thrush Mountain to deliver cupcakes to a grump who greets every visitor with the business end of his Remington."

"But he's a veteran," Helen said.

"Who lives in the middle of the forest and who doesn't give diddly-squat about Christmas charity."

"But—"

"I'll go," Zach said. It was one way to escape the day's planned festivities. Hard to justify indulging in a light-hearted sleigh ride, the community theater's rendition of the living nativity, and a candlelight wassail toast around the town Christmas tree while his comrades endured an-other dog day in hostile territory.

"It's a long drive," Helen said, looking worried, "and you'd have to take an old logging road, which could be rough given the recent snow."

"I'll manage."

"Your leg—"

"Won't be a problem. As for the snow, that's one of the benefits in owning an all-wheel-drive Hummer. Where exactly on Thrush?" he asked Dan.

While Dan rattled off specifics, Zach glanced at Maya, who seemed suddenly and unnaturally engrossed in slath-ering a muffin with orange marmalade. It triggered a lingering sexy memory, something Giselle had written about in one of her letters. Last night, in trying to recon-nect with his *pen pal,* Zach had touched on that fantasy. If Giselle had had any latent interest in him, she would have snatched up the flirtatious baton. Instead she'd veered off, avoiding the subject altogether.

"Depending on traffic and weather, it could take up to three hours to get there and back," Helen said. "You'll miss out on part of the fun. It's not fair—"

"Happy to do it," Zach said, still focused on Maya, whose brow was creased in deep thought. Was she angry with him for bailing on the sleigh ride? Worried about him driving that kind of distance with his bum leg? He kept waiting for her to volunteer to ride shotgun. To keep him company or to trade off driving. Delivering a cupcake care package to an isolated Scrooge, trying to inject some Christmas cheer into a lone soul's life, was right up her alley.

"You should invite Giselle along," Maya said, still focused on her muffin.

"Invite me along where?"

All heads turned as Maya's friend and business partner stepped into the kitchen. Zach knew from Maya's carefully worded excuse—*G's jetlagged and sleeping in*—that Giselle had slept in because she was hungover. Even so, she looked gorgeous—her dark hair sleeked into a high ponytail, makeup expertly applied. And even though she'd skipped any hokey holiday attire, she still looked festive in her tight jeans and emerald-green sweater set.

"Sorry I'm late," she said.

"Jet lag is a horrible thing, dear," Helen said. "No apologies necessary. I'll fix you a plate."

"Please don't go to the trouble," Giselle said as she took the empty seat next to Dan. "I'll just have a toast and coffee." She glanced at Maya. "Invite me where?"

"Zach's delivering a Christmas care package to a war veteran on Thrush Mountain. Kind of a long drive, but pretty. You said you wanted to see more of the countryside, so I thought—"

"I'd love to," Giselle interrupted, cheeks bright, "but I . . ."

"She has other plans," Zach finished for her. He didn't know for a fact, but given the way Giselle had hit it off with Adam and a few other locals last night, Zach wouldn't be surprised if someone had invited her somewhere to do something.

"What plans?" Maya asked, looking flustered.

Giselle thanked Dan for pouring her coffee, then tossed Zach an apologetic smile. "I thought you had plans with your family—a sleigh ride and a play. I sort of invited myself on this trip and I didn't want to intrude further, so I, well, Adam invited me to go snowmobiling and I sort of said yes."

Maya frowned. "Sort of?"

"Adam who?" Helen asked.

"Adam Brody," Zach said.

"Nice boy," Dan said to Giselle. "I'm sure he'll show you a good time."

Giselle's mouth twitched.

Maya choked on her muffin.

Zach smiled into his coffee. Since he and Giselle had traded intimate letters for several months, he should have felt a sting of rejection. He didn't. All he felt was relief. The last thing he wanted was to spend half the day trapped in a car with Giselle. She was nice enough, but they didn't click, as Maya would put it. He didn't want to pretend interest in whatever Giselle had to say or to make small talk if she fell silent for too long. Truth told, he was looking forward to some time alone to stew in his holiday funk.

"For the record," Helen said to Giselle, "you're not intruding. Any friend of Maya's is a friend of this family. If Adam has no plans for the evening, please know you're both welcome for dinner. Now," she said with a pat to Giselle' s arm, "what would you like on that toast? Apple butter? Jelly? Marmalade?"

"Dry is fine. I'm not big on sweets. Except for Maya's cupcakes, of course. I . . ." Giselle trailed off, traded a look with Maya, who'd just bitten into the second half of her marmalade-smeared muffin, then smiled over at Helen. "Although once in a great while, I do get a craving." She dipped her knife in the jar, glanced at Zach. "That trip of yours. Maybe Maya could tag along."

"That's a grand idea," Helen said, beaming now at Maya. "It will give you and Zach time to catch up."

Maya blanched. "Yes, but—"

"If anyone could crack Roscoe Marx's gruff shell," Dan said with a pointed look at Maya, "that would be you, princess."

Zach, who was contemplating the marmalade weird-ness, assumed Giselle had pushed Maya into the mix so that she wouldn't feel bad about jilting him—again. His aunt and uncle obviously didn't want him to be alone on Christmas Eve and were no doubt worried about him driving that distance given his bad leg. Maya . . . Zach couldn't guess her thoughts, but he sensed her discomfort. She didn't want to be alone with him. Why? Was she still angry with him for keeping her in the dark regarding his injuries? Had she sensed his sexual interest? Was she dis-gusted? Intrigued? Why did she keep trading cryptic glances with Giselle? And if Giselle wasn't keen on sweets, why had she teased Zach with a fantasy that involved sug-ary foreplay? He glanced at Maya, his groin tightening when she licked a glob of orange marmalade from her thumb. An innocent action that conjured the devil in him.

Any thoughts Zach had of privately wallowing in his misery fell by the wayside. He suddenly wanted nothing more than extended time with Maya. Time for a frank talk and he didn't plan on having it in the pantry.

"I'd appreciate the company," Zach said, robbing Maya of a chance to wiggle out of the drive. "Although maybe you should stay in the car until I get Marx to lower that rifle."

"He's yet to shoot anyone," Dan said. "All bark, no bite."

"Better safe than sorry," Zach said, throwing in his own cliché.

"You'll have to stop at Ethel's to pick up the basket," Helen said. She pushed to her feet. "I'll pack up some snacks and beverages for you two as well. Just in case the drive takes longer than anticipated."

"I'll help you," Giselle said, grinning at Maya before following Helen to the fridge.

"I've got a map in my den," Dan said. "I'd feel better if you took it along. Never know when a road's going to close and you might need an alternate route."

"I have a portable GPS in the rental car," Maya said at long last. "I'll get it." She didn't look happy.

She hurried out of the kitchen, and Zach ambled after. He caught up to her at the front door, where she was jamming her arms into the sleeves of her coat. She looked flustered and cute as hell in that goofy reindeer sweater. "If you'd rather not go with me—"

"Did I say I didn't want to go?" she snapped in a hushed voice.

His mouth twitched. "It's written all over your face."

"It's just . . ."

"What?"

"I wanted Giselle . . ."

"Stop trying to push us together, Maya. She's not into me."

"But you're into her. In your letters—"

"She showed you my letters?"

Maya backed away from him, easing into the threshold, reaching for the doorknob. As if she couldn't escape this conversation fast enough. "Maybe a few," she said. "Okay. All of them. Don't get bent out of shape."

He wasn't bent, but his wheels were turning. His libido was fired up, too—the image of Maya licking marmalade from her thumb was imprinted on his brain. "What did you think?" he asked while crowding into the door frame.

She blinked up at him—cheeks pink, eyes wary. "Think of what?"

"I was sexually explicit in some of those letters." He dipped his face close to hers, raised a brow. "Then again, so was Giselle."

Prompted by curiosity and the mistletoe hanging above them, Zach kissed Maya. She didn't balk. She didn't encourage. She just stood there, allowing him to sample. She tasted of sunshine and marmalade. Warm and sweet. *Addictive.* He wanted more, but he eased away, unsure of the moment. Unsure of the future. A one-night stand wouldn't cut it with Maya. Forever wouldn't cut it with him. Not when a person's days could be snuffed in an instant.

Never saw it coming.

Wide-eyed, Maya stared up at Zach. "Why did you kiss me?" she asked in a husky voice.

He smiled a little and pointed up.

She glanced at the mistletoe. "Oh." She cleared her throat, gave a nervous laugh. "Kind of a crazy tradition. I mean anybody could kiss anybody, not that it means anything."

"Mmm." He searched her pretty face, her expressive eyes, trying to read her mind and failing. He sensed her confusion, though, and her curiosity. Instead of making a quick escape, she lingered on the threshold—toe-to-toe

with Zach. Her gaze moved to his mouth, and his heart skipped in anticipation. A smart man would salvage their longtime friendship and back away. Zach's good sense must've taken a hit along with his legs. Instead of retreating, he willed her to make the next move, to initiate another kiss. But then she looked toward the kitchen and he knew she was inhibited by their surroundings. More than ever he wanted to get her alone. Away from this house—a place that rooted them in their childhood and old patterns.

Heart pounding, Zach buttoned Maya's coat, the exact opposite of what he wanted to do. The urge to explore her bare skin was intense. Almost as intense as wanting to lose himself in her goodness. Seducing Maya would be selfish and reckless and potentially hazardous to their friendship. Then again, Zach had never been one to play it safe. His body still hummed from their chaste kiss. Marmalade lingered on his tongue and tripped his imagination. He hadn't felt this alive in months. "Ready for an adventure?"

"Sorry?" she asked in a breathless voice, and he knew without a doubt now that the sexual awareness was two-sided.

"Roscoe Marx."

"Oh. Right. I . . . I'll, um, get my GPS."

"I'll get Dan's map."

Together, maybe she and Zach could find their way to wherever this new kink in their relationship was heading.

Seven

Maya was burning up.

In addition to thermal leggings and a matching thermal top, she was wearing jeans, her reindeer cardigan, thick socks, insulated boots, a knee-length down coat, a fleece-lined Santa hat (compliments of the Cupcake Lovers), and a matching wool scarf and gloves.

The Hummer's leather seats were heated, and multiple vents blew hot air. She could shed a few layers and she'd be more than comfortable, but she had this insane worry that if she as much as peeled off one glove she'd lose control and strip down to nothing. Ever since Zach had kissed her she'd had one predominant desire.

To get naked.

With him.

"Are you mad about the kiss?" Zach asked.

Startled by his voice, Maya glanced left. "What?"

"We've been on the road for half an hour. Aside from

the exchange we had while picking up the care basket from Ethel Larsen, you haven't said a word. Not that I mind Christmas music," Zach said while dialing down the volume she'd kicked up, "but I mind the tension."

"I'm not mad about the kiss."

"Ticked because you're missing the sleigh ride?"

"No."

"Because Giselle's spending the afternoon with Adam?"

"No. Yes." She shrugged. "A little."

Zach looked over the rims of his aviator sunglasses, catching her gaze before focusing back on the icy road. "Nash mentioned something about Adam going through a bad breakup a few months back. Hit him hard. Maybe you should be happy he hooked up with Giselle. Especially given the holiday. Beats cryin' in his eggnog."

"I guess."

"What's wrong, Maya?"

"Nothing. I just . . . I have a lot on my mind." She kept obsessing on that mistletoe kiss. The way she and Zach had cuddled on the sofa the night before. The fact that whatever had burned between him and Giselle because of those letters had since gone up in smoke. Face-to-face, they'd fizzled.

And the marmalade fiasco . . . Maya would bet her Disney Princess collection that Zach suspected the truth about who owned *that* particular fantasy. If she didn't know better, and she didn't, she'd think Giselle had slipped up on purpose.

"Giselle mentioned you've had an off year," Zach said while navigating the sparsely traveled back road. "And you've been on edge the whole time you've been in Sugar Creek. I know your party business is booming. So what's got you down? Charlie?"

Maya whipped around so fast, she nearly strangled

herself with the seat harness. "G told you about Charlie, too? Jeez, did she give you a tally of my financial assets? A rundown of my social calendar?"

"Don't get bent."

"I'm not . . . Okay. I'm bent. Why would she blab about Charlie?"

"I asked if you were seeing anyone."

"Why?"

"Because I was curious. Damn, Maya. Do I have to spell it out?"

Her heart pounded up into her throat, choking her silent. She stared at Zach's hard profile. Saw him work his jaw as if searching for words himself. She swiped off her merrymaking cap as her temperature shot through the roof. "That mistletoe kiss," she ventured.

"Wasn't half the kiss I wanted it to be," Zach finished. "I needed to know if my recent yearnings had merit. If I kissed you would I feel a spark?"

"Did you?"

He slid off his shades and glanced over, his gaze injected with a heady dose of lust. "I don't know what to do with this . . . attraction, Maya. Scratch the itch? Ignore it? You tell me."

"Pull over."

"What?"

She wretched off her gloves. Were her fingers smoking? "Pull over, Zach!" Her body burned as though thoroughly torched. She whipped off her scarf and was working the buttons of her coat when he peeled into an unplowed lot. She saw a silo and a crumbling barn and, beyond, a broken house. Abandoned or neglected, she didn't know. Didn't care. She saw no vehicles. No trucks. No tractors. No animals.

No signs of life.

She unbuckled her seat belt, pushed open the door . . . and took a header in a snowdrift in her haste to escape the suffocating Hummer. She heard Zach call her name, shook off the impact of the fall, and trudged toward the barn.

"Dammit, Maya! What the hell?"

"Don't curse," she yelled over her shoulder. "It's Christmas Eve."

"I know what day it is! What are you . . . Damn, woman," he shouted when she shrugged off her coat. "You'll catch your death!"

How was it, she wondered, that the snow didn't melt in her wake? Flames of passion licked at her soul, her mind. She burst into the dilapidated barn thinking she should slow down if she wanted Zach to catch her. His bum leg had him at a disadvantage. That one sane thought stopped her in her tracks. She turned . . . and practically slammed into Zach. How had he moved so fast?

"I'm sorry if I shocked you," he said, leaning on his cane while holding her discarded coat in his free hand. "I should have kept my feelings to myself. I should have—"

Maya launched herself at her oldest friend, backing him into one of several stables. The cane and coat dropped to the ground as Zach caught her in his arms. Wrapped around his hunky body like garland, Maya kissed him with a year's worth of pent-up passion.

Zap!

The connection was electric. Lust surged through Maya with a force that struck her dizzy. Light-headed, she stumbled back, stunned by the intense and heady sensation.

Zach jammed a hand through his hair, his expression stuck between shocked and pained. "I expected a punch in the shoulder."

"Are you sorry I kissed you?"

"I'm sorry you stopped."

"Did I hurt your leg?"

"You coldcocked my heart."

Seduced off her feet, Maya flew back into his arms, picking up where she'd left off—kissing Zach senseless. She told herself to take it slow this time, but her need was fierce, striking her stupid and clumsy. She tilted her head left, when she should have tilted right. She bumped his nose, clipped his chin. The openmouthed kiss was more teeth than tongue, and in her zeal she bit his lip, causing him to wince. Mortified, she dropped back.

"Okay. This is beyond awkward," she said. "I mean, I know how to kiss. Ask anyone. Well, not anyone. It's not like I've kissed everyone. Only a select few, but they'd tell you. Charlie would tell you. I'm one heck of a kisser. Usually. Just not today. Particularly not with you. Maybe that's a sign. Maybe—"

"Maya."

"What?"

"Shut up."

Zach closed in, and if he limped she didn't notice. Mostly she was aware of his raging aura. *Focus. Drive. Confidence.* He didn't falter when he took her in his arms. But she did. Her knees fairly buckled when he palmed the side of her face. He was definitely making a move. She just wished he'd hurry. The anticipation was brutal.

"Don't act," Zach said in a hypnotic, sexy tone. "React."

He kissed her then. A soft kiss that tickled her senses, a kiss that teased of something wondrous. Oh yes, on a scale of one to ten, ten being perfect, this kiss was a twelve. Maybe even a twenty. Maya melted against Zach's hard body and gave over to his sexy expertise. She responded to his touch, followed his lead, and suddenly they were making out like two star-crossed lovers intent on breaking all odds.

As his hand skimmed under her thermal tee and spanned her bare back, Maya envisioned her latest fantasy coming true: getting naked with Zachery Cole.

Merry Christmas to me.

She trembled with urgency, shivered in anticipation.

Zach eased away with a buzzkill of a frown. "This won't work."

Her stomach dropped to her toes. Not counting the awkward mistletoe peck, she'd fumbled their first two kisses and bombed on the third. "In other words, I don't light your fire."

Without a word, Zach pressed against her, contradicting her assumption. Her brain glitched with the knowledge that Zach was hard.

For me.

"So, um, what's the problem?' she asked, cursing the hitch in her voice.

Zach snatched her coat off the ground, shook out the snow, dirt, and straw, then wrapped it around her shoulders. "It's twenty degrees, if that. You ditched your coat, scarf, and gloves. Your hat. You might as well be naked."

"That's what I was shooting for."

His mouth crooked with the hint of a smile. "You thought we were going to do the nasty in a barn?"

"Can't say I was thinking at all. I was acting on impulse. As for the cold, I didn't notice." She wiggled against his erection and shimmed onto an emotional limb. "I'm hot for you, too."

"Since when?"

"I couldn't say, specifically."

"Generally."

She blushed, shrugged.

"Around the time you started reading my letters to Giselle?"

"Somewhere around there."

"Maya."

"What?"

"Giselle's not partial to marmalade. You are." He grasped her chin when she tried to look away. "Considering Giselle and I hit it off long-distance, I was puzzled by the total disconnect in person. Something tells me that's because it wasn't Giselle who captured my interest in the first place."

Maya squirmed, feeling trapped and jealous and all kinds of awkward. "G sent you several sexy photos of herself. She definitely captured your interest. I believe you penned the words 'smoking hot' and 'stunning.'"

"I'm not looking at Giselle right now. I'm looking at you. 'Smoking hot' and 'stunning' still apply—even in a reindeer sweater. Add to that 'sweet and engaging' and top it off with 'enigmatic.'

"It wasn't Giselle who explored my fascination with astronomy and fast cars," he went on. "It was you. Giselle didn't tell me about her dream trip to Hawaii. She didn't tease me with a fantasy that involved us licking marmalade from each other's bodies. That was you." He tucked her hair behind her ear, searching her face and making her flesh prickle with unease. "Why the pretense, Maya?"

Busted and embarrassed, she swung away. "I was going through my scrapbook. Giselle saw a picture of you. Instant infatuation," she blurted. "She wanted to strike up a flirtatious exchange and I thought, what the heck? I mean I knew you'd be physically attracted to her. All men are. She's a knockout. Only she had trouble penning conversational notes and asked for my help. I thought . . . That is, I wanted to provide you with a romantic distraction. Something fun and exciting, something to dwell on other than the danger and horrific situations you faced on a daily basis. At first I just embellished some of her thoughts, but then, well, I got sort of inspired by your responses."

"You mean turned-on?"

"I've always liked you, Zach. A lot. As a person. A friend. But then I got a glimpse of your sexy side and I got caught up and carried away with the fantasy. As if that wasn't enough, you charmed me with a few tender tales. It was that story about the dog you rescued, that picture, that did me in. I don't think I was fully aware of the impact it had on me until I saw you in person last night."

Leaning against a wooden pole, he massaged the back of his neck.

Fighting a chill now, Maya shoved her arms in her coat. "Are you angry?"

"Intrigued."

She fumbled a buttonhole and risked his gaze. "So we might still do it? You know. Fool around?"

"Make love?" Zach chuckled under his breath, shook his head. "How could I know you for so long and not know you at all?"

"You know me. Mostly. Just not my sensuous side."

"Speaking of . . . Where do you stand with Charlie?"

Talk about a buzzkill. She continued to button her coat. "At an impasse." Was Zach trying to shove another man between them? Or was this Zach's way of making sure he wasn't treading on another man's turf? Not wanting to muddy waters, she answered directly. "He wants to marry me and I'm not crazy about the idea."

"Not ready to settle down?"

"I'm ready." She'd been restless all year, anxious for her happily ever after. There had to be more to life than work, As much as she loved Cupcakes & Dreamscapes, the thriving business no longer filled her every need. She wanted more. A husband and kids. A family of her own. But not with Charlie Banks.

"Giselle described Charlie as a nice guy. Good job. Worships the ground you walk on. What's the problem?"

"I never wanted to get naked in a freezing-cold barn with Charlie." Her words had been heated, yet Zach iced over. She saw it. Sensed it.

His phone rang.

He eyed the screen, then answered. "Hi, Uncle Dan. . . . No. I wasn't aware. How far out?" Zach checked his watch. "We'll beat it. No worries. It's not like Marx is going to invite us in for a Christmas feast, right? . . . You take care, too. I'll check in later. . . . Yeah. Bye."

"What is it?" Maya asked as Zach thumbed through apps on his Android.

"A blizzard's blowing in."

"More snow on top of what we got yesterday?"

"According to the Weather Channel, an estimated twelve inches." Zach pocketed his phone and retrieved his cane.

Maya followed him out of the barn, mindful now of the freezing wind and a landscape already blanketed with several inches of glistening snow. The main roads had been adequately plowed. The back roads were another story. If this new storm hit hard and fast, some of the mountain roads would be perilous, if not impassible. Yes, Zach's Hummer was reliable, a veritable monster that ate up rough terrain. But what about if they got stuck? She thought about the physical aspect of digging or pushing their way out. Not knowing the full extent of Zach's injuries, she had to wonder what kind of toll that exertion would have on his body.

As if reading her mind, Zach glanced down at his cane as he opened the door for her. "If you're worried about me keeping you safe, I can take you back to Sugar Creek."

"I trust you to keep me safe, Zach." It was *him* she was worried about, but she stifled that thought, knowing it would hurt his pride. "If I'm concerned about anyone it's Roscoe Marx. He sacrificed who knows how much for our country. The least I can do is weather a storm for him." She buckled in and met Zach's gaze. "I don't care if he's the grumpiest cuss in Franklin County. Roscoe Marx deserves some Christmas cheer."

Zach leaned in then and brushed his mouth over hers. "You're killing me, Maya."

A barely there kiss, yet she felt it to her toes. "Back at you, Zach."

Eight

It blew in out of nowhere. A massive, blinding snowstorm.

"Son of a b." Zach kicked up his windshield wipers.

Maya dialed down the volume of the radio. A bouncy version of "Let It Snow" faded to background as fat swirling flakes obscured the mountainous landscape. "I thought you said the storm was several hours out."

"That's what Dan said and that's what I saw on the forecast." *What the hell?*

"Maybe there's an update on the local news station." She scanned the radio but was stonewalled by static.

Up until now, reception had been fine. "Storm interference," Zach guessed as Maya continued to search. She'd even lost the station they'd been listening to for the last hour.

Rather than hashing out what had happened between them in the barn, they'd tuned into a station featuring holiday classics. A mutual distraction while searching their souls. Did they or did they not want to pursue this attraction? More was at stake than scratching an itch and "doing it." Their friendship. The future.

Maya had given Zach a lot to absorb. *She* had written those sexy, engaging letters. She was hot for him, a wounded, unemployed former sniper. Not Charlie, the successful real-estate agent and Orlando-based pacifist. She was ready to settle down, which meant a home and family, and as near as Zach could tell, he was her prime target. It blew his mind on so many levels, he hadn't had a clear thought in an hour.

Now they were in the midst of a freak storm and he was suddenly razor sharp. Senses primed, he accessed the situation. Their position, their supplies. His goal was straightforward: Keep Maya safe. "Check the weather on your phone app."

"Okay. Wait. Oh no." She frowned at the screen. "Seriously?"

"What's wrong?"

"No signal."

Zach passed her his Android. "Try mine."

"Yeah. Okay. Not a superstrong signal, but it's something."

"What's it say?"

"This can't be right."

"What's it say, Maya?"

"That the storm's still several miles south of here."

That couldn't be right.

"I don't want to worry Uncle Dan," he said to Maya. "Call Giselle. Ask her what's happening weather-wise in Sugar Creek."

Zach half-listened to Maya making the call, the bulk of his focus on the inclement weather and worsening conditions. Surrounded by snow-laden trees, they were on unpaved terrain now an old logging road a quarter way up Thrush Mountain. Closer to Roscoe Marx's cabin than to Sugar Creek by far. No sense in turning back. Better to push on and take shelter.

"No snow at all?" Maya exclaimed. "Yeah. . . . Okay. . . . No. We're fine. Just checking in. So . . . are you having fun with Adam?" she asked in a near whisper. "Wow. No, I mean, great. . . . Yeah. We'll see you at dinner. Can't wait." She disconnected and glanced to the skies. "Please, God, don't strike me down."

"What are you talking about?"

"I'm not *really* looking forward to seeing G with Adam. It sounds like they really hit it off. She's having a blast. No complications. No concerns. Why is it always so easy for her?"

"Maybe it's because she doesn't run as deep as you."

"There's more to G than meets the eye."

"You don't have to defend your friend to me, Maya. That wasn't a judgment on her personality. Just saying some people are more sensitive than others. Life's harder for those who wear their hearts on their sleeves."

"I don't—"

"You do. That's why I'm reluctant to make love to you." He hadn't meant to be so blunt, but there it was. "I'm not ready for where it would lead. And I don't want to hurt you."

"Why does it have to lead anywhere?" she said, sounding annoyed. "Why can't it just be great sex? Scratch the itch, as you put it. Satisfy our curiosity and then go back to being friends."

"You're not built like that and you know it. Hell, I'm not built like that. Not when it comes to you."

He shouldn't have kissed her. He should have buried his impulses and ignored the mounting sexual tension. Instead, he'd indulged and now he was paying the price. He was pretty sure he loved Maya in a way that promised, or at least threatened, heartbreak. If he gave in to this, if he committed his all, and if he ever lost her . . . If she fell prey to an ailment or accident or, worse, malicious harm . . . He didn't think he could handle that.

He'd always thought himself impervious—until Ben had been cut down in front of his eyes. Not only had Zach failed to protect his partner; he'd been unable to save him. Worse, he'd been unable to carry the man's lifeless body safely down the mountain.

"Now I know what Helen and Giselle meant by 'broody,'" Maya said. "You're doing it now. Brooding. If the thought of sleeping with me troubles you so deeply—"

"For God's sake, Maya. I shoot people for a living."

"*Bad* people," she clarified. "And not anymore."

"Whether those soldiers or terrorists were *bad* depends on whose side you're on. And just because I'm retired, that doesn't erase my past. What I've seen. What I've done. As for the future . . . I can't promise I won't pursue an equally deadly profession. Or at least one that involves some form of violence. Do you really want to be a part of that? To live with that on a daily basis? You wouldn't be able to stomach it. Not even the thought of it. One of us has to be the realist here."

"I'm going to ignore the fact that you just pegged me as a flaky wimp and focus on your military background. You did what you did in order to protect civilians from harm. To combat evil. The intent would be the same if you were a policeman or security officer or, heck, a bodyguard."

"I don't know what I'm going to do with my life. That's part of the problem."

"You're welcome to stay with me in Orlando while you figure it out."

Instead of warming Zach, the offer struck him cold, making him feel useless and unfocused. "Soak in the sun while you peddle cupcakes and whimsical fantasies?" He blew out a breath, cocked his head. "I'm sorry. That came out wrong. You've done an amazing job with Cupcakes & Dreamscapes. You're a talented baker and astute business-woman. I just . . . I can't see us meshing. Not long-term. Not in a romantic sense."

"That's too bad," Maya said, looking at him with an equal dose of pity and frustration. "Because I can."

Zach's heart jerked and the earth shook.

No. That would be the Hummer ramming into a road-block.

Zach automatically shielded Maya with an outstretched arm as she lurched forward on impact.

Thank God, he'd been crawling at minimum speed. The hit hadn't been intense enough for the air bags to deploy, but it had shaken the occupants all the same. Zach looked into Maya's stunned-wide eyes. "You okay?"

She nodded. "You?"

"I'm good."

"Happened so fast I didn't even have time to scream," Maya said in a choked voice. "What did we hit?" She squinted through the windshield into the blinding snow. "Please tell me it's not a deer or moose."

"I think it's a felled tree." Hard to tell in the near-whiteout conditions. "Sit tight."

Zach bundled up and swung out of the vehicle, his booted feet sinking a good six inches into the mounting snow. The wind whipped and the snowflakes stung. The swirling flurries put Zach in the mind of a snow tor-nado. How could this storm not be on anyone's radar? Chin down, he shoved forward, inspecting the Hummer and a massive downed maple camouflaged by several inches of snow. He looked ahead and then behind them. "Damn."

Kicking into survival mode, he made his way to Maya's side.

She rolled down the window, squinting against the wind and snow. "A tree?"

"Yeah. And it's not going anywhere."

"What about us?"

"Not in the Hummer. Blocked in front. Snowed in from behind. According to the map and GPS, Marx's cabin should be just up and around the bend. We'll have to hoof it. Wait out the storm there."

"What if he won't let us inside?"

"He will."

"But—"

"He will." Zach had lived through too much to be intimidated by the "business end" of a hunting rifle. They'd weather this freak storm in the safety and warmth of Marx's cabin. Of that, Zach had no doubt. "Bundle up good. I'll grab some supplies from the back."

"We have to take the Cupcake Lovers Christmas basket," she said while looping her scarf around her neck. "That's why we came up here after all. To spread goodwill and cheer."

"Whether Marx wants it or not."

"One of these days Roscoe Marx will be touched by something or someone and he'll see the light." She smiled softly. At Zach. "There's hope for every Scrooge."

Nine

"I can't believe you kept our snowshoes all these years," Maya yelled over the howling wind.

"Not me," Zach yelled back. "Uncle Dan and Aunt Helen. They were hanging in the garage. Same place we always hung them. Saw them the other day. Tossed them into the Hummer before we left. You never know."

"And the utility sled! I can't believe you thought to pack it, too." Instead of carrying the heavy thermal care basket stocked with cupcakes, can goods, and a small cooked turkey, Zach had piled the Cupcake Lovers' "present" on a sled specifically made for hauling hunting or camping supplies. He'd also added the insulated tote packed with "snacks" by Helen and Giselle, along with two blankets, a high-powered flashlight, and a medical kit. "Always prepared!" Maya went on. "Like a Boy Scout."

"Or a Marine," he said with a wistful smile.

Maya's heart ached, as she knew Zach was feeling lost

now that he was no longer on active duty. How many civilian jobs were there for a sharpshooter? A professional sniper? Not counting a hit man. What if Zach never fully recovered from his injuries? Would he even qualify for a desk job with the police? He was smart, resourceful, and experienced. Surely he could land a job in an advisory or teaching capacity. But would he be happy? Fulfilled? One thing was certain: She couldn't imagine him hawking houses or cars or running an amusement ride at Disney. Not that there was anything wrong with those jobs, but they weren't Zach.

Strapped into the snowshoes she'd owned as a teen, Maya glided over the accumulating snowfall rather than sinking in. Once again she was teleported back to her youth when Zach used to take her and some of their other friends hiking in the winter. He'd always been an outdoorsman, always physical. Even now, even with his stilted gait, he navigated this storm with confidence. Since he was wearing a harness that was attached to the sled, his hands were free, enabling him to utilize the walking stick. He seemed to be leaning on it more than before. Trudging uphill in the deep snow while pulling the added weight of their supplies had to be brutal on his bad leg.

She wanted to offer to help, but she knew he'd take offense. Instead she held silent, allowing him to concentrate on their trek. She couldn't see twelve inches in front of her what with the blizzard, but he seemed to know exactly where they were heading. When she finally spied the small log cabin nestled in a copse of evergreens, her heart nearly burst with relief. Finally, Zach could get off his feet and she could warm up. Her cheeks and nose were so cold, they hurt.

Zach touched her arm as they neared the covered porch. "Hang back."

"Why?"

"In case he comes out packing that rifle and a bad attitude." Zach narrowed his eyes when she jutted her chin.
"Humor me."

"Hurry." Maya covered her face with her gloves and
blew into her hands, hoping to unthaw her nose. Her pulse
raced as Zach abandoned the harness and snowshoes and
stepped onto the porch. Daniel had pegged Rosco Marx
as more bark than bite, but who knew? If the man felt
threatened . . .

Zach whistled and motioned her forward.

She hurried across the frozen lawn, unsnapped the
straps on her snowshoes, and joined him at the door. "What
are you reading?"

"A letter from Marx. It was tacked to the door and ad-
dressed to the Cupcake Lovers." He passed it to her while
he tried the door. "Locked."

Maya read the scrawled note.

*SINCE YOU PERSIST IN FORCING YOUR
CHARITY ON ME, THIS TIME I TOOK MYSELF
OUT OF THE EQUATION. GONE HUNTING
OVER THE BORDER. WON'T BE BACK TILL
AFTER CHRISTMAS. GIVE THAT DAMNED
BASKET TO SOMEONE WHO NEEDS IT.—
ROSCOE MARX*

"How rude," Maya commented, then gasped when she
noticed Zack picking the lock with some pocket tool.
"That's breaking and entering!"

"Do you want to freeze to death?"

"Good point." As soon as the door gave, Maya pushed
into the dank, dark cabin. "Although it's not much better
in here." She flicked a switch. "No electricity."

"I'll check the generator. Hold tight." Zach went out front, then around back.

Maya dragged in their supplies. The way the storm continued to rage they could be here all night. She pushed open a curtain, allowing the waning daylight to filter inside. Furnishings were sparse and old and it smelled like stale cigarettes, but at least the place was tidy. Unfortunately, though not a surprise, there wasn't a holiday decoration to be seen. Not even a menorah or a Charlie Brown Christmas tree.

She thought about the Coles' home with its oversized, overdecorated spruce, the singing Santa, the army of nutcrackers. She thought about the pine and cinnamon scents. About the Christmas Eve dinner they'd be having without Maya and Zach. Being stranded in a stinky, cheerless cabin wasn't the holiday she wanted, and it didn't help that Zach had distanced himself. She didn't sense that he was wallowing in self-pity, but she did feel his intensifying cynicism. More than anything, she wanted to vanquish that troubling darkness.

Maya blinked with a vision and a goal. If she couldn't provide Roscoe Marx with cheer and goodwill, she'd gift the spirit of Christmas to Zach.

He clomped back into the cabin just as she shoved a log into the woodstove. "What are you doing?" he asked.

"Building a fire, Sherlock."

He grunted. "Funny." Moving in, he dumped an armful of chopped wood into the iron bin. "As it happens we're on the same wavelength, Watson."

She glanced over her shoulder. "No luck with the generator?"

He shook his head. "We'll have to make do for warmth and light from the woodstove and fireplace. Hopefully the flue isn't clogged."

"I'm thinking we're probably stuck here for the night."

"That'd be my guess."

"I know we brought that gift basket for Mr. Marx, but he doesn't want it and he's not here. We are."

Zach's lip twitched. "Thinking about filching Marx's Christmas feast, Maya?"

"I look at it as not letting good food and intentions go to waste."

He smiled full out then and her heart thumped against her ribs. Without another word he moved to the fireplace, and within a couple of minutes Zach had a fire raging in the cobblestoned hearth.

Maya's own efforts at the wood-burning stove were successful as well, and she didn't waste a second breaking into the Cupcake Lovers care basket as well as the thermal tote packed by Helen and Giselle. She arranged the booty on the kitchen counter while Zach ditched his damp outerwear and futzed with his phone. Not getting a strong signal, he switched to Marx's landline. Thankfully, that worked.

"Yeah. Hi, Uncle Dan. It's Zach."

Maya raided drawers and cabinets while listening to Zach fill his uncle in on their circumstance. She supposed she should have felt depressed, being away from her parents, the Coles, and Giselle. Being stranded on a mountain in a smelly cabin without an ounce of Christmas cheer. But instead Maya tingled with the thrill of an adventure. She hadn't had many adventures lately. And thinking back, she realized her most memorable adrenaline rushes had happened with Zach.

By the time he signed off with Daniel, the main living area, which included a basic kitchen, had heated up enough that Maya had stripped off her coat and scarf, although she retained her Santa hat—just for the fun of it.

"Dan said this storm's finally being reported on the news. Although it's being referred to as the Ghost Storm. No one can make sense of it."

"Mother Nature has a way of keeping us on our toes," Maya said, unaffected. Utilizing the wood-burning stove, she'd already started heating the turkey, boiled potatoes, and a can of green beans sprinkled with almond slivers. She held up two cans of soup. "Clam Chowder or Cheddar Ale."

Zach glanced from the stove to the table she'd set, using a pine-scented candle she'd found in the care basket as the centerpiece. Smiling a little, he looked at Maya, striking her weak in the knees. "You choose."

Ten

He'd told himself he wasn't going to pursue the attraction. That he cherished Maya's friendship too much to screw it up on the off chance that they might click in bed. But as the evening wore on his resolve crumbled.

Scents from the delicious dinner Maya had whipped up lingered and mingled with the smell of pine wafting from a lone candle and the pleasing aroma of burning wood. While she'd cooked, Maya had hummed and sung Christmas songs, an old-fashioned form of entertainment that had moved Zach deeply as he'd toured around Marx's cabin, acquainting himself with the grump of Franklin County via random pictures and keepsakes.

Marx was an army man. A veteran of Vietnam. And near as Zach could tell, Marx had never married. No evidence of a wife or children, ever. Just photos with a few fellow soldiers and a hunting buddy or two. Marx struck Zach as a loner. A man who dwelled in the past. Was he shackled to the war by personal demons? Mentally and emotionally incapable of letting go and moving on? Had he even tried to fit into civilian life? Zach commiserated and at the same time fought the notion of ending up like this himself. Alone and miserable for life.

Maya's singing helped to lift his spirits and he suddenly found himself clinging to her goodness and optimism like a lifeline. While they feasted on turkey, soup, and various simple side dishes, she shared several touching stories based on holiday parties she and Giselle had volunteered to cater for local homeless and women's shelters. Maya spoke casually, as if Cupcakes & Dreamscapes had only played a small role, and focused on the people in need and their heart-tugging stories. But Zach felt the depth of Maya's and Giselle's kindness and generosity to the pit of his soul. It certainly shed new light on Giselle and only made Zach love Maya all the more.

Oh yeah. He'd fallen for Maya Templeton in a way that made his mind swim and his heart ache. He was the moon to her sun, the rain to her rainbow. He was the exact opposite of what he wanted for her, yet he didn't want to miss out on what she offered him. Hope. Happiness.

Even if only for tonight.

"Thank you for helping me clean up," she said to Zach after they'd cleared away the remaining food and dishes.

"Sure." He watched as she dried her hands on a ratty dishcloth. Her long hair was still tousled from the wind. Sexy. Even the Santa hat was a turn-on. All she had to do was lose the reindeer sweater and a few more layers and he'd be a goner.

"Have room left for dessert?" she asked.

"Let me guess. Cupcakes?"

She smiled and his heart skipped. "Why don't we have them in front of the fireplace?" she suggested. "There's a bottle of red wine, too, although it has a screw cap. How good can it be?"

"Who cares? You get the glasses. I'll fix us a pallet." Trying to get in the spirit and wanting to make the evening as festive as possible for Maya's sake, Zach pulled Marx's bearskin rug closer to the hearth. He shook out the comforter and blanket he'd brought along, draping them over the furry hide, then nabbed the pillows he'd found on Marx's bed, shimmying them into fresh pillowcases he'd found in a closet.

"Oh, wow," Maya said as she joined him, wine bottle and two plastic tumblers in hand.

"I don't know about you, but I'm not high on sleeping in Marx's bed. It's cold in that room and it just feels wrong."

"I agree," Maya said. "This is great. Sort of like a slumber party."

Zach noted her bright pink cheeks. Flushed in anticipation of sleeping together? Or because of her close proximity to the crackling hearth? "I'll pour the wine," he said, freeing up her hands. "You get the cupcakes."

Pain shot up his left leg as he lowered himself onto their makeshift bed. Like always he ignored the discomfort. Even when he'd been hospitalized, both legs in traction, he'd never once complained. His injuries were nothing compared to his partner's loss of life. Zach took a bullet in his right thigh and left shin, and he'd broken multiple bones in both legs in a fierce tumble down the mountainside. He might've made a clean escape if he'd left Ben's body behind, but that hadn't been an option. Even though Zach had failed to complete that mission, he didn't regret the effort.

Pushing away dismal memories, Zach shed his boots and poured two tumblers of bargain wine.

Maya sank down beside him, placing a plate of assorted

cupcakes on the floor. She kicked off her own boots and swept off the Santa cap, looking more serious than she had all afternoon. "There's something I want to say."

"Okay."

"If I don't it will fester. I want to get it out there and then we can move on."

Heart thudding, Zach calmly passed her a tumbler of wine.

"I know you don't want to talk about it, Zach, and I don't blame you. But I want you to know I'm sorry about Ben."

Holding her tender gaze was tough, but Zach did it. "I feel like I failed him."

"Do you think he'd feel that way?"

Zach searched his soul. "No."

"From what little you told me about Ben, I think he'd be miffed if he knew you were struggling with guilt." She reached over and squeezed his hand. "You're a good man, Zach."

"So was Ben."

"All right then. Rather than mourn his death, why not celebrate his life." She raised her glass and crooked a tender smile. "To Ben."

Overwhelmed, Zack tapped his glass to hers. "To Ben." She and Zach both drank deeply, and even though the wine was bitter, a wisp of sweet serenity flowed through his tortured being. He waited for Maya to press for details regarding the ambush. When she didn't, his spirits lifted even more. Last night she'd told him she'd be available if he ever wanted to talk about it. At the time, he'd brushed off the offer. Now he tucked it away for the day he was ready.

He picked up the dessert plate and studied six festive cupcakes by the light of the fire. "What do you think we have here, O baking expert?"

She grinned. "Not sure. Let's taste and see."

They both took a cupcake and sampled.

Maya chewed and groaned. "*Mmm.* Mine's maple with a kick of cayenne. Butter crème icing."

Zach swallowed a mouthful of savory delight. "Chocolate."

She rolled her eyes. "We're talking the Cupcake Lovers here. Can't just be plain ol' chocolate." She leaned in. "Gimme a taste."

Zach fed her, his nads tightening when she licked icing from his fingers.

"Devil's food," she said in a husky voice. "With raspberry ganache and milk-chocolate frosting."

Logs crackled in the hearth, the flames flickering throughout the darkened room and bathing Maya's beautiful face in a soft, enticing glow.

Zach edged closer, accepting the invitation sparkling in her eyes. Coating his finger in chocolate frosting, he smeared the sticky delight over her lower lip, then savored. "Not marmalade," he said, slipping her sweater from her shoulders and eyeing her creamy skin, "but it is sweet."

Eleven

Maya woke with a start, bolting upright, senses whirling.

"What was that?"

"Just a log crackling and shifting in the hearth," Zach said. He placed a strong hand at the base of her bare back. "You're safe, honey. Go back to sleep."

"I don't know that I can." She couldn't believe she'd drifted off in the first place, but she'd been so sated from their lovemaking and the wine, somewhere in the night she'd fallen asleep in Zach's arms. "What time is it?"

"Not even midnight."

"I can't believe that storm's still at it." She hugged a blanket to her chest, shivering as the wind howled and the windowpanes rattled. "Ghost Storm is an apt name. It's downright spooky."

"It'll pass." Zach pulled her back down on the soft pallet. Braced on one elbow, he gazed down into her eyes. "How are you feeling?"

Her sleepy pulse tripped. "You mean about what we did?"

"Any regrets?"

Her body hummed in memory of Zach's sensuous touch. "Only that it ended so soon."

He frowned. "You weren't satisfied?"

"I *was*," she teased. "But that was then and this is now. Call me shallow, but the way those flames are dancing over your hunky body I'm feeling sort of frisky just now. Plus, I could use a distraction."

"From the storm?"

From my thoughts. Now that she was awake, her mind churned with the realization that she'd fallen in love, true love, with Zachery Cole. Maybe she'd always loved him, but it hadn't fully blossomed until they'd made love. She didn't want tonight to end and yet she knew it would. The question was, what would tomorrow bring? Dare she hope for a Christmas miracle? For a happily ever after with her tortured best friend. "I never knew it could be like that. I mean, it's not like I'm a virgin, but I've never felt that kind of connection. That kind of intense pleasure. I mean I had three orgasms. *Three.*"

He grinned. "I know. I was there."

"Was it good for you?"

"Never better."

Maya's inner thighs tingled when he hovered and soul kissed. Amazing how he could fire her up with mere kisses.

"Maya."

She blinked up at his handsome face, her stomach fluttering with a thousand butterflies.

"I don't know about the future, honey. I can't think beyond now."

She brushed her fingertips over his worried brow.

"That's okay. We'll figure it out tomorrow. Or the day after." She could sense his doubts and concerns, and even though she didn't have all the answers herself, she did at least have faith in their deepening relationship. Something this good, this special, couldn't be doomed to failure. "I'm thinking you're the one in need of distraction now."

Heart full, Maya rolled on top of Zach and rained kisses down his chiseled torso. "Let's see if I can top *never better.*"

Zach's eyes flew open, startled by a sound. No. Not a sound. A *presence.* He reached for the handgun he'd hidden nearby. He hadn't mentioned the weapon to Maya. She wouldn't approve. But Zach believed in the right to protect. He wouldn't think twice about defending Maya. Yet when he trained his Glock on the shadowy figure sitting in a nearby chair, Zach's heart seized. "Ben?"

"Yo, dude. I've already been shot once." He waved off the revolver. "Do you mind?"

Zach lowered his weapon and looked down at Maya. She was fast asleep. He looked back to Ben. Still there. "Am I dreaming?"

"Maybe. Maybe not." Dressed in bloodied cammies, Ben motioned to Maya. "She's something special."

"How would you know?"

"I've been watching."

"From where?"

Ben pointed up.

Zach licked his lips, raised a brow. "From heaven? What are you now? An angel?"

"A messenger."

Heart pounding, Zach spared Maya another glance. She hadn't budged. She didn't hear them talking? Of course

not. Because he had to be freaking dreaming. He looked
back to his dead friend. "I'll bite. What's the word?"

"Don't be a wuss."

Zach laughed. "That's the message from above?"

"In a nutshell." Ben leaned forward, bracing his forearms on his knees and affording Zach a better look at his
grease and blood–smeared face.

Zach felt sick and mesmerized at the same time. "Are
you going to haunt me, Ben?"

"Nope. This is a onetime visit. I saw you screwing up
and begged for this chance. A chance to say thank you and
good-bye, and to give you a kick in the ass. Step up to the
challenge, Zach. There's more than one way to make this
world a better place. Just ask Maya."

Sweating now, Zach palmed Maya's shoulder, hoping
to connect with reality. *Oh yeah.* She felt solid and
warm, which freaked him out all the more. He'd played
along with Ben, thinking he was dreaming, but if he was
awake . . . He glanced back to Ben, but the angel, the ghost,
the messenger, whatever . . . was gone.

Zach fell back on the pallet, temples throbbing.

He closed his eyes, willing his nerves steady. Maybe
he'd been hallucinating. Too much cheap wine. A bit of bad
chowder. He didn't believe in ghosts. Dead was dead,
right?

He rolled away from Maya, toward the comfort of the
fire. He wondered if Marx kept any hard liquor in this
cabin. He could sure use a shot. He opened his eyes and
found himself face-to-face with his mom.

"Holy hell."

"Don't curse in the presence of women, Zachery."

"Sorry." His long dead mother was lying on her side,
propped up on an elbow. She hadn't aged in fifteen years,

and she was still wearing her waitress uniform. "How can you be here, Mom?"

"You needed me."

"I've needed you lots of times."

"Not like tonight." She pushed up a couple of inches and looked over his shoulder. "I always liked Maya."

Poleaxed by the surreal feeling of being caught between reality and a dream state, Zach flashed back on the holiday movie he'd watched with Maya. He knew Maya thought he was cynical. Had he twisted things in his mind so that he was Scrooge, putting Ben and his mother in the roles of the ghosts of Christmas past and present?

Damn.

"Do you have a message, Mom?" he asked, wanting to hurry this nightmare along but at the same time wanting her to linger.

"I do. But not for you. For Maya. Tell her I said you'll make beautiful babies."

"Mom—"

"I love you, Zach," she said, and then she was gone.

The next time Zach awakened, sunlight was spilling through the cabin windows and Maya was looking down at him with a big, cheery smile. "Merry Christmas, Zach."

He smiled up at her sweet face, palmed her cheek to make sure she was real. "Merry Christmas, Maya."

"Storm stopped. At least the wind died down. I'm almost afraid to look outside. There could be six feet of snow out there."

"I doubt that, although the drifts could be fierce. I'll check it out." He brushed a kiss across her mouth, experiencing a moment of pure joy, before pushing to his feet.

Though he managed a poker face, his muscles ached and his leg hurt. What bothered him more was the fuzzy feeling in his head. "Remind me to steer clear of that brand of wine in the future."

"Are you feeling hungover?" she asked as she pulled on her undies and jeans. "You didn't have that much."

"Not hungover, but, I don't know. Disconnected. Groggy. Had a couple of weird dreams."

"Want to talk about them?"

"They're sort of fuzzy. Maybe some fresh air will help." Zach dressed quickly, angling his head when he heard a rattle and a hum.

"Is that the generator?"

"Sounds like it's trying to kick in."

"That would be awesome." Maya pulled on that reindeer sweater and whisked into the kitchen area. "I think I saw some oatmeal and coffee. I'll see if I can whip us up a quick breakfast. We'll need energy to dig out. Oh, and maybe we should call Daniel. See if he can get someone up here with a plow and—"

"Maya."

"What?" She turned away from the cabinets and teetered into Zach.

He steadied her, frowned. "Are you babbling because you're excited about Christmas Day? Or because you're anxious about us?"

She smiled a little. "Both?"

"Like you said last night, we'll sort things out today. Or maybe tomorrow."

"No rush."

He grinned now. "Liar." Backing away, Zach nabbed his walking stick and limped toward the front door. "Make that coffee strong!" he called over his shoulder.

He stepped onto the porch and shoved on his shades. Unlike yesterday, the sun was beaming full out. There was a lot of snow, but nothing like what Zach had expected. Had it blown and drifted on the other side of the cabin? Navigating knee-deep snow, he rounded to the back . . .

And saw an old white-haired man leaning over the generator. He was dressed in hunting garb and sporting a scowl. Zach recognized him from the photographs inside. "Roscoe Marx?"

"As you live and breathe."

"I thought you were in Canada until after Christmas."

"So did I."

At first Zach thought Marx was hunched over the generator, but on second glance he looked plain crooked, his posture bent at an unnatural angle, sort of like a question mark. Zach looked over the brim of his glasses for a clearer look, but the glare off the glistening snow was blinding. "Name's Zachery Cole."

"Gunnery Sergeant. United States Marine Corps."

Zach pulse thrummed. "Not anymore."

"Once a Marine, always a Marine, son."

"I know the code." Zach shifted his weight, frowned. "How do you know me, sir?"

"Let's just say we're kindred spirits. Or at least we will be if you maintain your present course. You can languish in the past or grab the future by the horns. Choose wisely. I did not and look how things turned out for me."

Was he referring to his hermit-like existence? What the hell? Who was he to advise . . .

A shiver stole down Zach's spine as words echoed in the back of his brain.

Don't be a wuss.

You'll make beautiful babies.

"Lookin' a little green there, soldier," Marx said.

"Bad storm. Rough night. Spent it in your cabin. Coffee?"

"I like it strong." Marx went back to tinkering with the generator.

Zach heard a pop and a whir as he rounded the corner. What the hell was going on? He ambled back into the cabin, anxious to check in on Maya. She was sitting in a kitchen chair, holding her phone and looking stunned. "What's wrong, honey?"

"My phone. I have a signal. I called Aunt Helen to check in and she told me . . . well, I mean it's just awful. And on Christmas Eve, no less."

Zach's stomach turned.

"Roscoe Marx was killed last night in a car accident."

Twelve

Maya couldn't figure Zach out. His giddy mood was plain weird. She hadn't expected him to break down over the news of Roscoe Marx's demise—he didn't know Marx. *She* didn't know Marx. They'd never even met. Naturally, with that kind of emotional distance it was easier to disconnect. But at least she was sorry Marx had died. Zach had looked shocked for all of five seconds, and then he'd gotten a goofy grin on his face. He'd swooped her into his arms and spun her around with a childlike glee that reminded her of the scene in *A Christmas Carol* where Scrooge rediscovered the spirit of Christmas. She would have been charmed and thrilled if not for the inappropriate timing.

Zach had hurried her along, saying Marx wouldn't want them missing Christmas Day with the Coles. Which didn't sound to Maya like the Roscoe Marx Daniel had described—the same grump who'd left the rude letter for the Cupcake Lovers. Regardless, it was difficult not to be affected by Zach's lightened heart.

Presently she and Zach were backtracking through the forest. Although there was a lot of packed snow, the trek was easier since they weren't being slammed by wind and flurries. Maya could actually see where she was going, and the scenery was magical, to say the least. A veritable winter wonderland.

"I was thinking of maybe moving back to Sugar Creek," Maya blurted as they neared the snowbound Hummer.

"I was thinking of moving down to Orlando."

Her heart nearly burst through her ribs. She touched Zach's arm, urging him to stop. "What's going on with you?"

"You wouldn't believe me if I told you."

"Try me."

"Maybe later. I need to simmer on this a little more."

"Simmer on what?"

He tugged on her Santa hat, then shrugged. "A Christmas miracle?"

"Okay. You know what? You're freaking me out. This isn't you talking."

"Not the old me, no."

"What's that supposed to mean?"

"There's more than one way to make a positive difference in this world. You're doing that with Cupcakes & Dreamscapes."

She palmed her brow. "You want to make cupcakes?"

"I want to make a difference. Thought I could hang out with you while I figure out how."

"Hang out?"

"Marry me, Maya."

Knocked dizzy, Maya slumped against a tree trunk.

Zach moved in, bracing his arms on either side of her head. "Mom said we'll make beautiful babies."

Something Daisy Monroe had said about Zach and Giselle. *But Zach's mom is dead.* "When did she say that?"

"Last night."

"What? In your dreams?"

"Something like that." He kissed Maya then. One of those kisses that shimmied throughout her entire body, leaving her weak-kneed. He served a death blow with a breathtaking smile. "Marry me."

Maya gave him a whole five seconds to take back the proposal. He didn't. "Okay. You know what? I'm going to say yes, because I think you've gone a little screwy and you need someone to look after you."

"Any other reason?"

Heart full, Maya pushed her hands through Zach's messy hair and rested her forehead to his. "I love you, Zachery Cole."

The besotted look in his eyes seduced her soul. This time Maya initiated the kiss and she was certain the heat they generated would melt a path leading them back to Sugar Creek.

Instead a car honked breaking the silence, if not the magic.

Still holding Maya in his arms, Zach eyed the logging road. A monster vehicle with a plow was pushing its way toward the Hummer. "Looks like Adam's truck."

A dark-haired woman shoved her body out the passenger window and waved. "And G," Maya said with a smile.

"Ah, Giselle. The woman who talked you into penning her letters. Remind me to thank her."

"For misleading you?"

"For gifting me with the woman I love."

Have Yourself
a Curvy Little
Christmas

Sugar Jamison

One

Don't Want a Lot for Christmas...

Sleigh bells ring. Are you listening?

Dina Gregory had heard that song no less than twenty-six times on her five-day bus ride from California. Twenty-six. Freaking. Times and now it was stuck in her head like some kind of brain-eating ear worm.

A beautiful sight. We're happy tonight. Walking in a winter wonderland.

She had never thought about winter being wondrous. Or beautiful. She had always thought it cold and dark and depressing. That's why she had escaped to LA for two years. But as she walked up the steep driveway to the Windermere mansion she had to amend her thought. A fresh snow had just fallen, leaving the trees and ground covered with beautiful, shimmery snow. There were no footprints or tire tracks to muddy it. It was beautiful. The stuff that Christmas cards were made of.

And if she weren't cold, pissed off and carrying a

twenty-pound baby, she might be able to enjoy her surroundings more.

"Ma?" Her ten-month-old son, Dash, touched her cheek, pulling her out of her head for a moment.

"It's okay, lovey," she said to him as she held him a little closer to shield him from the wind. "We're almost there. Just a couple million more feet until we reach the top. Hopefully Mommy won't have a heart attack before we make it. I'm not sure what these people were thinking when they built this place. Surely a moat would have been good enough to keep the riffraff out. Or a dragon. I think building a house on top of a mountain was just a way to keep chubby people out. They should just have a sign that says: 'No Fat Chicks Allowed.' But they don't know your mommy, do they, baby? They're not keeping me out."

Her son grinned at her, one of those happy baby grins, like he knew what she was babbling about, and it kicked her in the heart. Good God she loved him. He was the reason she was here. He was the reason she had spent five days on a bus with people who looked like they had just been released from mental institutions. He was the reason she was huffing and puffing her out-of-shape ass up this steep hill. He was the reason she kept going.

There were just thirteen days until Christmas. Normally the holiday would pass as just another day to her, but this year was different. This year was special because it was Dash's first Christmas. She didn't want anything for herself. Somewhere along the line material things stop mattering. If she had one wish it would be to give her son the world.

That's why she was back in New York, a place she had been too afraid to show her face in the past year and a half. Her family lived just a few towns over, but she couldn't face them. Not after what she had done. The best gift she could give them was to never darken their doorstep again. But she would gladly darken Windermere's doorstep.

She was here to face Dash's father. Virgil Worthington Rowe. The man who knocked her up and disappeared the day after she told him about it.

Asshole.

At first she didn't bother tracking him down. The pregnancy had been a wake-up call for her. The thirty-four years of her life before she became pregnant with Dash had been spent partying too, much, destroying too much, not caring enough. Dash had changed all that. He made her want to become a better person. He made her want to stand on her own two feet.

But Dash didn't deserve to live in squalor just so she could prove a point. He was innocent in all of this. And his father had more money than he knew what to do with. She was going to get some of that money. And if she couldn't she was going to kick his no-good ass. With the fifty pounds she had put on during her pregnancy she was pretty sure she could take him.

Another blast of icy wind smacked her in the face, reminding her that her poor nose was going to fall off if she didn't get inside soon. She wished she could have taken a cab right to the front door to save them from some of this brutal cold, but in the tiny village of Sleepy Ridge there were none. Virgil had to be here, because it was too damn long of a walk back to town to leave with nothing.

She had looked for him all over LA. She called around to the hotels he liked to stay in, checked in all the bars they used to frequent. But he wasn't there. Nobody had seen or heard from him in months. The coward was probably hiding from her.

She finally came to the front door, her hand raised to knock, and she froze.

She was nervous.

Shit.

Nerves were the one thing she hadn't planned on. She had been too pissed to be nervous before, but now that she was facing the front door of this huge mansion nerves snuck up on her and grabbed her by the throat.

"Can I help you, ma'am?" The southern-accented voice that came through the intercom caused her to jump.

Duh, Dina. They probably saw you coming as soon as you stepped foot on the driveway.

"Ma'am, is there something I can do for you?"

"Um . . ."

"Ma?" Dash called to her, reminding her of her purpose. Reminding her that this trip was about him.

"Yes. My name is Dina Gregory. I'm here to see Virgil."

Benjamin Rowe sat in his office staring at the stack of legal documents and bills that he had just inherited. Thirty-seven thousand dollars for a hotel bill. Fourteen thousand on a bar tab. The money just kept adding up and he wondered how one person could waste so much. Not the money. In the end money was nothing. Ben wondered how one person could waste so much of their life.

He shut his eyes, unable to look at the mountain in front of him any longer. With each bill he paid, with each lawsuit he studied, his stomach sank even further.

Disappointment. It was a familiar feeling to him. It was all he had felt when he thought of his brother for the last few years. He wished he didn't. He wished he could just wash his hands of the whole mess. He had a team of lawyers and accountants at his disposal. All of this could be sorted out in less than a week. He wouldn't have to think about it. But he couldn't let it go. He couldn't let somebody else handle this. This mess was too personal, too revealing. If he let somebody else fix it he knew he would be letting down his father.

You've got to be a man now. Protect your little brother. You're the only one he's got.

He had tried to protect Virgil. Their mother had died when they were just little boys. Their father had died when they were just barely men. They had money. They had employees, people who called themselves friends, a company worth billions, but they only really ever had each other.

Now all Ben had in front of him was a pile of debt. His brother was gone. He'd pulled away from Benjamin a long time ago. Virgil didn't like being controlled. He balked at his brother's guidance. He didn't like rules or limits or expectations being placed on him. He wasn't cut out for a life of hard work. All he had ever wanted was freedom. Ben almost couldn't blame Virgil. It was hard being a Rowe man. It was hard running a billion-dollar company, living up to the extremely high example set by their father and grandfather. There were times in his life when Ben wanted to be like Virgil, when he just wanted to be free too. But he couldn't.

And now Virgil was gone and it left Ben wondering would he still be here today if Ben hadn't cut him off?

"Sir?"

He looked up to see Miguel, his assistant and personal security guard, standing just inside of his office door.

He hadn't heard the man coming. He was too deep in his thoughts.

"Do you have a brother, Miguel?"

Miguel, who was usually unflappable, was taken off guard. "No, sir. Three sisters. All younger."

Ben studied the young former Marine who had been

with him for nearly eight years now and realized that he wasn't so young anymore. "Do you have a father?"

"Yes, sir."

"What's he like?"

"Sir?" Miguel frowned. They had never had a conversation in all the years Miguel had been there. But Ben trusted this man with his life. He should know something about him.

"I want to know what your family is like."

Miguel blinked at him, hesitation clear on his face. "My family lives in Texas. My parents own a food truck that runs six days a week. My sisters Angela and Marielle are both married with babies and my younger sister, Carmen, is in college."

"When's the last time you saw them?"

Miguel looked guilty for a moment, but he shouldn't have. It was Ben's fault. Ben worked, so he made his entire staff work. He never paid much thought to holidays. Holidays stopped having any meaning for him when Karen got sick nine years ago.

"It's nearly Christmas, Miguel. Maybe you should go see them."

"But, sir—"

"The last time I saw my brother was nearly three years ago. You can't be like me. Go see your family. I don't want you to come back until January second."

"But that's too long."

"You deserve it. You put up with me for eight years without a complaint. I think I owe you some vacation time."

"I get ten days a year. This is too much."

"Go tell Dovie and the whole downstairs staff that they have off too."

"But you'll be alone." The way Miguel said it, the way he looked at him with a little bit of pity in his eyes, made Ben pause. He would be alone, but then again he had been alone for years. The presence of people didn't change that for him.

"I'm nearly forty. I think I can manage. Now go. I've got to get through this."

Miguel turned to leave, but he stopped. "Sir? I came here for a reason. There's a woman at the front door. She's here to see your brother."

"Send her away." Ben put his glasses on and picked up the document on top of the stack. Lots of people came to see his brother. They usually wanted something from him. But Virgil had nothing left to give.

"We will, but we wanted to check with you first."

"Why? I trust your judgment."

"Her name is Dina Gregory and she's carrying a baby."

"Mr. Rowe will see you now."

The enormous mansion door slowly swung open, causing a delicious wave of warm air to touch Dina's face. For a moment she just stood there, absorbing the tease of warmth. She also stood there because for the first time she realized she didn't have a plan. Well, she did have a plan actually. But a life plan. Get support for Dash, find a job teaching dance and then open her own dance studio. But she had no idea what she was going to do when she faced Virgil. Too many emotions ran through her whenever she thought of him

"Are you coming in, ma'am?"

Dina almost didn't notice the woman who had answered the door. She was a tiny older African-American woman with skin the color of fresh-baked bread, startling white hair and the most delicate set of cheekbones she had ever seen. "Holy shit. You're beautiful."

The woman's eyes widened, as she was clearly offended by Dina's potty mouth.

"I'm sorry." She shook her head. "I've been on a bus for five days and the little bit of class and poise I had was probably left somewhere in the Midwest."

"It's quite all right, ma'am. Please follow me."

"You betcha," Dina said, which earned another curious look from who she presumed must be the housekeeper. It was then she decided to keep her mouth shut until she saw Virgil. There was no need to waste her energy when she was going to need it to confront him.

The bastard knew she was pregnant when he disappeared. When she told him, he glanced at her stomach and sneered with disgust.

Too bad. You had a really nice body. Maybe you can get it back after you give the kid up. I know you aren't thinking about keeping it. I wouldn't allow you to care for my goldfish. There is no way you can care for a child.

Up until that moment she had thought about giving her child up for adoption. There were a lot of lonely couples who wanted children. Her own parents had adopted a child. Her little sister, Ellis, had turned out pretty damn good. But when Virgil said she couldn't care for a child, she knew she had to prove him wrong. She knew she had to prove everyone wrong. She was capable of good things. She could be a good mother.

"Mr. Rowe's office is on the third floor. Will you be able to manage with the little one for three flights? There is a service elevator in the back if that would be better."

"This house has an elevator? Well, damn." She took in her surroundings and realized that she shouldn't have been surprised. The house was enormous, practically museum-like. She felt out of place in it, like her dirty boots shouldn't be allowed to touch the floor. "I can carry him. The piece-of-crap stroller I got from the thrift store broke a month after Dash was born. I have to carry him everywhere. I've got arm muscles that can rival any professional wrestler's."

The housekeeper gave her another look and discreetly glanced at Dash before she ascended the stairs.

"I know I probably won't be staying long, but I would feel a little better if you told me your name."

"My name is Dovie, ma'am."

"Dovie! What an awesome name. It suits you. It's sweet and delicate. Unlike my name. I always hated 'Dina' growing up. My real name is Adina, but that's not much better. There's no romance in it, but I was named after my mother's great-aunt. My stepfather got to name my sister. Her name is Ellison. She was named after his grandfather. But her name is kind of cool. People always remember a girl named Ellis."

"That's quite interesting, ma'am."

"I'm babbling. I know." She pressed a kiss to her son's smooth cheek, hoping that it would soothe her frayed nerves. It did slightly. There was nothing that smelled better than a clean baby. "I've haven't seen Virgil in a very long time. I'm surprised he agreed to see me."

"Yes, ma'am." A sad look crossed Dovie's face before she turned away and continued up the stairs.

Dina stopped talking and tried to gather her thoughts before she faced him again. This meeting was too important to screw up.

Dovie stopped at the top of the stairs and gestured down the long hallway. "Mr. Rowe is just through that set of double doors, ma'am. His personal office is the first door on the left."

"You're not going in with me?"

Dovie smiled gently at her. "Miguel will assist you from here." She walked away leaving Dina feeling truly alone.

Stop it!

She shook her head, trying to shake herself out of her stupidity. She had to do this. Dash deserved it.

So she walked down the long hallway, taking in her surroundings as she tried to ignore the fact that her heart was nearly pounding out of her chest. This part of the house felt different. A little more modern. A little less warm, with its dark mahogany wood and tasteful modern art lining the walls. She couldn't imagine Virgil here. His quarters. His office. When she had known him he had never worked. Never had a place he called home. Hotels seemed to be his preferred residences. Maybe he had changed in the past year. Change was possible. She knew she had undergone some. Maybe that's why he agreed to see her. Maybe he was ready to take a role in his son's life. Or maybe Virgil was going to throw her out on her ass. It wouldn't matter if he did. She wasn't going away easily.

She walked through the double doors, finding a handsome man wearing a dark suit and tie. Even though he stood straight, almost regally, she knew he was no butler. He almost reminded her of one of those Secret Service men, or some kind of trained assassin. He looked like he didn't take any shit from anybody, and that's why she smiled when he began to walk towards her. She couldn't picture this man spending any time with Virgil. Virgil was a man who hated order and rules. This man looked as if he lived by them.

"Ms. Gregory." He approached and gave Dash a very long look.

She knew Dash didn't look very much like Virgil. He had dark brown hair and dark eyes. Skin that was almost olive. His father had been light, angelic looking, with hazel eyes and sandy blond hair. She would go for a DNA test if she had to. Virgil had been the only man she had been with for a very long time. Dash was his son, even if Virgil wanted nothing to do with him.

"Please follow me."

They walked through a set of double doors, past a tiny room with only a bed in it, before they walked into a wide-open space. At first all Dina could see was books, shelves and shelves of them, but it was only when she heard the doors shut behind her that she noticed the man sitting behind a simple sleek black desk.

"Ms. Gregory." The man didn't look at her. His eyes were only focused on her son, who was looking back at the stranger. But he was no stranger to her. She knew him because she had spent two long awkward days in his presence. He was Benjamin Rowe, head of Rowe Steel and Rowe Communications and about a half-dozen other businesses that had made him a billionaire. He was Virgil's brother and he hated her.

Shit.

Virgil she could face, Virgil she knew, but Ben was one of those men who were hard to read. He was humorless and serious and responsible. All the things his brother wasn't.

Ben stood up and walked towards them, and Dina had to force herself to not to step back. He was huge and even though he wore a refined three-piece suit and glasses there was something a little dark about him. Not dangerous, but dark. She had the same reaction to him now as she did when she met him nearly two years ago.

"You're not Virgil," she managed to get out.

For some reason she didn't expect to find Ben there. She always pictured him as a man who traveled the world.

London one week, Paris the next. But she remembered what Virgil had told her about Ben. That he was nearly a recluse. That his wife's death had sucked what little life he had left out of him.

"Look, if he sent you to deal with me save your breath. This is between me and him."

"This boy . . ." Ben never bothered to take his eyes off Dash. "This is Virgil's son."

"Yes." Dina was surprised that there was no question in his voice. Like he knew it was a fact. "You believe me."

She looked at Dash and then up at his uncle. It struck her then how similar they looked. Dash was dark like Ben. They had the same eyes. The same-shaped nose. Ben could be his father. How had she never noticed before? But then again she tried never to think about Ben.

"I may have had a few hazy nights these past few years," Dina said, "but I know I have never slept with you."

"No." Ben's eyes finally snapped to hers. And in the warm room a chill—no, more like a tingle ran down her spine. Two years ago she hated when he turned that intense stare on her and she hated it now. Nobody ever had that kind of power over her, the power to make her feel . . . Self-conscious. That's why she fell for Virgil and his lazy glances. Virgil had a kindness about him. He had a way about him that pulled people in. Not Ben. No wonder why the man lived in hiding.

"What can I do for you, Ms. Gregory?"

"I-I," she stuttered, still a little flustered by his long observation of her. "I need to see Virgil."

"I'm afraid that's not possible."

"Oh, you better make it possible. I spent five days on a bus with a ten-month-old baby to get here. Five days. I'm sure you've never ridden a bus, so you have no idea how much they suck. You tell that bastard that I'm not going anywhere until I see him. He needs to do the right thing by his son."

"I wish I could make him do the right thing." Ben looked weary for a moment. "More than anything I would like to make him accountable for this."

"I can make him accountable. I'll go to court. I won't let my baby suffer."

"The courts won't help you, Ms. Gregory. I'm afraid Virgil is dead."

TWO

I Have No Gifts to Bring...

Ben watched Dina pale. She stumbled backward, as if the news of Virgil's death was a physical blow. He reached for the child, for the nephew he never knew about, and took him from his mother before she fainted. "Sit down," he ordered, wrapping his free arm around her body and guiding her to the couch near the window. He couldn't help but take note of the scent of her hair. Like strawberries and cream. Even though she looked like a homeless person at the moment, she smelled like something he would like to eat.

What a strange thought.

Especially coming from him, especially about Dina. He didn't like her when they first met two years ago. She talked too much. She laughed too loud. She said the wrong things, but there was something about her that kept him watching her the entire time he was near her. He looked at her now, at her pale face and big sad eyes. Dina must have loved Virgil. He didn't think so then. He thought she was just going to be another one of Virgil's girls, but he was wrong. He was wrong about many things.

"Take off your coat. It's warm in here."

"Would you stop barking at me, jerk face?" she said, but she obeyed him, her hands shaking a little as she unzipped the ugly puffy green jacket she was encased in.

"Ma?"

It was then Ben realized that he held a child in his arms. He had never held a baby before and stared at the small powder-scented boy with wonder. He had always wanted children. He and Karen had tried for years, but they never got their wish.

"I'm okay, baby. Can you please take off his hat?" she said to Ben. He did as she asked, revealing a mass of dark curly hair. He looked just like Ben did when he was a baby. There had been women who claimed that Virgil had fathered their children. Each time a paternity test was issued, each claim had proved to be false, but this time when Ben saw the little boy who was supposed to be his brother's, he knew this woman told the truth.

He tossed the hat on the couch and carefully unzipped the boy's coat. He was dressed nicely in a little sweater-vest, blue corduroy pants and a button-down shirt. Much better than his mother, who looked as if she had gone shopping in a dumpster.

"What's his name?" Ben asked, looking at his nephew again.

"Dash."

"Dash?"

"I thought he looked quite dashing when I saw him." She looked from her son to Ben. "I hate to admit this, but he looks just like you."

"I noticed the resemblance."

"Is that why you believed me? I thought you would have had a doctor here to do a DNA test by now."

"That's not necessary, Ms. Gregory."

"Dina," she corrected. "Geez, you make me feel like I'm back in grammar school when you call me Ms. Gregory." She drew in a couple of slow deep breaths, trying to calm herself before she looked at him with wide eyes. "What happened to Virgil?"

"Skiing accident." He looked at Dash and then back to his mother. "Vodka and the slopes don't mix."

"Ski accident." She shook her head. "What a rich people way to die."

"Excuse me?"

"It's just that you never hear of regular people dying that way. 'John Smith, plumber from Toledo, died in a tragic ski accident today on the slopes of Aspen.' But Virgil . . . That seems just like the way he would go."

"Does my brother's death amuse you?"

"Of course not." Her eyes flashed. "He was the father of my son and I may be mad as hell he walked out on me, but I would never be happy that he's gone. And you can go to hell if you think that."

He stared at her for a moment, his respect for her going up slightly. No one had ever told him to go to hell. They never had the guts. "You were with him for six months. I know you must have cared about him."

"Yeah. He could be an asshole, but he was my friend too."

Ben nodded; somehow in her inelegant way she expressed exactly how he felt about his brother. "You look very different than the last time I saw you."

"You try having a baby and not gaining any weight. I know I'm a little more bountiful than usual, but I like me and if you don't you can shove it."

"I didn't say you weren't beautiful. I just said you didn't look the same. I prefer you this way."

She was taken aback by his comment. He hadn't meant to say those words, but they weren't a lie.

"I always thought you looked a little gaunt before," he said to cover how he truly felt.

She was beautiful then but even more so now. Despite her ratty clothes and messy hair, he had a hard time pulling his eyes away from her. And his body—it reacted to her, wanting to move closer when his brain told him to back away. She was lush. Her skin was peachy. Her wild auburn hair was thick and healthy. He imagined what she would look like all cleaned up. He imagined her on his arm. Which was an odd thought, a dangerous thought, because he had promised himself that after Karen there would be nobody else.

"My, my, sir. If you keep up with those outrageous compliments you might swell my head." She rolled her eyes. "So what now?" She stood and took little Dash out of Ben's arms and kissed her son's face. "I guess I need his death certificate."

"For what?"

"I can get Social Security from the government. Right?" She looked so unsure. "I think I heard that. Because Virgil is dead, Dash is entitled to those benefits."

He nodded.

She pursed her lips. "Do you think it will take very long? I rented a motel room for tonight, but my bus leaves the day after tomorrow and I have to get back to work soon or I'm going to lose my job. And I can't afford to lose my job. Do you think you can get the certificate to me by tomorrow?"

"I'm not giving it to you."

"What?" She looked up at him in shock. "I need that.

I need it for him. Listen, I'm not asking you for anything except what my son deserves. I know you hate the fact that I tainted the Rowe line with my blood, but get over it. My kid is part of your family whether you like it or not."

Ben felt himself grow extremely angry with his brother. He'd abandoned her. He'd put his son, the only person left who could carry on the Rowe name, into destitution. If Virgil weren't already dead Ben would kill him. "Miguel!"

"Are you seriously kicking me out? Dude, your brother said you were an asshole, but I never thought you would throw a lady and a baby out in the street!"

"Sir?" Miguel burst through the door, immediately searching for the source of trouble.

"Tell Dovie to take Ms. Gregory and her son to the east wing. She'll be staying here."

"Sir?" Miguel frowned in confusion. Ben knew he was questioning his judgment and he had a right to do so. Ben didn't know this woman. She could be a scam artist. He shouldn't trust her. But part of him did. He knew that Dash was his brother's son.

"Tell Dovie to put her in the pink room and give her whatever she needs. But make sure they are both fed first."

Ben looked back at Dina, who was staring at him, her wide hazel eyes filled with confusion and maybe a little bit of fear. "You are not taking my nephew to a cheap motel. You will not be traveling with him, on a bus. Your destitution ends here."

"You're shitting me?"

"I shit you not."

Dina smiled at him and she ceased to be just beautiful. She was gorgeous. She looked happy. It had been a long time since anybody had been happy in this house.

"Ben!" She launched herself at him, pressing herself and her baby into his chest. "I'm totally sorry that I called you an asshole. You're not an asshole." She kissed his cheek. "We promise we won't bother you. We'll be on our best behavior." She kissed his cheek again, her full, soft lips leaving a trail of warmth on his face. "Thank you. Thank you."

Ben stood there for a moment frozen. No one touched him anymore. Only the occasional handshake. He hadn't been hugged in years, kissed in even longer than that. It was almost a foreign feeling. But not an unwelcome one.

He gently set himself away from her. Immediately he noticed the loss of the warmth provided by her soft body. "You don't have to thank me. We'll discuss your future later."

"Of course." The smile faded from her lips. "I'll see you later."

"Ma'am?" Miguel called to her. "Please follow me."

Dovie took Dina to the pink room, which turned out to be an enormous luxurious bedroom that her apartment could have fit into three or four times. It had a distinctively different feeling from Ben's quarters, from the rest of the house. There was something warm about the room, with its cheery yellow drapes and its plush carpet. It was a room that somebody could spend a lot of time in.

To say she had been relived when Ben offered to put her up was an understatement. She dreaded the thought of going back out into the cold. She dreaded taking her son back to that small, dark motel room. But now she was left with the realization that she would be under the same roof as him. As Ben. She, who never found herself uncomfortable around men, found herself uncomfortable around him.

"The bathroom is over there, Ms. Gregory," Dovie said,

distracting Dina from her troubling thoughts. "I can run a bath for you if you'd like."

"Oh." It had been years since Dina had a good bath. Her apartment in LA only had a shower, and even if it had a tub she wouldn't want to leave Dash unattended for long.

"I can watch the little one until you get out," Dovie said, reading Dina's thoughts. "I won't even leave the room with him if you'd like."

Dina's eyes filled. She wasn't a crier, but suddenly the past week had caught up to her. It had all been too much. She was exhausted. Mentally. Physically. Her soul felt weary.

"Oh, ma'am, don't cry." Dovie rushed over and patted her back. "It'll be okay."

"I'm fine." Dina swiped at her eyes. "I'm just over-whelmed. Who knew the thought of a hot bath would bring me to tears?"

The older woman smiled gently at her. "Go on, honey. You get undressed and have a nice long soak in the bath-tub. I can give your boy a bath too while you're in there, so you don't have to worry about him."

"You don't have to." She held Dash closer to her. "I can bathe him."

"Of course you can, but there hasn't been a baby in this house since Mr. Rowe and Virgil. Old Dovie doesn't have so much to do anymore. I would like to feel useful again."

"Of course." Dina handed her son over, feeling stupid for being so protective. "Knock yourself out. I bathe him in the kitchen sink because my apartment doesn't have a tub. Do you think he'll be okay in a full-sized tub?"

"We've got a whole bathroom in the nursery, ma'am. It's just right for little ones."

"There's a nursery here?"

"Just right down the hallway. I won't take him far."

Dina nodded, forcing herself to let him go for a little while.

"Would you like me to run your bath before I go?"

"No, thank you. I can manage."

"There are fresh towels on the shelf and a new robe on the back of the door. All of your washing products are under the sink."

"Thank you, Dovie. I appreciate your help."

"My pleasure, ma'am. Will you be needing anything else before I go?"

"Yes." She looked around her plush surroundings once more. "Why do they call it the pink room? There's nothing pink in here."

"No." Dovie shook her head. "Mr. Rowe had everything torn out and redecorated about seven years ago."

"Why?"

"I'm not sure, ma'am, but after his wife died he ordered the room changed."

His wife, Dina thought. *How could any woman agree to spend the rest of her life with Ben?*

Ben knocked on Karen's door. And then he realized that it wasn't Karen's door anymore. This room, this part of the house, stopped being hers nine years ago. It was then she retreated from him, retreated from the world and holed herself up in a small sitting room on the other side of the house. Keeping herself from him. Keeping her secrets from him.

He mentally shook himself. Now was not the time to think about his wife. Dina was in there. The woman who had loved his brother. The woman who was going to keep the Rowe name alive. He knocked again and waited, but there was no answer. She was in there. He could hear sounds coming from the room, baby sounds. Dovie had reported to him that his guests were fed and bathed and that she took the liberty of sending for Dina's things at the motel. The memory of his former nanny's report amused him. She seemed almost excited, happy that there was going to be another child to take care of for a few days. She said it would bring some life back into her. She was right. Dash would bring a little life back into the entire house. It had felt somewhat like a mausoleum these past few years. Quiet and dark and lifeless.

Ben knew he should have sent Dovie away years ago, paid for her to enjoy her retirement someplace warm. He had promoted her to housekeeper, but there wasn't much to do. He wasn't a man who needed much, but he couldn't seem to part with the old woman. She had raised him. They rarely interacted anymore, but knowing she was in his home brought him some comfort.

He knocked once more, his only answer a loud baby coo. He entered to find Dina asleep on the bed. She was curled up on her side, her, hand resting under her chin. Her wild auburn hair spread across the pillow. She looked so peaceful that he couldn't take his eyes off of her. He also couldn't help but notice that she wore a just a T-shirt and a pair of pink cotton panties. Her long legs were shapely, her thighs thick, her hips curvy. She looked . . . soft. Womanly. He could just imagine how she would feel wrapped around him. It had been a very long time since he had a woman wrapped around him and the thought of sinking into warm curves awakened something inside him that he thought had died a long time ago.

It was a pull. That was the only way he could describe it. He felt it the first time they had met, but he denied it then. He could never be attracted to her, to one of Virgil's girls. He could never entertain the thought of being with anybody but his wife, but there he was, watching this beautiful woman sleep and feeling the pull all over again.

"Bah!"

Ben shook his thoughts away from the inappropriate and he peeled his eyes away from the boy's mother and placed them on Dash. He should be in the nursery. Ben and Karen had the room completely remodeled the first time she had gotten pregnant. Unfortunately, the room had never been used, but all the furniture was still there and Ben made sure the room was dusted once a week. Dash could stay in there. There was no reason the room should be empty. Besides, Dina was exhausted, in a sleep so heavy that she didn't hear him enter the room. Maybe it was time she had some undisturbed rest. She deserved it.

And he needed some more time to figure out what the hell he was going to do with her. He wanted her gone. Out of his life. Out of his mind forever. But then there was the boy. The last Rowe man. Ben couldn't live the rest of his life without having his nephew near him. He approached Dash quietly, lifting him off the bed as carefully as possible so not to hurt him, but the boy was sturdy. He would grow into a strong young man. Ben only hoped Dash's mother would be able to raise him to be a good young man.

He left the room, but suddenly the nursery seemed too far away, so he took Dash next door to his old bedroom, another room that was rarely used anymore.

He sat on his bed, Dash on his lap facing him. He knew he shouldn't just stare at the boy, but he was amazed at how much he looked like the Rowes.

He should say something, talk to his nephew, but what did one say to a baby?

"What's up, kid?"

Dash giggled at him, showing off his four-tooth grin. It caused Ben to smile, something he hadn't remembered doing in a very long time. "Did that sound as ridiculous to you as it did to me?"

Dash let out a long line of unintelligible baby jabber.

"Is that so? Well, what would you like to talk about?"

"Ma Ma?"

"Your mother?" Ben nodded, understanding the boy's meaning. "She's very tired right now. It's best if we let her sleep."

"Bah Bah?"

"Bah Bah," he repeated. "Bah Bah?" He searched his mind for meaning and then it dawned on him. "Are you thirsty? Would you like your bottle?"

"Bah Bah."

"What a smart boy you are. Of course you can have a bottle." Ben went to get up and get it and then realized that he didn't know where the bottles were or if they had any at all. He didn't want to disturb Dina or leave Dash alone, so he did the only thing he could think of. He called for help. Within moments Rebecca, one of his maids, was at the door.

"Sir? Can I help you with something?" His staff were well trained and usually showed no reaction to any of his requests, but Rebecca couldn't hide her shock. She kept looking at Dash as if she wanted to save him.

"My nephew is thirsty. I need a bottle."

"Oh, sir, I can give him a bottle for you. You don't need to trouble yourself."

"Bring me a bottle, Rebecca." He glanced at Dash, who looked like he could go for a snack. "And some pudding."

"Sir?"

"We don't have pudding?"

"I made some myself for you this morning. Butterscotch, from scratch just like you like."

"Then what's the problem?"

"Are you sure about this?"

"Go."

She hurried off and Ben returned his attention to Dash. "What is it babies like to do for fun?"

Three

Blue, Blue, Blue Christmas...

Dina woke up with a start. Her baby wasn't there. She didn't even have to open her eyes to know that he was gone. She couldn't feel him beside her. She couldn't hear him or smell him. She slept beside him every night. He was like an extension of her and he was gone. She bolted out of bed and searched the room. Her backpack was gone too. All of her things, his things, were gone, like they were never there in the first place.

She took a deep breath and forced herself not to panic. But it was hard for her. Dash was the only thing she had left. Maybe she shouldn't have trusted Ben. He was a Rowe after all. And Rowes couldn't be trusted. Virgil proved that. They probably stole her baby to sell on the black market. She knew the idea was ridiculous, but who would just take her baby without asking? She headed down the hallway towards the nursery, but Dash's voice stopped her. Her heart lurched. He was close. She turned towards the sound.

He wasn't alone; a deep rumble of a male voice followed her baby's.

"You really need to work on your eating habits, son." Ben had Dash in his lap and a washcloth in his hand. He was gently wiping what looked like pudding off Dash's face. "It's on your toes too? How the hell did it get there? I must not be an expert at this feeding business. You can't be this messy all the time."

Dash babbled happily while Ben cleaned him up.

"Oh, you are? Then your mother must spend a fortune just to clothe you."

"Bah Bah?"

"Yes. Here, drink your milk." He cradled Dash in the crook of his arm and gave Dash his bottle.

Dina smiled at the picture the two made. She didn't want to. She wanted to continue thinking that Ben was a cold, humorless bastard, but she couldn't. There was a gentleness about him. He was down to just his starched white shirt and slacks. His feet were bare. He had just a hint of five o'clock shadow showing and he was covered in brown goop. But there was something very sexy about him. She didn't know what it was, the fact that he kind of had a Rock Hudson thing going on or the fact that he was holding her son in his lap. He was treating Dash with kindness, like he was a part of Ben's family. It wasn't what she had bargained for when she came here. She thought she would get some money, an agreement from Virgil for child support so she could spend more time with her baby and less time doing double shifts as a waitress. She didn't expect to find him dead or his brother so willing to accept her son.

"He has very cute little feet, don't you think?" she said when she noticed Ben stroking Dash's little toes.

Ben looked startled for a moment but recovered quickly. "I've never seen anything so small."

"You should have seen him when he was born. He was so tiny. I thought I was going to break him."

"He's a sturdy boy."

"He is."

"Ma Ma!" Dash dropped his bottle and clapped his hands, cheering her arrival.

"How's my baby?" She crawled onto Ben's huge four-poster bed and collected her son. She settled next to Ben, not ready to take her son from his only uncle. They were just a few inches apart, their arms nearly touching. She could feel the warmth radiate off his body. She could smell the butterscotch on his skin.

"I was just trying to get to know him a little," Ben spoke, breaking the silence. "I came to talk to you, but you were sleeping and . . . Well . . . He seemed alone."

"How long was I out?"

He glanced at her bare legs before he looked into her eyes. She was too panicked when she got up to even notice that she didn't wear pants. But now she was in his bed her long legs stretched out before her. Even with the added weight she never minded when a man looked at her, but when Ben did . . . she couldn't describe it. It was more than just self-consciousness. But she refused to fold her legs beneath her. She refused to care what he thought about her body.

"We've been together for a little over an hour. I don't know how long you were asleep before I came to see you, but if I had to guess it's been a long time. It's nearly eight p.m."

"Oh. I'm sorry." She felt stupid for letting her guard down for that long. "I was exhausted."

"Don't apologize. I know the past few days have been difficult for you. I want you to feel comfortable here."

Comfortable? She was alone in a room with him. Comfortable was the last thing she was feeling at that moment. "So what did you want to talk to me about?"

"Did you really name him Dash?"

"Well, yeah." She looked up at Ben's frowning face: "You don't like it."

"No."

She shrugged. At least he was honest. "I think it's a cool name. It kind of goes with Chip and Muffy and Scooter. All those names you rich white folks like to give your offspring."

"I've never known anybody with any of those names."

"No?"

"No." He took Dash's small hand in his, touching each one of his small fingers. "What's his middle name?"

"Walter. I named him after my stepfather."

"Where is your family? I take it you didn't turn to them for help."

She looked down at her son's head. "I can't go to them. They don't like me."

"Why? I can't imagine anything that you could do to make them turn their backs."

A dull pain throbbed in her chest. The same pain she thought about whenever she thought about her family. "I was a bitch, Ben. Before I had my kid I was a stupid, selfish bitch. They don't like me for the same reasons you don't like me and frankly I deserve it."

He let go of Dash's hand and took hers, stroking his large thumb over her palm. "I never said I didn't like you. But obviously you didn't like yourself."

She looked up into his eyes, surprised by his gentle touch, surprised that he pegged her so quickly.

"Are you a better person now that he's here?"

"I would like to think so. I'm sure trying to be."

Ben nodded. "Then you will be." She didn't know how

it happened. She didn't know if he moved or she got closer, but there was no longer any space between them. Their sides were pressed together. His strong shoulder was supporting her head and he still held her hand. She couldn't remember the last time any man had simply just touched her. Without expecting more. Without trying to pressure her into sex. To most men that was the only thing she was good for, and for a while she had believed that.

"Are you gay?" She tried to break the bubble around them, the odd closeness that she felt. It couldn't be real. This couldn't be happening.

"No." He didn't act all huffy like she expected. He didn't jump with wounded male pride. All he said was, "Why do you ask?"

"You keep looking at my legs."

"Normally when a man looks at a woman's legs the last thing she accuses him of is being gay."

"I don't know. I keep thinking that you are looking at my chubby legs and judging them. Like you are dreaming up exercises that I can do to make them smaller."

"I keep looking at them because they are quite nice to look at and because it's been a very long time since there has been a bare-legged woman in my bed."

"Are you a leg man?"

He shifted his head to look into her eyes. "I'm more of a tits and ass man, but since you aren't walking around here with those things bared I haven't had the chance to look at them."

"Ben!" She was shocked by his words and yet laughter bubbled up inside her. Dash giggled too as if he were in on the joke, and Ben smiled.

Ben smiled and she realized how beautiful he was for the first time.

"I'm a man, Dina. I appreciate beautiful women. Even ones who think they have chubby legs."

"What kind of women do you date?"

"I don't date."

"Why not? You could get any woman you wanted."

"I loved my wife very much. After she died, I didn't want anybody else. I don't want anybody else." The raw pain in his eyes was undeniable for a moment, but then it disappeared so quickly Dina wondered if it was ever there in the first place. "You have to understand what it's like to be the head of Rowe and Son. People don't want to get to know me for who I am. They want to know me for what I can give them."

"What made you fall in love with your wife?"

"We went to school together. We met at when I was ten and she was eight."

"How long has she been gone now?" She didn't want to pry, but looking at him, hearing that strange catch in his voice, made her feel like she was mourning with him.

"Nine years."

"Nine years? But-but . . . hasn't the pain dulled yet?"

"Some pain never goes away. We weren't in a good place when she died and it was my fault. I should have done more to keep her happy." He fell quiet, gazing down at sleepy Dash's little face. "I'm not sure why I told you that. I don't speak like this with anyone."

"It's because now we are BFFs."

He frowned. "BFFs?"

"Best friends forever. We should wear matching friendship bracelets or something."

"I was thinking more along the lines of tattoos, but whatever you want."

She grinned at him and he smiled back at her, looking

into her eyes. She realized how much she liked him in that moment.

"What was she like, Ben?" She didn't know why she asked, but as she got to know, Ben she saw glimpses of a man a woman could love. She wanted to know what kind of woman could cause a man to love her so much that he still heavily mourned her nine years after her death.

He stiffened. His expression hardened. "I don't want to talk about Karen anymore."

"Oh," Dina said. And just like that, the bubble popped, the closeness she felt disappeared and they were back to that awkward tense state she was so used to with him.

"I think it's past my baby boy's bedtime."

"Oh, of course." He looked down at Dash, his expression going soft. "I hope I didn't keep you awake too long."

"Say good night to your uncle." She handed Dash to Ben while she got out of his bed.

"Good night, son."

Ben looked like he wanted to hug or kiss Dash but seemed unsure of how to connect.

"Good night, Uncle Ben." She pressed a kiss to his cheek. She wasn't sure why, but she felt like she needed to, like this man was as starved for affection as she was sometimes. "Uncle Ben, ha-ha. Uncle Ben. Get it? Just like the rice."

He frowned at her. "Hysterical."

"Good night, Ben."

"Good night, Dina."

She made the short trip back to her room her mind buzzing with thoughts. Her conversation with Ben had brought up a lot of things for her. Her family was one of them. She missed them. She missed her outrageous loudmouth mother, she missed her awkward genius stepfather, but most of all she missed her little sister. The person she loved and hurt the most. She glanced at the phone by her bedside. Ellis's cell phone number never changed. Dina called it sometimes when she was lonely. She called it sometimes just to hear her sister's voice, but they never spoke. She always wanted to. She always wanted to say, *I miss you. I love you. I'm sorry.* But the words never came out. But now, tonight, the need to speak to her sister overwhelmed Dina. She wanted to tell Ellis about Dash and Virgil and Ben and how she had held down the same job for two years and how on weekends she helped teach dance classes at the community center. And how much she liked working with little girls and how much she wanted to open her own studio one day.

Before she could think she put Dash down, grabbed the phone and dialed her sister's number.

"Hello?"

"Hi," Dina said before her voice broke.

"Dina? Is that you?"

And somehow in that moment she lost her nerve. She wasn't ready to speak to her sister. She couldn't bear the rejection. "No-no. . . . It's, um, Amy. I was looking for Carla."

"Oh." That little word seemed to be filled with disappointment. "I'm sorry, but I think you have the wrong number."

Dina hung up before another word could be said. She wasn't ready yet. She just wasn't ready.

The next morning Dina woke up earlier than her usual time. It was pitch-black out, but her stomach was rumbling with hunger. She had been so overwhelmed yesterday that she didn't manage to swallow more than a few bites. In fact, she hadn't been eating much the last few days, so afraid for her son's future that even the thought of food made the knot in her stomach bigger. But today for the first time in a long time she was hungry.

It was odd. It was as if her brain had finally given her body permission to relax, but it shouldn't. Her future wasn't any more settled than the day before. She had no idea what Ben's plans for them were. And she had to get back to work or she was going to lose her job. But she knew that whatever happened he wouldn't let his nephew go without. Ben wasn't that kind of man. She crawled out of bed knowing that there was no way she would be able to get back to sleep. It wasn't 5:00 a.m yet. Dash wouldn't be up for another two hours or so, and her stomach was growling so loudly she might wake the whole house if she didn't put something in it.

She walked into the hallway, in just her T-shirt. Her clothing was gone, either in the laundry or thrown out by one of Ben's efficient staff. Nobody was awake to see her thighs. And she wanted to keep it that way. She hoped to be down to the kitchen and back up to her bedroom before anybody noticed, but when she walked past Ben's bedroom she noticed that the door was open and by the dim light in the hallway she could see that he wasn't in his bed. Had he slept there? Curiosity got the better of her and as she walked down the hallway she decided not to head to the kitchen. Finding out more about Ben was suddenly more interesting.

She found that special wing of the house that was his domain. It was where his office was, where he seemed to spend most of his time. Ben looked like the type of man who liked to work, like he lived for it, like he wanted to be buried with his computer and smartphone when he died. She could just imagine him sitting behind his desk already, in his three-piece suit, making big decisions. It was so opposite of her.

She had never enjoyed working. It was just something she did to pay the bills. It never brought her any joy. But then again it was hard to find joy standing on her feet for twelve hours in a restaurant. Her sister loved her job. Ellis ran a clothing store and bridal boutique in Durant. It was her dream come true. Dina wanted her dream come true too, something she could wake up excited to do. That's why opening her own dance studio one day was so import- ant. She didn't know how long it was going to take to get there, but she would get there one day.

She walked down the hallway towards Ben's office, but that tiny room caught her eye again. She noticed the bed in it yesterday and thought little of it. But today the bed was rumpled, unmade. Curiosity getting the better of her, she walked into the room and that's when she spotted Ben on the floor. Doing push-ups. He was shirtless, slightly sweaty and throwing out pheromones like a pitcher during a perfect game.

It all caused Dina to stumble backward. She had noticed yesterday that Ben was in good shape, but she never imag- ined he would look like this. There wasn't an inch of fat on him, no softness either. She gawked at the ripples in his back, and the bulge of his biceps, and the dark hair that sparsely decorated his chest.

Hot damn.

There was that beat of attraction again. She tried to shake it off. It must be because she hadn't had sex since she had gotten pregnant with her son. Yeah, that had to be it. She had enjoyed sex immensely before Dash. Her body was just missing what it had gone for so long without.

Yeah, that must be it.

She shook her head. This was a bad idea. Watching Ben like he was a live version of a dirty movie was a bad idea. She should have just gone to the kitchen like she was planning to. She took another step back, trying to escape the room as quietly as possible, but her back connected with the door frame, causing a nice loud thump. Ben jumped up off the floor and was before her in an instant.

"What are you doing here?" he snapped.

"You don't sleep in your room," she said, not really having an explanation to why she was there. "I wanted to talk to you."

"And it couldn't have waited until a decent hour?"

Her stomach betrayed her, letting out a mighty rumble.

"You're hungry." His expression softened a bit. "Come on. Let's feed you."

"How do you like your eggs?"

She watched Ben pull out a frying pan and turn on the stove from her spot on the counter. He was still shirtless. She tried not to watch the way his muscles worked beneath his skin as he moved, but she couldn't help it. He looked edible.

"Dina?"

"Um . . . Over easy. You know you totally don't have to do this. I can settle for a couple of pieces of bread or some fruit. I like fruit. I should probably just eat fruit. I should probably go on a diet. Or maybe I should have cold cereal or oatmeal. I could even heat up some leftovers. I'm not picky."

He looked over at her and frowned. "Are you done talking?"

"I can be if you want."

"I want." He went over to the fridge and took out eggs,

butter and cheese. He worked quietly and efficiently. She was surprised. She thought a man like him wouldn't know a kitchen if it jumped up and bit him in the ass.

"I know you want me to be quiet, but I can't be quiet. Quiet makes me nervous."

He left the stove and walked over to her. She froze as he reached behind her, his arm brushing against her bare thigh.

He grabbed the bread and stepped away from her. She noticed that his eyes touched her legs before they returned to her face. "What would you like to talk about?"

There were a million things, like why she had felt so close to him last night, or why he didn't put a shirt on before he came downstairs or why she felt things for him that she shouldn't feel for her ex-lover's brother. And most important, she wanted to talk about what he was planning on doing about her and Dash, but she couldn't blurt any of that out. "I didn't think you could cook."

"I can't. I can do basics. Eggs, sandwiches, pasta."

"Why would you ever have to cook? It seems like your staff would break their necks to serve you."

"I keep odd hours. I don't sleep very much. It would be wrong of me to expect them to stay up just in case I have need of something."

"Virgil wouldn't have cared. He once had a hotel wake up their chef at two a.m. so he could have beef Wellington."

A muscle in Ben's jaw ticked. "That explains the four-thousand-dollar bill I got for dinner at the Frances Hotel."

"Did he die in debt?" she asked carefully.

"Half a million dollars' worth."

"Oh." She fell silent. Half a million bucks and now a kid. Even after Virgil was gone he was still leaving behind his mess for Ben to clean up.

He toasted four slices of bread before he assembled two

sandwiches and handed one to her. She took a bite, not sure she was feeling hungry anymore, but as soon as the combination of toasty bread, fluffy eggs and melted cheese hit her mouth she moaned.

"Is it to your satisfaction?" he asked, handing her a glass of orange juice.

"Thank you." She felt her cheeks burn. Ben stared at her for a moment. His eyes lingered on her mouth before he turned his attention to his own meal. They ate in silence for a few minutes. "Ben? Do you think I might be able to have my clothes back?"

"No. I'd prefer to keep you naked and chained to a wall."

"Was that a joke?"

"Yes," he answered, not smiling. "You're going to get new ones today. Dovie will take you shopping later today. You are to get yourself and Dash whatever you need."

"Oh. Thank you." Ben had just confirmed once again that he was going to help, but she didn't know for how long. "Ben?"

"Yes?"

"What exactly are your plans for me and Dash? We have to leave soon and I don't want to disturb your life any more than we have. If you can just assure me that you'll help me with Dash I can be out of your hair soon."

"I don't want you out of my hair soon. I plan to marry you."

Four

I Really Can't Stay.... Baby, It's Cold Outside...

Ben almost laughed when he saw Dina's big, beautiful hazel eyes bulge, but he didn't because he knew he had just dropped a bomb on her. He had just dropped a bomb on himself. He never thought he would get married again, never thought he would share his life with another person after Karen died. But he couldn't let Dash walk out of his life. Or Dina for that matter. He didn't know what made him offer marriage. It might have been the time he spent with Dash last night. It made him remember how much he wanted to be a father. It made him realize how empty his life had become these past few years. It made him not want to go back to the way things were. He stared at Dina. She sat before him with shock and uncertainty etched on her pretty face. It could have been her too. His brother had treated her badly. Her family wasn't a part of her life. She was just as alone as he was. She didn't have to be. She shouldn't have to struggle or be unsure of her son's future. He could do that for her. He could protect her. Protect them.

He couldn't keep Virgil alive. He couldn't save his brother, but he could keep his son safe. He could give the boy everything and in the process gain the family he always wanted.

Marriage seemed to be the only way to do that.

"Hold up." She hopped off the counter and poked him in the chest. "What the hell do you mean you plan to marry me? I may be a poor unwed single mother with no job, no home and no prospects, but I'm still a woman and a feminist. The least you could do is ask me. I'm going to say no, but a girl likes to be asked. You don't even love me and let's not mention the fact that I've been here less than twenty-four hours and that I am the mother of your *brother's* son and that that is the craziest idea that anybody has ever thought of ever. Plus—"

He grabbed her hand, gently squeezing her fingers in order to stop the endless stream of words that were coming out of her mouth. "Are you finished yet?"

"Well, I don't know. You got any other crazy-ass ideas rolling around in that head of yours?"

"Just the one and it's not so crazy." He motioned to the table, inviting her to sit. "Will you listen?"

"Do I have any other choice?"

"Yes. Your other choice involves me throwing you out of here in just your underwear and that T-shirt."

She sat down and crossed her long legs, irritably jiggling her foot. "I guess we're about to have this conversation."

He felt the corner of his lip tug. He wanted to smile again. She made him want to smile again. He hadn't had a reason to for a long time. "I've always wanted children," he started. "But my wife, Karen, had a very hard time getting pregnant and when she did she always miscarried. We went through three of them and one stillbirth in seven years of marriage. That last time was extremely hard on her. . . ." He trailed off, trying to stop the painful memories that sometimes invaded his thoughts. "After she died I couldn't bring myself to remarry. I loved her too much to try and replace her with another woman. And for a long time I thought my chances of fatherhood had died with her, but then you showed up yesterday with Dash. He needs to be supported, Dina, and I know you could do a fine job of raising him yourself, but I think every boy needs a father. I would like the chance to be his."

"I see," she said softly. "But why do you want to marry me? I want you to have a role in his life."

"Having my only blood relation raised three thousand miles away is not acceptable to me. I want him to grow up here. I want to see him every day. You come with him and it would better for him if the world saw him as the product of a married couple than Virgil's discarded offspring. I want him to have a real father."

"I need another reason, Ben." She looked him in the eye, searching for something he couldn't figure out. "I-I just need more."

"If you marry me people will stop thinking I'm a reclusive hermit. Having people think I'm the next Howard Hughes is bad for business."

She grinned at him. "Try again."

He looked away from her, from her pretty full lips and soft smile. "I think we could be friends. This house gets to be a lonely place sometimes. You and Dash could be my family."

She looked so unsure. He didn't want to push her. He knew how crazy this sounded, but she had come into his life for a reason.

"If I married you, what would you require of me?"

"To raise my son. To be my companion and accompany me places sometimes."

"What about sex?"

"What about it?"

"Would you expect me to have it with you?"

"No," he said, although last night for the first time in years he felt . . . awareness of her as a woman. It had been so long since Karen had died, so long since he had been around another woman; it was only natural for his natural urges to reappear. "I just want to be your friend."

She said nothing.

"You don't have to decide right now. Stay with me until Christmas. That's twelve days. If you don't like being here you can leave with no hard feelings."

"And what will happen to Dash if we go?"

"I'll send you a check each month until he comes of age."

"And if we stay?"

"He'll be raised as a Rowe. He'll have everything you have ever wanted for him and more. And you too. If you stay, Dina, you'll be my wife. You'll never have to work or struggle again."

She was quiet for a long moment. "I know this is going to sound crazy to you. Hell, it sounds crazy to me, but I don't just want to be somebody's wife. I have dreams too, you know. And surprisingly none of them involve being supported by you."

It wasn't what he expected to hear from her, but her words made him more curious about her than ever. "What are your dreams?"

She seemed surprised by his question. "I used to be a dancer. I was good at it, I really was. I moved out to LA because I thought somehow I might have a shot of making it, but it seems nobody wants to hire an over-thirty-year-old dancer for a music video. I learned very quickly that in the dance industry over twenty-five means over the hill. I didn't dance again for a long time, but after I had Dash I walked into our community center and this lady was teaching ballet to little girls. I don't know what happened, but I sort of fell head over ass in love with them. They had little pink tutus and cute faces and they were so happy to be there. It reminded me of how I felt when I first went to dance class. So I started to help out with classes on the weekends and putting the little money I got from teaching into a savings account. I want to open my own little studio one day. I want something that I can build from the ground up." She looked down at her hands, looking bashful for a moment. "It probably sounds like a silly dream to you."

"No, it doesn't. It's a nice dream and if you marry me you can have it as soon as you wish. If you marry me you wouldn't have to work so hard. You could spend more time with Dash. You can have everything you ever dreamed of for him."

Five

We Need a Little Christmas…

But would she have her freedom?

Two years ago she would have jumped at the chance, but she didn't want to be dependent on Ben. She didn't want to be a user. She could support herself. She could make her own dreams come true.

And marriage? She knew she had been unlucky in the love department, but she held out hope that one day she would fall in love. That one day she could have the kind of marriage her mother and stepfather had. She wanted her own happy ending.

But how could she deny Dash the chance to have the world? She knew alone, even with child support, she couldn't give him everything. She couldn't be both his mother and father. She could raise him alone, but he deserved a father. She knew from her own childhood how hard it was to go without one.

"Oh, sir!" Rebecca came into the kitchen. "What are you doing in here cooking for yourself? You should have called for me." She rushed forward looking more distressed than Dina had seen anybody be in a very long time. "I would have gotten anything you like. What can I do for you?"

"Well," Dina said, "you can start by congratulating us. We just got engaged."

"What!" She put her hand over her heart. "Excuse me. I was just surprised. Congratulations. Please, miss. Is there anything I can do for you?"

"She's kidding, Rebecca. We don't need anything. You may go." He turned back to face Dina. "You'll stay?"

"Yes. For twelve days. If I don't like you or if I find out anything freaky about you, like you like to wear wedding dresses in your free time or you have a booger collection, I'm taking me and my kid out of here so fast your head will spin."

"Okay. That sounds agreeable. We can discuss this more later if you would like." He stood up and walked away.

"Ben," she called when his foot hit the threshold. "Just one more thing?"

"What is it?"

"Can you show me how to get back to my room? I'm not sure how."

Six hours later Ben sat alone in his office. The house was empty, as he had just sent his entire staff home for the holidays. It might have been a crazy move with a strange woman and baby in the house, but if he was going to be Dash's father he wanted to spend time with the boy like a real father would. That meant no servants hovering around trying to do everything that he was capable of himself. He wanted time to get to know Dash.

"Sir?" He looked up when he heard Dovie's voice.

He looked at the woman who was more his mother than his servant. She had barely come to see him anymore. Dash's arrival had changed that. "Why do you call me sir? You know I don't like it."

Dovie lifted her head proudly. "Because it is proper. You are the head of the household. It's a sign of respect."

"You've given me a bath; you've changed my diapers. I think it would be all right if you called me by my given name like you used to."

"I don't think so."

"Even if we are alone?"

"Fine." She smiled at him. "Ben, I've come to tell you that I'm in love with that little boy. He looks just like you were when you were a baby. I could swoon."

"I'm glad to hear that."

"I took him and his mama shopping today. We got some really nice things for Ms. Gregory. Wait till you see her. The woman looks like Ava Gardner when she's cleaned up. And Dash! Well, he really will be dashing when he wears the little suit she got for him to wear on Christmas day. She didn't even spend a lot of money on it. She found it on the clearance rack. In fact, she barely spent any money at all. I think she's a good woman, Ben." Dovie looked into his eyes. "I was thinking since you don't need me so much, maybe I could go live with them and help raise him."

No. He didn't say the word, but it seemed his entire body stiffened at her request.

"I've invited her to stay, Dovie. I would like to raise Dash as my own."

"Do you now?"

He wondered what was going on in Dovie's mind. She clearly had an opinion she wasn't willing to share. "I do. I also gave the entire staff the holidays off. I want you to go back to South Carolina and visit with your family."

"But I don't want to go there. There's hardly anybody left anymore." He couldn't ignore the sadness in her eyes.

"Then where would you like to go? I'll send you anywhere on the planet."

"If it's all the same to you, sir, I would rather stay here. With everybody gone who's going to do all the cooking and cleaning?" She got up shaking her head. "You need me to stay. I'll come back and the house will be in shambles. Oh no. I can't let that happen."

His eyes followed her as she left the room still mumbling to herself and he spotted Dina standing just outside the doorway with a small smile on her face.

"Hello," he greeted her.

She walked into the room much more dressed than she had been the last two times he saw her. She wore an unadorned gray dress that probably would have looked plain on another woman but suited Dina very nicely. It hugged her lush-looking body and flattered her curves. Her thick hair was neatly brushed and braided and she looked . . . perfectly appropriate. But he kind of missed the sight of her long bare legs and the hint of pink underwear he saw every time she moved.

"Hi." She walked in the room seeming almost shy around him. "I wanted to bring Dash up, but the shopping trip wiped him out. I don't think he likes to cruise the sales racks as much as his mother does."

"Maybe next time you can leave him here with me."

"Maybe." She walked towards him, a small piece of paper in her hand. "I wanted to give you this."

He unfolded the paper to find that it was a receipt from

her shopping trip. Dovie was right; Dina barely spent anything at all. Just over two hundred dollars for her and Dash at a discount department store.

"What's this?" He looked up at her. "When I sent you to the store to buy things you needed, I expected you to buy things you needed."

"I did," she said quietly. "Okay, so maybe I didn't need the nail polish, but the rest of the stuff is legit. I need to wipe Dash with the hypoallergenic wipes or he gets a rash. I know they are more expensive, but—"

"I don't care about the wipes. I expected you to buy more. If you are going to be my wife I expect you to be clothed in an appropriate manner."

"We aren't married. We might never be. I don't want you supporting me. And minus the things I bought for Dash, I owe you seventy-five bucks."

Her statement surprised him so much he didn't know what to say.

"Besides, I think I look pretty good." She did a dramatic turn and he got a glimpse of how her dress really curved over her backside. "This dress only cost seven dollars and I got the boots on sale for nineteen." She turned back to him, her face serious. "You don't like the way I look?"

She was beautiful in her seven-dollar dress and cheap boots. Just as beautiful as she was in her ratty T-shirt. "You look fine, but that's not the point. I wanted you to get whatever you wanted. For these next two weeks I don't want you to worry about money."

Her eyes lit up for a moment, but she briefly closed them as if she were putting out her own flame.

"What is it?"

"There is something I want. But it's not something I can get from the store."

"Tell me."

"This is Dash's first Christmas and I want it to be special for him. But this house." She looked around her. "It doesn't feel like Christmas. I want it to feel like Christmas for him."

Dina didn't know what she expected from Ben when she told him what she wanted. She half-expected condescension or laughter or snark, but he got up from his desk, took her by the hand and led her out of his office without a word. They traveled through the long quiet hallways of the house in silence. She knew she should wonder where they were going, but instead she was focused on the way Ben's hand felt around hers. Nobody simply held her hand. She never thought of herself as a hand-holding girl, but feeling his big, warm fingers around hers was kind of nice. She felt almost protected when she was with him, and she didn't know why. He was a stranger to her. A stranger who offered her marriage. She didn't trust him. She shouldn't trust him. So why was there a part of her that felt like she was safer here in this museum-like house than she had been anywhere else in her life?

"Where are we going?" she finally asked as he led her up a narrow, dark staircase in a part of the house she didn't know existed.

"To the attic."

"Are you going to chain me to the wall?"

"Not today."

"Are you going to show me your large collection of sex toys?"

"I keep that in the basement." He looked back at her and for the first time she saw a little mischievousness in his eyes.

"I find basements are too damp for my sex toys. Mold is a bitch."

He shook his head at her comment before coming to a stop at the small door. "I haven't been up here in years, but I imagine that everything is still the same."

He stepped aside to let her in. The room was vast, running the length of the entire house, but all she saw was white dust sheets from floor to ceiling. She looked back at him, unsure of what his purpose was.

"This is where Christmas is." He looked around the attic. "Somewhere up here."

"You mean, we are going to have to look through this big, huge, dusty attic to find the Christmas decorations?"

"No, you are. I'm going back to work. Good luck." He turned away from her.

"Hey!" She grabbed his suit coat. "You can't leave me up here."

"No?"

"Well, you could at least send some of your servants."

"I can't. I sent them home for the holidays an hour ago. Except Dovie, and you don't expect a seventy-five-year-old lady to go digging through boxes, do you?"

"It's just you and me here?" She didn't know what to think of that. He must have sent the servants home every year for Christmas. There could be no other explanation as to why he would make it so they were practically alone.

"Not just you and me. Dash and Dovie are here too."

"Well then, buster. I suggest you take off that pretty suit jacket, because you might get blood or dust on it."

"Blood or dust?"

"Dust from the attic if you stay or blood from your nose if you don't."

"You threatening me, Dina?" He smiled at her, fully smiled at her for the first time, and she was blown away by how his whole face changed. Before she thought Virgil was the charmer, but Ben, there was something about Ben too.

"Yup." She nodded. "I think I am."

He slid his jacket off and she watched as it dropped to the floor behind him. "Just for the record, you're not big enough to take me."

"Oh no?"

He took a step closer, studying every inch of her body, and if she didn't know any better she would say she could feel his gaze like it was a touch. But she did know better.

He looked in her eyes. "Not a chance in hell, little one." He turned away from her, breaking eye contact, leaving her feeling a little bereft. "Let's start in the middle. You take the left side; I'll take the right."

An hour later they were still searching with no luck. "Why can't we just go to Walmart like everybody else and get decorations?" she complained for the third time.

He turned from the box he was digging in and frowned at her. She smiled at him. He was pretty cute when he frowned.

She went back to looking through the boxes. In actuality she didn't need to look through the boxes—once they took the dust sheets off she could see that the boxes were labeled and stored together by function, old furniture in one section, old books in another—but it was fun to look through other people's stuff. She was learning more about Ben, Virgil and the Rowes just by seeing the things that they kept for so long. A small box marked "Photos" caught her attention. There were hundreds of them, snapshots, baby pictures, the Rowes' family history, all without frames, just left in a box to fade. Suddenly she felt sad, for the forgotten pictures and for herself. She didn't have very many photos of her baby. Just a few that she had snapped with her shitty cell phone. But the Rowes were different. Their whole lives seemed to be documented in photographs.

She dragged the box over to an antique settee she had uncovered some fifty feet back and sat, pulling a handful of pictures out of the box. It was the picture on top that intrigued her. She stared at the beautiful blond woman in black and white who was sitting so elegantly on a checkered blanket. Dina could tell that the woman, even sitting in the grass, had more poise in her little finger than Dina had in her whole body. She tried to ignore the feeling of inferiority that crept up inside of her, but she knew she didn't belong there in her seven-dollar dress and cheap boots. She would never truly be comfortable in a life that was so different from the one she had led.

Ben sat next to her, his big body taking up all the remaining space on the settee, his side pressed against hers, and she quickly lost that train of thought. He gently took the picture from her hands and stared at it. "My mother," he said in a quiet voice. "She was very young here. My father used to consider himself somewhat of a photographer when we were young, but it seemed like most of the pictures he took were just of her."

"Your parents loved each other?"

"Yes," he said, looking down at the picture, his thumb lightly stroking over his mother's face. "More than they loved anything else on the planet."

"Oh," was all Dina could say. There was pain there. She could hear it in his voice. Something had happened to her. Virgil had never talked much about his family except to complain about Ben. It now struck her that she had spent six months with a man, given birth to his child and never known anything substantial about him. "What happened to your mother?"

"She died."

"Ben . . ."

He looked up at her, knowing that she needed to hear more from him. "Aneurism. I was eight. Virgil was five. Things were never the same after that."

"I'm sorry."

"You shouldn't be." He looked back down at the picture. "I'm glad you found this. I hadn't seen her in a very long time."

There were no pictures up, Dina suddenly realized. Not in his office. Not around the house. It was so different from her own childhood home, where her mother would frame every photograph and school picture and drawing and hang them until there was no space left on the walls.

Dina picked up another picture, this time of two tiny boys snuggled together in a rocking chair.

"Virgil was six months old there," Ben said quietly. "He looked so much like our mother even then."

She looked away from the picture and up into his handsome face. "You two look very happy here."

The corners of Ben's mouth turned up a bit. "I guess I was. I so wanted to be a big brother." He fell quiet for a moment still gazing at his younger brother. "I wish I could have protected him better."

"How can you protect somebody from themselves, Ben?" She had known what it was like to be self-destructive and selfish and have the world try to save her. But in the end she was the only one who could pull herself up. Virgil was the only one who could have saved himself.

"I wish I knew."

"Can I have some of these pictures?"

Ben blinked at her, surprised by her request. "Why would you want them?"

"For Dash. I want him to know about his family."

Ben nodded slowly and searched her face as if he was searching for the truth. "I would like that."

He looked away from her down to the stack of pictures in her hand. The next one was of another elegant blond woman, but this photograph was much more recent than the others and when Ben looked at it she felt his entire body grow tight.

"I think we looked at these enough," he said tightly.

"Is this your wife? Is this Karen?"

"Let's find these decorations so I can get back to work."

"Why won't you talk about her?"

"Because I can't!" he snapped.

He moved to get up, but something inside of Dina screamed, *No! Not yet!* She didn't want him to walk away just yet even though he had barked at her. She grabbed his arm and pulled him against her in a tight hug. He might not have wanted it, but he needed it. And she needed to be the one to give it to him. There had been so much loss in his life. His parents, his wife, his brother.

"What are you doing?"

"Um . . ." How could she explain it to him when she couldn't even explain it to herself? She was holding on to a man she didn't even like. Only that wasn't so true anymore. She was holding on to this man because she knew what he was feeling. She knew what it was like to feel loss. "Stalling. I really don't want to look through any more boxes."

"Fine." He pulled himself away from her. "Then I am going back to work."

Six
Deck the Halls...

Ben couldn't sleep that night. He didn't sleep much these past few years, but tonight the exhaustion that usually overtook him failed to come. He didn't know what to call the feeling that was rolling around in him, but if he had to name it he would call it guilt.

He had disappointed Dina. He saw it in her face the last time he looked at her before he walked away, but he had to get away from her. She had pulled up a picture of his wife, of Karen. She looked so happy there because it was the day she found out she was pregnant. Two months later that happiness died; two months later the woman he had fallen in love with had started to disappear. He hadn't wanted to think about it then because he had spent years thinking about Karen and how their marriage had fallen apart. He wanted to escape that moment, but then Dina hugged him, she held him to that warm, lush body of hers and a whole set of unwanted feelings rushed him. He wanted more of her. He wanted to sink into her warmth, and smell her smell and taste her skin and feel her beside him at night and that alarmed him. How could he feel such a heavy attraction for her, the woman who loved his brother, when he was still in love with his wife? This wouldn't work. A marriage of convenience, of simple friendship, wouldn't work if he wanted Dina, and he knew in that moment he had to get away.

He found himself going to the nursery. He had learned through Dovie that Dina agreed to let Dash sleep there at night. He was glad for that. The room was meant for children, not to sit empty forever. It had been a very long time since he had been in this room. He avoided it on purpose. But Karen had spent time here. Days. It was almost sick, but when he walked in and saw little Dash in the crib all of those thoughts melted away. He reached down, stroking Dash's soft cheek with the back of his finger, amazed by how connected he felt to this little person he had just met. This boy was the only piece of Ben's family left and he needed to keep Dash in his life. Seeing this boy grow up was something that had to happen or else he would regret it for the rest of his life. That meant he needed to keep Dina around.

"I like to watch him sleep too," he heard from behind him. "I'm not sure why it isn't creepy for people to sneak into rooms and watch babies sleep, but if I snuck into Daniel Craig's bedroom to watch him sleep they would have me thrown in handcuffs faster than I could blink."

He turned to look at Dina, who was dressed for bed again, only this time she wasn't in a T-shirt. She wore a tiny baby blue cotton nighty with thin straps whose only purpose was to keep the dress on her body. She was braless. He could see her nipples through the fabric in the chilly room. Her hair was loose. Her long legs were bare and he felt more than attraction when he looked at her. He felt himself grow hard.

"Daniel Craig, huh? Personally, I could never get on board with a blond Bond, but I can see you have a type."

"Type? My only specifications for a man are two hands and a p—"

"Dina!" he barked.

She grinned at him. "You couldn't sleep?" She stepped forward and stood next to him, the scent of her shampoo making him want to get closer.

"No, what about you?"

"I've never slept more than five feet away from him. I kept thinking something bad was going to happen to him. And then I heard you on the baby monitor. You better be glad I couldn't find a weapon and gladder that I recognized you, or your brains might be smeared on the carpet."

"Bloodthirsty."

"No, I'm a mother. It's how we are."

"He's safe here, Dina. I promise you that. He's safer here than anyplace else."

"This place feels too big. I grew up in a tiny house. I couldn't sleep unless I heard my little sister's radio through the wall. I can't sleep knowing he's so far away."

She was right. The house did feel too big. It felt isolating, but it was his home. "He's a boy, Dina. He's going to need to sleep in his own room eventually."

"When he's thirty." She bent over the crib and kissed Dash's cheek. "I'll let him stay here. This room is too beautiful to go unused." She leaned against Ben for a moment, her bare skin touching his. "He doesn't seem to care about being away from me. Look at him. I've never seen him so peaceful."

"That's because you snore. It's probably the first good night's sleep he's gotten since he was in the womb."

"That's not true. I don't snore!" She gave him a sideways glance. "Do I?"

"No." He smiled at her and she smiled back. For a moment they just looked at each other.

"Why don't you sleep in your bedroom?"

"I don't know," he said truthfully. Sometime in the past few years the room had stopped being functional for him. "I work in my office. I eat in my office. It just makes sense for me to sleep there."

"I don't want you to."

"What?"

"I don't want you to spend your entire life in your office. Because that's no life at all." She reached up and set her hand on his shoulder. "If there's any chance that this is going to work, you have to be near us. I grew up in a family. I want Dash to have that. I took my family for granted and I lost them. But now it seems that we both have been given a chance to start over."

"And me sleeping in my bedroom is going to accomplish that?"

"Yes. You want to be his father. I want you to eat with us and play with us and shop with us. I want you to have a life with us. It's a lot to ask of you, I know, but you asked a lot of me too. You asked me to give up half of my son."

"Okay, Dina."

"Okay?" She looked into his eyes so hopefully. It was a very long time since he had seen hope in anyone's eyes. He couldn't have disappointed her if he wanted to.

"Okay." He nodded.

"Thank you." She stood on her toes and leaned in, giving him a lingering kiss on his jaw. "I know you don't like hugs. Hopefully my kiss wasn't too icky for you. Good night, Ben." She walked away then and he watched her go, hips swaying all the way.

* * *

Dina woke up the next morning to the sun shining through her bedroom window. She had slept past 5:00 am, but she didn't feel any more rested that she had the day before. She couldn't sleep last night, at first because she was missing her baby and later because she was thinking about Ben. Ben who walked around at night shirtless. Ben who watched her little boy sleep. Ben who had asked her to marry him yesterday.

Was that just yesterday? It seemed like a million months ago. She knew her life was going to change when she had Dash, but she never expected this to happen. She never expected to be here. She got out of bed, grabbed the baby monitor and walked to the window to look at the snowy landscape below. Dash must still be asleep. She held the monitor to her ear and listened carefully. She thought she heard the sounds of the soft baby noises he sometimes made in his slumber, but she couldn't be sure. In her mind she knew he was fine. She knew that Ben was probably right, that Dash needed space from her, but she was still his mother and she could peek at him if she wanted.

She opened her door ready to rush down the long hall to get to her baby, but there were boxes stacked in front of it. Boxes . . . Boxes with labels on them. Outside decorations. Lights. Ornaments. There must have been twenty of them there.

Ben. He did this for her and for a moment she was torn between going to her son and rushing to Ben's room to thank him. First she went to her son, who was sleeping peacefully, and then she went to Ben, who was also sleeping peacefully. In the bedroom next to hers. Just like he promised.

She jumped onto his high bed and pressed a loud

smacking kiss to his cheek. This time she didn't linger. She remembered last night. The way her lips felt on his hard jaw. The way he still smelled like aftershave even hours after he last touched a razor to his face. "Thank you, you sweet mushy grouchy man." He didn't stir and this time she kissed him on his forehead. There was something sweet about him in his sleep that reminded her of Dash. And she was amazed that a man she had never been with could look so much like her son's father. She was amazed that Ben would want to be Dash's father.

Ben moaned a little, grabbing her arm and pulling her down on the bed. She yelped and before she had time to think or respond she was underneath his hard body. Underneath all that heavy, smooth, soap-scented muscle. "I missed you," he murmured.

It was then she knew he was dreaming. He was thinking about his wife. Dina knew that was who was in the picture she had found yesterday. She knew he must still love her very much even so long after she had passed away.

"Um, Ben." She lifted her hand to his shoulder to wake him, but he shifted her body, taking her legs and wrapping them around his waist.

"Ben?"

He buried his face in her neck. He touched his lips to her skin. His long fingers trailed up the back of her thigh, cupping her behind in his large, warm hands.

"Ben," she said again, but this time it came out more like a moan than anything else.

"Mmm. You feel really good. Better than I thought." He pressed a kiss in the soft spot behind her ear that made her melt. "You're so damn beautiful."

She was too stunned to speak, too turned on to stop him. Men weren't like this with her. Sex wasn't like this with her. It had been wild and adventurous and fast and emotionless. But he was so gentle, and slow and kind. She never thought the man she met just two days ago wearing a frown and a three-piece suit could be so—so damn sexy. But of course it wasn't her he was thinking of. He could never think of her that way. It was her son he wanted, the continuation of the Rowe name. She only came as part of the bargain.

He moved his lips to the column of her throat and left a soft, hot, wet kiss behind just as clarity was about to fill her. A moan escaped her lips. Her body shook with sensation and that's when he brought the lower half of his body right against hers, rubbing her through her underwear. She flooded, like a rainy day during monsoon season.

Holy freaking hell.

It was then she came to her senses. Not that she wanted to, but she had to. She couldn't sleep with him. That was the last thing they needed. It was the last thing he wanted.

"Um, Ben?" She tapped on his head.

"Dina," he mumbled, and then froze. "Dina?" He lifted his head and looked down at her, his expression horrified, and a little piece of her confidence died. "What the hell are you doing here?"

"Um . . . I came to thank you for getting all the boxes from the attic. It must have taken you hours. You're probably going to be sore. I know how sore I was when I moved, and I only had like three boxes. But I wanted to say thank you and then you pulled me down and then you were on top of me and I thought it would be rude to stop you so I didn't, but then I did because I figured you would probably be mad when you realized it was me you were trying to have sex with, but for the record I wouldn't have minded so much, because you really know how to work a girl into a pile of mushy jelly."

"Stop talking," he said, and rolled away from her.

She looked down into his tortured face. She hadn't meant for this to happen. But just like always, disaster seemed to follow her wherever she went. "You don't have to look so miserable. I know I'm not as gorgeous as some of the women you've been with, but I'm not a leper either. And I swear I got my cootie shot before I came here."

"Dina, I need you to leave this room right now," he said very calmly.

"Why? It's no big deal." She shook her head. "Are you mad at me? I didn't—"

He pulled down the sheet that was covering him and revealed to her the tent that had sprouted in his boxer shorts. "I. Need. Time. Away from you. Now please."

"Oh . . . Wow." She felt herself blush. She never blushed. "That's really impressive. I think I should be flattered."

"Get out!"

"Okay. Okay." She hopped out of his bed. "But if you ever need somebody to take a closer look at that thing, you know where to find me."

Dina. She drove him crazy.

He had spent the better part of an hour in his bed waiting for his body to calm down. But it wouldn't. Every time he closed his eyes and tried to focus on something else he kept thinking about her. About her curvy body beneath his, how good her skin smelled, how soft it felt beneath his lips and how she moaned when he kissed it and how she moved her body so it fit just right with his. She was the only person on the planet who had the power to make him feel uptight and comfortable at the same time.

What the hell was happening? Yes, he was attracted to her, any red-blooded man would be, but he had been attracted to women before and he had been able to control himself. He wished he could have blamed what happened between them that morning on him being in a deep sleep, on his dreaming, but he knew who he was touching when he touched her. It was her he was dreaming about when he dreamed.

Nine years had been too long to go without sex and he had made the mistake of inviting a woman into his home who could make a priest give up his vows.

Ben finally forced himself out of bed and into an icy shower. He had to face her. He had promised her he would spend time with her and be with Dash and act like part of the family she wanted. He had asked her to marry him. As crazy as that was, as much as a possible disaster as it could be, he still wanted to go through with it. He wanted a son. This was his last chance for it.

When he opened his door he found her sitting on the floor in the hallway between their bedrooms. Dovie sat near her in a rocking chair holding Dash. He gave her a silent hello before he turned his attention back to Dina, who was so engrossed in looking through the boxes that she didn't notice he was there.

"Oh, Dovie, look at this." Dina held up a silver and white antique glass house ornament that he had seen every year on their Christmas tree when his mother was alive. "I'm not sure I've ever seen anything so delicate."

"It's lovely, child."

"You think Ben would mind it if we had more than one Christmas tree? I would like to put a little one in the nursery with some of these special ornaments. They are too nice to go on a big tree. They'll get lost."

"You can have whatever you want, Dina."

She looked up at him, smiling happily as if she was glad to see him. There was no awkwardness coming from her, no shyness. "Come." She held out her hand to him.

He hesitated for a moment. There was a world of memories locked inside of those boxes. Memories of his mother and Christmas days with his family and of good times. He should be eager to look through them with Dina, but if he let the memories flood the bad ones would come too and he would remember the first Christmas without his mother, and how life had changed so much for them after that and how the holiday had lost all meaning for him when he was so young.

"Bring Dash," she prompted him softly.

"Yes, sir. Take him," Dovie said, handing Dash to him. "I need to get you a cup of coffee. Ms. Gregory, would you like something?"

"Ms. Gregory?" Dina dramatically looked around the empty hallway. "I don't see any Ms. Gregorys here. There's a Dina here and a Ben and a Dash, but there are no Ms. Gregorys."

"*Dina,* can I get you something?"

"Yes, Hugh Jackman on a bed of lettuce. No? You're all out of that? Maybe a glass of water then."

Ben watched Dovie walk away shaking her head, but she was smiling. It was something he hadn't seen from her in a long time.

"Pop a squat." Dina patted the floor beside her.

"Pop a squat?"

"That's my low-class way of asking you to sit." She blinked at him for a moment. "You are totally not going to want to marry me after Christmas. You can't take me anywhere. I'm too much like my mother."

That wasn't true. If he didn't marry Dina it wouldn't be for that reason.

"Hi," came from his arms. He looked down to see Dash staring up at him, a curious look in his eye.

"Did he just greet me?"

"Yes." She smiled proudly. "He's a genius. Sit down, Ben."

He obeyed, setting the boy on his feet after he did so he could just look at him for a moment. He wore a tiny red sweater with a reindeer on it and little blue jeans. Ben was still so amazed that this little boy had come into his life. And at Christmastime. There was no better present. "Hello, son. You look very festive today."

"He's freaking adorable." Dina leaned over and kissed her son's cheek. "We have to get you a matching sweater so we can take pictures."

Matching sweaters? Pictures?

"I'm glad you're here. I need your help sorting this stuff out. What do you want to go up?"

The woman was somewhat of a whirlwind. He looked at all the decorations she had pulled out of the boxes and then to Dina, who was happily sorting through them. Things he hadn't seen in years. After his mother died, Christmas stopped being a major event and over the years the displays got smaller and smaller until one year his father told the staff not to bother with it at all. That was a sad day, especially for Ben, because it was the day he felt like his mother had finally fully slipped away for him.

"Whatever you want, Dina," he said, feeling a lump in his chest.

"You keep telling me I can have whatever I want. You're going to regret that one day."

"We haven't had Christmas here since I've been an adult."

"Not even with your wife?"

"No. We always spent Christmas day at her parents' home." She had never made Christmas into a big event. He thought she might when they were first married. He had hoped she would bring the splendor back to Windermere, but the holiday never seemed very important to her.

"My mother is Jewish, but my stepfather is as Waspy as they come, so we had a big Christmas every year. Eggnog and mistletoe and even a goose."

"A goose?"

"A Christmas goose. Just like in *A Christmas Carol*. He ordered it special every year. My mother is a strict vegetarian, so he and my little sister would spend hours in the kitchen on Christmas day cooking it."

He didn't miss the wistfulness in Dina's voice. She missed her family. It was a shame she couldn't be with them. "Where were you during that?"

"With my mother. She liked to go shopping the day after Christmas and spent hours on Christmas strategizing which stores she was going to hit first."

"When's the last time you saw them?" He knew he was prying, but he wanted to know about her; he wanted to know her.

"Two years ago." She picked up a small wooden soldier and cradled it in her hand. "The detail on this thing is amazing. It must have been hand painted. It makes me sad that nobody makes things like this anymore."

It made him sad that she lost so much time with them. "They've never met Dash?"

"No."

"You've been totally alone this whole time?"

"Yes." She offered him a small smile. "But not for much longer. Some crazy guy might want to marry me."

She was smiling at him, but he could feel her sorrow, the shame hanging over her. He wanted to tell her that it was never too late to make up with her family to right whatever wrong she thought she did, but he couldn't give her advice. He couldn't keep his family together either.

He leaned over, surprising himself by pressing a kiss to her forehead. "Would you like to come out with me today?"

Seven

It's the Most Wonderful Time of the Year...

Dina watched Ben as he adjusted Dash's hat over his ears and fussed with his coat. Dash just kind of stared at Ben in wonder as they walked through the quiet, snowy streets of the small village that surrounded Windermere. Dina looked at him in wonder too. He cared about her son. The cynic in her really wanted to distrust Ben, like she distrusted all men. He was a stranger. But there was something about him. He was good with Dash. And for the first time in his young life Dash had somebody else who was willing to love him. That was one of her fears as a single mother. That her son would grow up with only her to love him.

And then Ben came along. And even though they had just met, even though the circumstances were crazy, she was starting to feel a little something for him. There was something about him.

"I grew up about a half hour from here, but I've never been to this town. I never realized how lovely this place is."

Ben looked down at her. "You grew up near here?"

She nodded. "In Durant. Tell me about this place," she said so she wouldn't have to tell him about the home she hadn't seen since her little sister got married, about the place she wasn't worthy of returning to.

"My great-grandmother was from the village. She met my great-grandfather when he was up here scouting places to build a steel mill, but he fell in love with her instead. My grandmother was willing to give up this town and move her life to the city. But my grandfather saw how much she loved this little village and instead of building a mill he built a Windermere for her. He moved his life here for her."

"That's very romantic. People don't do things like that anymore." She shook her head. "Well, maybe that's not true. My brother-in-law would do anything for my sister. He quit his job and went into a huge amount of debt just so he could make her dream of owning her own business come true. And my stepfather, he turned down a high-paying job at Stanford just so he could be with my mother. I guess people do crazy things all the time in the name of love. I guess I just haven't had anybody want to do something like that for me."

She stopped talking, feeling foolish for revealing so much of herself to Ben. She could hear the sadness in her voice. Feel the heaviness in her chest. It was something that she tried to avoid, thinking about her family. She had caused the rift between them. Their absence was her fault. She missed them and yet she wasn't ready to face them. Not until she could show them that she could stand on her own, that she could make something of herself. She just wished she knew how long it would take until she got there.

Ben gently looped his arm through hers and led her

through the center of town. This place felt like Christmas. It looked like Christmas with the pristine white snow and the clean-smelling air and the old-fashioned decorations. It was so different from LA. This was the type of place she would like to raise her son in. Even if things never worked out between her and Ben, she didn't think she had the heart to take Dash away from him. She might have to settle in this little town so Dash could be near him.

Ben stopped in front of a large evergreen in the town's square. "Look, son." He pointed to the top and Dash's eyes followed. "You see that star? They are going to light it in a few days. It's a tradition here. A week before Christmas the entire town comes out to light the tree and sing carols. When it's very quiet I can hear the celebration from the house and from my office I see the tree. I would like to show it to you this year, Dash. If your mother allows you to stay up that late."

"Wouldn't it be more fun to come to the tree lighting instead of watching it from your office?"

"You want to go?" He looked surprised.

"Yeah. Why not? It sounds like fun."

"I haven't been since I was very small. Not since my mother died."

"Oh." She stood closer to him, leaning against him for a moment. It was an involuntary action. This was a hard time of year for him, just as hard as it was for her. Maybe they were thrown together for a reason. Maybe they just weren't meant to be alone at Christmas. "I think we should make a new tradition. I would like Dash to go to his first tree lighting with you."

"It was always cold those nights," Ben said with a small, almost wistful smile. "My mother would dress us in our warmest pajamas and down coats and Dovie would pack us a huge thermos of hot chocolate. I remember being so excited. I didn't get to go to school with the other kids, so it was one of the few times we got to play with the local children. We would run around and throw snowballs and just as we were about to drive our parents crazy the ceremony would start and the whole town broke out into 'Silent Night.' And when it was over my parents would take us home and feed us shortbread cookies and for that one night we got to sleep in front of the fireplace. It was my favorite time of year."

"Why did you stop going?"

"My mother died right before Christmas when I was eight. Nothing was ever the same after that."

"No," Dina agreed. "It wouldn't be, but that doesn't mean we can't make Dash's Christmases as happy as yours once were."

"I would like very much for Dash to have happy Christmases."

He looked at her son before pressing a gentle kiss to his forehead. Dash closed his eyes as if he were savoring Ben's affection as if it was something he had been missing out on his entire life. Dina felt a large lump form in her chest. It choked her. He needed this. They both needed this.

"I would like to get some pie now," Ben said to her. "There's a little place not far from here that serves the best apple pie on the planet. I would like to buy you some."

"And I would like to eat some. Let's go."

Ben watched Dina's eyes grow wide as the waitress set her slice of pie down in front of her. After minutes of agonizing over the menu and questioning him about every flavor she had settled on cherry, his second favorite.

"This looks amazing," she said before she thanked the waitress. Dina's smile was wide. Her eyes practically danced with enjoyment. Never had he met anybody so excited about a piece of pie.

"My little sister loves cherry pie," she said more to herself than to him.

"Ellis?"

"Yeah," Dina answered, but that one word was filled with so much heaviness that it caused him to feel her sadness too. "I was so mean to her when we were kids. I loved her, only God knows how much I did, but I was always picking on her. If I ever have another kid I hope Dash isn't as mean to them as I was to her."

"Why did you tease her?"

"Because her father loved her and mine didn't." She tried to shrug the statement away like it was nothing. "It took me a long time to figure it out, but I've got daddy issues." She gave him a wobbly smile. "My parents divorced when I was two. My mother remarried and when I was ten my real father stopped coming around. So I took it out on Ellis and my stepfather, Walter. I was evil."

He shook his head, not believing that was true. Hurt? Yes. Jealous? Absolutely. But he could never see her as evil. "I hated Virgil sometimes," he admitted for the first time aloud. "He seemed to get everything without even trying. Friends would flock to him when I had to work hard to make connections. Things just fell into his lap when I spent hours trying to get ahead. He was more popular and smarter and more handsome then I could ever be and sometimes I hated my brother. I was jealous of him."

She reached across the table and gently locked fingers with Ben. "For the record. I don't think he was more handsome. But then again, I got a thing for grouchy-looking dark-haired men who buy me pie and don't run away when I spill my guts to them."

"Ma!"

She looked over at Dash, who was staring at her. "Did you want some pie, baby?" She unlinked her fingers from Ben's and he missed the sensation immediately.

She slipped one of the soft cherries out of her pie and fed it to her son, who shuddered and scrunched his little face with disgust. "I'm guessing he's not a cherry pie fan."

Ben smiled at him. "That's okay. There will be more for us." He dipped his spoon in his ice cream and fed it to Dash, whose reaction was much less dramatic this time. "A vanilla ice cream man, I see. A man after my own heart."

Dash smiled at him and lifted his arms. Without thinking Ben pulled the boy from his high chair and settled him in his lap. "Do you want more ice cream, son?"

He felt Dina's gaze on him and he looked up to find her staring at him with a curious expression. "Is this okay? I should have asked you first."

"You don't have to ask." She smiled softly at him. "Of course it's okay."

Eight

It's Beginning to Look a Lot like Christmas...

The only thing missing was a real-live tree, Dina thought as she stood back and admired her handiwork in the formal living room. It had taken three days, but the house finally felt like Christmas. She used every decoration from the boxes Ben took down for her. The small hand-carved nativity scene, the antique nutcracker, the ornament Ben made when he was just six years old. She had hung stockings on the fireplace and lit cinnamon-spiced candles and probably gone overboard with it all, but the house was beautiful. And even though just the four of them were staying there it didn't feel so empty. It felt like a home should feel.

She wondered if Ben minded. She wondered how he really felt about her taking over his home, his space, and changing everything around. But she did it all for Dash, for his first Christmas. She might not be able to give him a hundred presents, but she could make his surroundings beautiful. She could make this year memorable.

She turned to face Ben, who was lying on the sofa with his hands folded over his chest. Just a little while ago Dash was with him, but Dovie had taken him off for a nap, leaving the two of them alone. He hadn't said a word to her since he entered the room, just watched her as she zoomed from thing to thing tweaking and hanging and fixing. Normally the quiet would bother her. She was a busybody by nature. She always went from job to job, from man to man, from hobby to hobby. She thought she had needed noise, needed action. That's why she was attracted to Virgil. He was like her: never stopping. But quiet Ben was the opposite. And for some reason she found his presence calming.

"Are you going to say something or are you just going to stare at me?" he said, startling her from her thoughts.

"I have to say something to you? You stare at me for hours every day and never say a word."

"That's because I'm staring at your ass. It often leaves me speechless."

She grinned at him, unable to help herself. It always took her by surprise when he said things like that. There was a little mischievousness to Benjamin Rowe and she liked it. "It's big," she said.

"Who said big is bad?" He sat up, his big body no longer taking up so much space, and patted the couch beside him. "Come here."

She who always balked at taking orders obeyed his and sat beside him. The couch was warm with his body heat, the air smelled of his aftershave and something about him made her want to get closer. She shouldn't. He only wanted to be her friend. He was still so in love with his wife. If she stayed she knew that she would never be more than just the woman who brought Dash into his life. She had always been second place or third place in every relationship she had ever been in; she didn't know if she could live like that again.

Ben's fingers touched the nape of her neck and then ran through her hair. It was a soft touch, a sweet one, and she was so surprised by it her breath caught a little. "Relax," he soothed. "I've been watching you hop around this room for the last hour. Just sit here for a while."

"I could never sit still. It's probably why I failed at every desk job I've ever had. My mother used to say I had ants in my pants and that I ran around like my butt was on fire. She threatened to turn the fire extinguisher on me a few times. Once she even chased me around the house with it."

She missed her mother. Sometimes so much that an overwhelming ache came over her and she was paralyzed with it. She e-mailed her from time to time just so she would know she was alive, but she didn't offer much information about herself. She never called. She knew her mother was disappointed in her. She knew her mother would never truly forgive her for what she had done, but she still wanted to hear her voice so bad it hurt.

"What's going on in that head of yours, Miss Dina?"

She shook her head. "I would like to get a real tree for this room."

He nodded. "Tomorrow. What else?"

"That's it," she lied. "You know, I've never had a real tree before. My mother is a crazy hippie and said that the slaughter of millions of trees every year for a holiday that had been too commercialized and lost its meaning is outrageous. She forbade us from ever bringing one into the house. So we used a fake one, but I would like a real one if it's okay with you."

He cupped her face in his large, warm hands and looked into her eyes. "What's wrong, Dina?"

Her eyes welled. She tried to turn away so that she could hide her tears from Ben but he wouldn't let her look away.

"What is it, sweetheart?"

"I've been called a lot of things in my day, but nobody has ever accused me of being sweet." She attempted to smile at him, but her mouth just wouldn't work right.

Ben pulled her forward until her chest was touching his and her face was so close to his that their lips nearly brushed together. "Please tell me." He smoothed his hand down her back, each touch causing her to unravel a little more.

"I miss them," she finally said, and the moment the words escaped her mouth the tears rolled down her cheeks.

"Your family? Why don't you go see them?"

"I can't."

"You can. You're just afraid. You still have them, Dina. They may be mad at you, but you still have them. I have nobody. Everybody I have ever loved has died. I would give everything I own to have them back just for a little while. But you don't have to give anything; all you have to do is show up. They still love you. How could they not?"

She shook her head, unable to speak, and Ben didn't force her to. He just pulled her closer and held her while she cried. Even though her misery was so palpable she could taste it, even though thoughts of her family churned in her mind, she was very aware of Ben, very aware that he was holding her and comforting her and there for her. Nobody had just been there for her. No one had ever held her while she cried. No man had ever cared enough. She had only known him for five days and yet this man had been sweeter to her than all the men she had dated combined.

She lifted her head to look at him, his face expressionless but his eyes full of concern. She didn't know what made her do it, but she pressed her lips to his and when simple contact wasn't enough she kissed him a little deeper, a little harder, a little longer. He didn't kiss her back, but he didn't push her away either. He just held her a little tighter, let her take from him all that she needed, and when she broke the kiss he didn't chastise her or react or say anything at all. And that's when she knew she had done the wrong thing.

She shouldn't have kissed him. She shouldn't have begun to feel for him. It would only mean disaster for her and her son. She wasn't what Ben wanted. She would never be what he wanted.

"I need to check on Dash." She got up, unable to look at Ben anymore, and fled the room, ignoring him as he called after her.

Ben sat there for a moment after Dina fled. He was stunned. His whole body was literally stunned. She had kissed him. He had been kissed after having nine years of no physical contact with any woman and it did something to him. He loved his wife, for years she was the only thing he could think about, but Dina's kiss was like nothing he had ever experienced before. Dina's kiss spoke to him. It told him that she needed him, to protect her and care about her and care for her. It told him that he needed her, that he needed something more in his life than what he currently had.

But you still love Karen.

And he felt guilty. And he felt like he couldn't trust his heart. Five days in the company of one woman and he was already thinking about the promise he had made to himself that he would never allow himself to love again, that Karen would be the only woman who ever had him.

But it's been nine years.

Yes, it had been nine years. Nine years was too long to mourn. But could he really move on? With Dina? He hadn't bargained for this when she walked through the door. He hadn't expected that her reappearance would change him this much. Maybe asking her to marry him was a mistake. He could do it if he had no feelings for her, but he did. Every day he felt a little something more for her. It wouldn't be fair to her to go into this when he was so confused. Maybe he couldn't go through with it. Maybe he couldn't marry Dina at all.

Nine

O Holy Night...

Dina walked into the nursery later that night prepared to give her son a bath. She knew he was in the room. She could hear his soft baby sounds, but he wasn't in his play-pen where she had left him. She followed his noise and the sounds of a soft, deep, murmuring voice to the bathroom to see Ben on his knees besides the tub. His sleeves were rolled up. His shirt was wet. He had bubble bath on his chin. He was smiling down at Dash, and Dina felt herself slipping a little in love with him.

Shit.

There was no way she could marry him now. She sucked at relationships, at making someone else happy.

He doesn't love you.

There was that too. She knew if she ever entered a marriage, a forever, it would have to be with someone who loved her as much as she loved him.

She sat on the floor behind him, her back resting on the

vanity. He turned to look at her, never taking his hand off of Dash.

"I decided I wanted to try my hand at giving him a bath. Is that all right with you?"

"No, Ben. It's not all right. How dare you spend time with your son and take care of his basic needs at the same time. I'm totally offended."

He turned back to Dash, brushing his hand over his head. "My son. Have you decided to take me up on my offer and be my wife?"

I can't marry you, she wanted to say, but the words just wouldn't come out.

"I thought you said I have until Christmas to decide."

"You do. But you called him my son. I thought—"

"He needs a father. But you don't need me as a wife. You could fall in love again. If you let yourself. You could find a younger wife than me to give you lots of kids. A younger, hotter wife, without cellulite on the backs of her thighs."

He looked at her for a long moment and for the life of her she couldn't tell what he was thinking. "The tree lighting is tonight. Do you still want to go with me?"

"Yeah. Why wouldn't I?"

"Because you kissed me, then went all chickenshit on me and hid in your room all day."

"Oh, that?" She grinned at him. "That was just a case of hormones. Don't mind me."

He smiled back at her. "Good. Go get ready. Dress warm. I'll finish up with Dash."

She returned to the room a few minutes later, finding Ben still with Dash, working her son's tiny feet into snow boots. Ben's face was scrunched in concentration. He took the task so seriously it caused a smile to form on Dina's lips and a lump to form in her throat.

She knew that if she married him she would find some

way to screw it up. But not being his wife . . . She wouldn't ever be able to turn off her feelings for him.

You could build a life with him. You can be happy.

She internally shook her head, not sure that would be possible.

You could make him happy. He needs to be loved.

She could give her love. She could give and give after so many years of taking.

"I took a dry sweater out of your closet. I hope that's okay," she said when Dash was finally shoed.

Ben gently set her son in his playpen and came to her, surprising her by taking her in his arms. She involuntarily leaned her head against his hard chest. *This is nice,* she thought, *to have somebody there just to lean on.*

"You seem sad. What's wrong?"

"If I tell you then you'll really know what kind of nut job I am."

He buried his fingers in her hair at the base of her neck. "Knowing how crazy you are will only make me feel better about having the largest collection of celebrity body hair in the country."

Her eyes snapped up to his. He was grinning at her with that naughty bad-boy smile and she damn near melted. "You're a huge weirdo, with an odd sense of humor."

"So are you. That's why I like you so much."

"You like me? I think I can die happy now."

He smiled softly at her again as he smoothed her hair back into place and looked into her eyes. "Are you going to be warm enough?"

"Yes, I think so." She was warm enough right now. She was so warm with his touch she thought she never might feel cold again.

"I want you to wear one of my scarves and a hat just in case. It's a long way into the center of town."

"I should be fine. We're not walking to town. Are we?"

He said nothing, just kissed Dash's forehead and then hers. "Let's grab our coats."

Ben didn't say a word to Dina as they bundled up in their warmest coats. An unfamiliar feeling rushed through him as he watched her dress. Excitement. He hadn't remembered feeling this way since he was a small child. And he had Dina to thank for it. She gave him something to look forward to and he wanted to repay her.

She stood quietly at the front door, Dash in her arms. He could tell she was lost in thought and he wished he could be inside her head for a little while. He wanted to know how she really felt about being here, if she was really ready to give half of her son to him, but that was a conversation for another time. Right now the only thing he wanted to do was give her a good Christmas.

He took the scarf he had grabbed for her and wrapped it around her neck. As he did, she shut her eyes and smiled.

"What?" he asked her, wanting to know the source of her happiness.

"It smells like you."

The strong urge to press his lips to hers struck him. He wanted to kiss her smile, to taste her warmth, to relive some of the feeling that overtook him this afternoon when she touched him, but he tamped it down and stepped away from her. He couldn't kiss her. Not now.

"Are you ready?"

"I've got enough layers on to climb Mount Everest and not catch a chill."

"And Dash?" He looked down at the boy as a tiny bit of concern passed through him. "Do you think he's warm enough?"

"I think he's going to roast if we don't get him outside. Don't worry, Ben. He'll be fine."

Ben nodded and opened the door, leading them into the driveway.

Dina screamed. She turned to him in wide-eyed disbelief. "You didn't?"

He took a bewildered-looking Dash from her. "Their names are Olaf and Barnum. They are the two best looking Clydesdales in the state. The driver's name is Terrence. He's been giving carriage rides for over twenty years."

"Hello, ma'am." He tipped his hat to her and climbed down from his perch. "Can I help you up? It's a nice evening for a ride."

She was smiling. Smiling so much her cheeks hurt. She couldn't remember a time that she had felt so—so—so . . . damn happy. There was something magical about the night. She was sitting in a horse-drawn carriage looking up at a night sky that seemed to be filled with a million stars. She had her baby in her lap and was snuggled under a thick blanket with a man who went through a lot of trouble to make the night special for her. A man who made her want to forget about the rest of the world.

"Are you warm enough?" Ben asked her as he touched her cheek. "I had Dovie pack us a thermos of cocoa. It might be a little bumpy now to have some, but as soon as we stop I can pour you a cup."

"I'm fine." She leaned against him. "And if I forget to thank you later for tonight, thank you."

Once they got to the lighting Dina wanted to get out and stand with the crowd. She had rung in the New Year in

Times Square. She had been in the stands when the
Yankees won the World Series. Both crowds had some
sort of amazing electricity running through them, but
there was something different about this crowd, something she really wanted to be a part of. Maybe because it
was made up of families drunk on happiness and hot cocoa instead of booze. Or maybe it was that this gathering
was what Christmas was really about.

"It hasn't changed much since the last time I was here,"
Ben said, breaking her from her thoughts. "It's almost like
I can feel my mother here. I haven't felt her in a very long
time."

Dina looked up at Ben, who was looking away from
her at the unlit tree. She thought she saw tears in his eyes
for a moment, but when she looked again they weren't there.
Seeing him miss his mother made her miss hers; it made
her wonder what her family was doing that night. It made
her think about seeing them again. She slipped her hand
into his seeking comfort. Their fingers locked. But that
wasn't enough for either of them, it seemed, because he
pulled her closer, wrapping his arms around her. She had
never been hugged like this before. Held so close to somebody that she didn't know where he ended and she began.

Suddenly people around them began to count down. He
let go of her then. She missed his warmth, but it was only
for a moment. He lifted a sleepy Dash from his stroller so
he wouldn't miss the magic and pulled her close to him
again just as the tree lit. And as if on cue everyone around
them starting to sing "Silent Night." Even Ben in his beautiful baritone. Dina was speechless. She had never experienced anything like this and she didn't want it to end. She
didn't want to go through the rest of her life without feeling this feeling again.

Ben looked at her, took her chin in his free hand and

pressed his mouth to hers. She gasped at the contact, but he didn't move away; instead he deepened the kiss, allowing her to taste the hot chocolate still on his lips. It was the sweetest kiss of her life and another thing that she didn't want to end.

She loved him. In five days she had fallen totally and completely in love.

Dina was quiet the entire ride home, but the small smile never slipped from her face. He knew he had made her happy. The carriage ride was a nice touch, but he knew she would have been happy without it. It was the tree lighting, standing there in the cold night with the entire town, feeling the excitement in the air. He could see the wonder in her eyes. They mirrored how he was feeling.

"Ma Ma Ma." Ben looked down at Dash in his arms. The boy had being speaking long sentences of baby babble the entire ride home and clapping his hands and bucking his little body. He was still wound up from all the festivities, a squirmy little ball of energy. Ben couldn't blame him, though. It was exactly how Ben felt when he returned from tree lightings as a kid.

"He's never going to sleep," Dina said with a smile. "You're a little party animal, aren't you, baby?" She kissed his forehead and looked up at Ben. "Would you mind watching him for a little while so I can take a shower?"

"Take as long as you need. We'll be in my bedroom."

She looked at him for a long moment, placing her hand on his arm. "I didn't realize how hard it was to raise him alone until I met you. You've been wonderful with him. I don't know how to thank you."

"I haven't done much."

"You took me in, a stranger that you didn't know from

anywhere, and you were kind to me and my son. That's a hell of a lot more than anybody has ever done for us."

He didn't know how to react to her gratitude, to the emotion in her eyes. He didn't take her and Dash in to help them. He took them in because he was a selfish man. He took him in so he could feel a little bit of the happiness that eluded him for so long.

"Go take your shower," he said, feeling uncomfortable with her gratitude. "We'll be here when you get out."

He walked into his quiet room, immediately noticing that it felt so different to him than it used to. It was no longer just an empty room to keep his extra clothes in. It felt lived in. It felt like a place he could truly feel comfortable. It didn't feel lonely anymore. He set a still-babbling Dash on his bed and looked at him for a long time. He couldn't help himself. The boy looked so much like his grandfather, like Ben, that it was hard to see any traces of Virgil in him at all. Ever since Dash had showed up he had been thinking about Virgil, about what he would think of all this, about how would he feel about Ben taking his place.

But he knew his brother well enough to know that Virgil never wanted this, a family of his own, a son.

It all made Ben think that things happened for a reason. That Dash was supposed to be in his life.

"Hi," Dash said, shaking Ben from his thoughts.

"I'm staring at you again. I know. I can't help it." He brushed his hand over Dash's soft hair. "I've become that creepy uncle. I'd much rather be your overprotective father. But what should I do about your mother?"

Dash gurgled something at him and then threw himself back on the bed and began to have a conversation with the ceiling. Ben lay next to him, holding his little hand as he let his thoughts overtake him.

Being with her at the tree lighting, seeing her happiness that night, had caused him to come to a realization. He didn't *want* Dina to stay. It had gone way past that point. He *needed* her to stay. To fill up his days. To make him feel things again. If she left he couldn't go back to the way things were. He would feel empty. He would miss his family.

"Is he sleepy yet?" Dina walked in. Her hair was loose around her shoulders. She wore a short pink nightgown, her longs legs bare and soft looking. He watched her walk closer, her hips swaying slightly as she did. He wondered if she had any idea what he really thought about her. If she had any idea what she did to him every time she walked into a room.

"I'm afraid not. He hasn't stopped talking since you left. I'm afraid the boy is a blabbermouth just like his mother."

"Hey!" She climbed onto Ben's bed, her nightgown rising up, giving him a glimpse of her supersoft-looking thighs. "I'm not a blabbermouth. I just have a very highly developed vocabulary. I scored very high on that part of my SATs. I bombed the math part, though. Bombed it. With a capital *B*. I was surprised that I got into any college at all. But then again, when both your parents teach at the university it's really hard for them to deny you. I wonder how many favors they had to pull to get me in there. I bet you my mother had to turn tricks just so they would pass me. Getting Dumb Dina through college must have taken a lot of them. No wonder they were so relieved when my sister got into two Ivy League schools."

"You see, son," Ben said to Dash. "She can't help herself." He looked up at her. "You're not dumb. You're just hyper."

"A little," she conceded. She climbed under his covers,

lifting Dash up to snuggle with him. "Get in here with us, Daddy."

He undressed, slipped into his sleep pants and settled in beside them. Even if he wanted to stay away from her, he couldn't resist her pull tonight. He wanted to be near her and near Dash and nothing was going to change that.

"I feel like this night should end with something special," she said. "Like we should watch *It's a Wonderful Life*. Or . . . I don't know. How did you end this night when you were a kid?"

"We fell asleep on the floor in front of the fireplace." He lifted his hand to her cheek. "You want to do that?"

"Would you?"

"If you wanted to."

"You're insane, you know."

"I know. I normally would wait seven days before I let a strange woman and child into my bed."

She grinned at him. "I always was fast."

They grinned at each other for a moment before Dina returned her attention to Dash. "I think he's finally settling down."

"He should be. It's been a long day." Ben could see the sleepiness in her eyes too. He knew how hard she had worked to make the house look and feel like Christmas. "For you too, Mommy. The house looks beautiful."

"You don't think I went overboard? It looks like Christmas threw up in here."

He shook his head. "Sometimes overboard is just enough."

They fell quiet then, the day finally catching up with them. Dina's eyes fluttered closed first and then Dash's. Ben watched them sleep for a little while. Dash looked so much like a Rowe, but Ben could see Dina in him too. His forehead, the shape of his nose. The way he slept with his hand nestled against his cheek.

Ben lifted Dash away from his sleeping mother and put the boy to bed in the nursery. Dina didn't wake then, nor did she when Ben returned to his bed and settled beside her. She moved closer to him in her sleep, pressing her warm, soft body against his, curling her arm around his chest like it was the most natural thing in the world.

In the back of his mind he thought about waking her up, about sending her to her own room, about sleeping alone, but he knew he couldn't do that. He couldn't send her away. So he gathered her closer.

She woke up then and blinked at him. "I dreamed I was in bed with a very sexy man. How disappointing to find you here."

He grinned at her smart-ass remark, noting that she didn't move away from him. If anything she got closer.

"I guess I should head to my own bed now."

"Or"—he sat up, pulling her along with him—"you could stay here."

He pulled her nightgown off over her head. She was nude underneath, no underwear in sight. He pushed her back on the bed, pulling the blankets away from her so that he could look at her body. He couldn't take his eyes away from her. Smooth skin, soft belly, a body made up of nothing but curves. His mouth watered. His erection strained against his pants and for a moment he was paralyzed, because it was almost too much for him.

He bent and pressed a kiss to her stomach. She trembled, looking up at him with wide eyes. "Are you okay with this, Dina?"

"What? Being made love to by a man who turns me on just by talking? Yup." She nodded. "I think I'm okay with that."

"Good." He knelt between her legs, wrapping each long limb around his waist. He smoothed his hands over her hips and groaned. She felt like a woman should feel, like a culmination of all his teenage fantasies and adult dirty dreams.

"You really like this?" she asked, surprised.

"What? Sex? It may have been a while since I've attempted it, but I like sex very much."

"The way I look. I'm not the same girl I used to be."

"I'm supremely glad you're not the same girl you used to be. I like your weight. I like your curves. I want to eat you like an apple."

"Oh?"

He slid his hands up her torso, lightly cupping her breasts in his hands. She moaned a little, and when he brushed his fingertips over her nipples she arched her body towards him. "I don't know where to start with you. Every bit looks good."

"You could kiss me."

"Where?" He pressed his lips to the undersides of her breasts. "Here?" He took her nipple into his mouth, enjoying the gasp of pleasure she made as he suckled. "Is that where you wanted to be kissed?"

He shifted himself so he could lift her long leg. He kissed the sole of her foot and then her ankle. He brushed his lips over her calf and the sensitive space behind her knee. He pressed his face to the inside of her thigh, smelling her sweet smell, wanting to taste her, but she stopped him.

"Is it my turn yet?" She reached for him, pulling his hard body on top of hers, rubbing her naked chest against his. "I need to kiss you." But instead of connecting her mouth to his she kissed his Adam's apple, and the seam of his jaw. She kissed his nose and eyelids and cheeks. He had never been kissed like this before. All over. With such sweetness. He never thought he wanted to be kissed like this, but now that he experienced it he knew he couldn't go back to living his life without it. He had been feeling that way a lot when it came to her.

"You're just what I needed, Benjamin Rowe." She slid her lips to his and kissed him. And it all became too much. Her taste, her smell, the way she made him feel, what she did to his heart.

"Dina," he whispered. He felt frantic, the need to be with her, inside her, overwhelmed him and he shook, his hands, his body. She seemed to realize this and hooked her fingers into his pants, pulling them down as she pulled herself closer to him. But he couldn't wait; as soon as he was free he pushed into her slow and hard. She cried out and dug her fingers into his back and wrapped herself around him so tightly he didn't think she was ever going to let go. And he didn't want her to. For the first time in a very long time. He was exactly where he wanted to be.

Dina woke up the next morning with her limbs tangled with Ben's. Their chests were pressed together; his hand was buried in her hair; their lips were inches apart. She had never slept like this before, completely wrapped up in another person, but she liked it. She liked it because she was wrapped up in Ben. There was nobody else she had felt this close to.

"Stop staring at me," he said in a rough, sleepy voice. "It's creeping me out." She smiled at him as he leaned closer and sealed his lips to hers. "Your smile," he said into her mouth. "It looks so good I could eat it."

"Now who's being creepy?"

He rolled her on her back, covering her body with his. He was ready to make love again. She could feel him against her leg, but he made no move. He just cupped her face in his hands and smiled down at her. "You bring it out in me."

She reached up and ran her fingers through his dark hair, needing to feel that much closer to him. "How are you this morning?"

"A beautiful woman let me make love to her for hours last night." He shrugged. "All in all it was a normal Friday night for me."

"Oh, lord." She rolled her eyes. "You sound like Virgil when you say shit like that."

He froze at the mention of his brother's name. She hadn't meant to bring him up, especially now, but his name had slipped from her lips.

"Did you love him?"

"No." She shook her head. "I feel guilty about it sometimes. He gave me Dash, I should love him, but it wasn't like that. Who knew I would end up in bed with his brother?"

He didn't say anything at first, just buried his nose in her neck.

"Ben?"

"Hmm?"

"Will you tell me about her?"

"Who?" He lifted his head to look in her eyes.

"Your wife. I want to know about Karen."

He rolled away from her onto his back. She felt him go rigid again, but this time he wouldn't look at her and she knew she had hit a nerve.

"I don't want to talk about this now."

"Why not? She's part of your life and now so am I. I think I should know about her."

He shook his head, continuing to stare up at the ceiling. And she realized that maybe she wasn't going to be a part of his life like she thought, like she had hoped. He wanted her only for her son. He would never fully let her in.

"She had cancer. Cervical cancer. She knew she was sick. She knew she was dying, but she never said a word to me. I didn't find out until after she died. Is that enough to satisfy your curiosity?"

"Yeah. Thanks for sharing." She got out of bed, finding her discarded nightgown on the floor before she walked out.

Ten

It's That Time of Year When the World Falls in Love...

"Have you seen Dina?" Ben asked Dovie after fifteen minutes of searching the house. He hadn't seen a sign of her or Dash since he dragged himself out of bed over two hours ago.

Dovie looked up from the tiny blanket she was just starting to quilt. "You did something, Ben."

"Did I?"

"The girl hasn't said a word all day, and since she usually is unable to stop talking there must be something wrong with her. And since the two of you spent all night and half the morning in your bedroom I think you might be the cause of her silence."

"Shit."

Dovie raised one of her white brows at him, but he didn't apologize. He knew his silence this morning bothered Dina, but he couldn't talk to her about Karen. He felt guilty. The wife he sworn he would be devoted to slipped out of his mind when he was with Dina, and so did the heavy sorrow that came along with every thought of Karen. He didn't think about her once last night.

She had been gone nine years and in that time there had been other women around him. The opportunity for him to move on had passed him half a dozen times, but he never did. He never thought he could. But now was the time. He could finally do it with Dina. If he could only convince her.

"Where is she?"

"She took Dash and headed out the door fifteen minutes ago."

"She left?" Panic rose inside him. "But her things are here. Did she take a cab? Why didn't you find me?"

"I didn't say she left. I said she went outside. Is there something you want to tell me about you and Miss Dina?"

"Only that I want her to stay."

He left Dovie then and headed outside to find his family.

He found them in the back of the house, in the formal gardens where the dahlias grew in the summertime. Dash was bundled in his down coat, snowsuit, boots and hat. Ben could barely see Dash's little face, he was so covered, but he couldn't help but notice what the boy was sitting on. A wooden toboggan that Dina found in the attic. It used to be Ben's. But he hadn't been sledding since . . . since . . . He couldn't remember.

"There's my boy!" He lifted Dash off the toboggan and tossed him into the air, causing Dash to giggle. "There's a really great hill for sledding just beyond those trees back there." He grabbed the sled and took off towards the hill. "When you get older I'll take you up to Flagman's Slope. That's where all the daredevils go when they want to have a little more fun."

"Ben?" He heard Dina's footsteps crunching in the snow

behind him, but he didn't acknowledge her. He saw her when he first walked up, bundled up just like her son, only she was wearing Ben's scarf and hat. His scarf that she said smelled like him. His hat when he knew she had her own. It told him something about Dina Gregory. It told him that there was a chance for them despite the tiny bit of hurt he noticed in her eyes.

"Ben, where the hell are you taking my baby?"

"For a little ride."

"On that thing?" She caught up to Ben as they approached the hill. "Down that hill? No freaking way."

He looked back at her for a moment. She looked alarmed, but the hill wasn't as steep as it looked. He used to go down with Virgil when he was just a little older than Dash.

"Ben, don't you dare."

He sat on the toboggan, Dash snugly tucked in his lap, and pushed off. It was just like Ben remembered, maybe a little less thrilling than it was when he was a small boy, but the wind on his face, the feeling of freedom, the warmth of holding a smaller body against him as they flew down the hill, was the same.

"You bastard!"

He hadn't seen Dina rushing down the hill after them until they were nearly at the bottom. But Dash was laughing and clapping and bouncing in his lap. "Did you have fun, little man? You want to do it again? I'll take you if your mother lets me live."

Dina's scream snapped his attention back to her, only she wasn't on her feet anymore. She was tumbling down the hill. He set Dash in the snow and was on his feet just as she came to a stop.

"Dina?" He stood over her. Her eyes were closed. She lay still in the snow. "Dina?" He knelt in the snow, his face hovering over hers. "Honey, are you hurt? Dina, open your eyes. I'll never forgive myself if something happens to you."

"You should have thought about that before you took my baby down this death hill," she said as she smashed a fistful of snow in his face.

"Holy shit." He recoiled as the icy snow touched his skin, but she didn't stop her assault. She was on her feet pelting him with snowballs faster than he could recover. "Stop it, devil woman."

"No." She pegged him right in the forehead. "You scared the shit out of me. You took years off my life."

"Look at him. He's fine. He's happy."

"Only by the grace of God." She pelted him with two more snowballs in rapid succession.

"What are you? Some kind of snow ninja?" He launched himself at her, knocking her off her feet, pinning her hands to the ground. "I would never do anything to hurt him. I love him."

"I know!" Her eyes watered. "I just got so scared."

"My poor baby." He cupped her face in his hands and gently kissed her. "My poor worrywart crybaby." He kissed her again only longer this time.

"Your stupid face is cold."

"Whose fault is that?" He rubbed his numb cheeks against her soft skin. "Even though I'm fairly sure my nose is going to fall off, I have to compliment you on your skills. You are an excellent snowball thrower."

"Thank you." She smiled at him. "I was really on my game today."

"Forgive me." He kissed the corner of her still-smiling mouth.

"Okay."

"And for this morning too." He kissed the other side of her mouth.

She blinked up at him, a little bit of her hurt returning.

"Please," he said, kissing her mouth again. "I couldn't talk about her this morning when I was with you like we were. It's hard for me to think about my past and my future all in the same moment. Does that make sense to you?"

She searched his face for a moment, looking for truth. "I think so."

"So say you'll forgive me."

He pressed his lips to her cold cheek and she shut her eyes. He felt her body go slack beneath him and he realized that spending the rest of his life with this sweet, soft girl was much more alluring than anything else.

"I'll forgive you, but only if you take me to get my Christmas trees."

"Of course."

"And out to lunch afterward."

"That goes without saying."

"Ma?" Dash crawled over to them.

"Hello, baby. Are you okay? The mean man didn't scare you half to death?"

"Up." He pointed to the top of the hill.

Dina looked back at Ben. "And to the mall. I'll need new boots if we are going to be playing in the snow."

"As long as we can pick up another sled."

"Yes," she sighed. "We can't forget the sled."

Dina watched Ben as he surveyed a six-foot tree. He had an axe in his hand that was supplied to him by Jollytime Tree Farm. They had passed hundreds of beautiful precut trees, but Ben wanted to cut his own. He was determined and, while she was fairly certain that he had never cut a tree down in his life, she said nothing to discourage him.

He looked so cute in his jeans and black knit hat. He looked so manly with that axe in his hand, like a well-dressed lumberjack. She swooned a little just looking at him.

He looked back at her, grinning. He was happy. He didn't *look* happy. *He was* happy. She could feel it. Maybe that's what good sex did to a man. "I can hear you thinking. You want to share your thoughts with me?"

"Nope." She smiled back at him. "I want to see you go all butch on me and chop down that tree."

He stepped towards her. "Give me a kiss for good luck."

She sealed her lips to his, savoring the touch. She had six days until she had to make her decision. Six days to decide to become his wife. She still didn't know what she was going to do. She loved him. She knew that because no man had ever made her feel this way, but he was still so in love with his wife and Dina wasn't sure she could be his wife unless it was for real. Not for convenience, not just for her son, but because Ben loved her as much as she loved him.

"Hey!" Dash protested their closeness, and Ben dropped the axe, lifted him from her arms and tossed him in the air.

"I'll kiss you for good luck too." Ben gave her son a loud smacking kiss on the cheek and Dina realized how deep her dilemma was. Ben needed to be Dash's father. No man could ever step in and take his place.

"I think your son is trying to talk your husband out of cutting down that tree. Lord knows I'm trying to talk my husband out of it. There are three hundred perfectly good cut trees just waiting to be strapped to the car."

Dina turned towards the familiar voice. It was a good thing Ben had taken Dash, because she would have dropped him. She was shaking so badly.

"Dina?"

She didn't expect to see her. Not here. Not yet. She had so much to make up for.

Ellis, her little sister, rushed towards her. Ellis, the little sister she had hurt so terribly, came at her and cupped her face in her hands. Ellis, the sister she hadn't seen or touched or spoken to in two years, was right in front of her.

"Dina Gregory." Ellis's eyes brimmed with tears. "Tell me that it's you. Tell me you're here."

She couldn't speak, so she nodded, feeling the hot splash of tears running down her face.

"I've missed you so much." Ellis broke in the moment and let out a sob. Dina wasn't expecting their first meeting in two years to be like this. She didn't expect her little sister to grab her and hug her so tightly that she couldn't breathe. She wasn't expecting forgiveness.

"Ellie . . ." She pulled away and opened Ellis's coat, placing her hands on her sister's large, rounded belly. "You're going to have a baby!"

"I am." Ellis smacked Dina's arm hard. "You already had one." She looked back at Ben, who was holding a bewildered-looking Dash. "You had a baby!" She smacked her again. "And you didn't tell me or Mom, or anybody." She smacked her with each word she spoke. "We were so worried about you. Why the hell did you stay away from us? Do you know how hard this has been on Mom? She's been trying to track you down."

"But I e-mailed her."

"Three months ago, Dina."

"I didn't think you ever wanted to see me again. I thought you hated me."

"Sometimes I hate you, most of the time I'm mad at you, but I never wanted you out of my life. You're my sister."

"I'm so sorry, Ellie." She grabbed her sister into a tight hug, both of them crying so hard that they couldn't speak.

"Ellis, honey." Mike, her husband, gently pulled her away and wrapped a protective arm around her. "You're going to make yourself sick." He placed his hand on his unborn child. "Please, calm down a little."

"I can't, Mike. I found my sister. And she had a baby."

"I know. Hello, Dina. It's good to see you again."

Ben came to her side and smoothed a kiss to her forehead. "Are you okay?" he whispered in her ear. "She looks like she hits hard."

"She does, but I deserved it." She leaned against him for a moment, needing his strength to hold herself up. "This is my son, Dash." She took her baby from Ben and presented him to Ellis. "Dash, this is your aunt, Ellis."

"No." Dash turned and buried his face in Dina's shoulder.

"Oh, come on, baby. She's our family." As Dina said those words she realized that she actually had a family. Not a group of people she disappointed, but a family who loved her. A fresh wave of tears fell down her cheeks.

"It's okay, Dee. I'm the hysterical pregnant woman that beat up his mother. I get his hesitation." Ellis stared at Dash, tears clouding her eyes. "He's gorgeous. He's perfect." She tentatively reached out and touched his little hand. "I'm so happy you have him."

"He's changed my life, Ellie." She looked up at Ben, who was still standing protectively by her side. He had changed her life too. In five days he made her want things she never dreamed of. "This is his father—"

"Benjamin Rowe. Good God, how the hell did you end up with him?" Ellis shook her head. "I don't want to know." She stepped forward and kissed her sister's cheek. "You got chubby. Am I evil to admit how happy this makes me?"

"No, feel free to mock me."

"Mock you? I think you are more beautiful than you

have ever been and I hate you for it." She stepped back and studied Dina, a smile on her face so bright that Dina could only compare it to the sun. "I can't believe you're here." She swayed on her feet a little. "I can't believe how woozy I feel."

Mike, her husband and the subject of the sisters' falling-out, wrapped his arms around her and held her close. "We need to get you home. Okay, baby? I don't want you to get sick."

There was such tenderness in the way he looked at her. It made Dina felt guilty for what she had done, all over again. It made her wonder how Ellis could forgive her.

Ellis looked back at Dina. "You are going to call me later. Mom and Daddy are out of town right now, but you and I are going to do some serious catching up. My baby and your baby are going to grow up together."

"Yes, Ellis."

"Promise me," she demanded.

"I promise."

Eleven

Celebrate Me Home...

Dina had disappeared after dinner that night. She had been quiet since her sister had left and Ben understood why. The reunion was dramatic and happy and sad and he couldn't imagine how he would feel if Virgil had reappeared in his life again. He would welcome him too. No matter how difficult their relationship had been, he would welcome him. And if he were here right now Ben would thank him for bringing Dina and Dash into his life.

Ben walked into Dina's bedroom to find her curled up on her side, her hand resting on her chin. She looked so damn fragile in that moment that something inside of him broke open.

It felt a lot like being in love.

He crawled in bed beside her, wrapping his body around hers, bringing her as close as possible. "How are you, sweet girl?"

"I don't know. I didn't expect her to still love me."

"I knew she would. She would be crazy if she didn't."

"You don't understand what I did to her. I was cruel."

He turned her around so that he could see into her eyes. "What did you do?"

"I don't want to tell you. You won't like me anymore."

"I will. I promise. Your ass is far too good to give up."

She gave him a wobbly smile, then sobered. "I was always horrible to her. I took joy in tormenting her growing up, but I loved her, you know. My mother had her new husband and her career and another kid, but the only thing I really had was my little sister. And then Mike came along. And instead of being happy for her I was jealous. I thought he was going to take her away from me and I couldn't stomach the thought of being alone. So I got drunk one night at a party and I kissed him. I didn't want him. I just wanted to break them up. I couldn't bear the thought of her loving someone more than me." She stared up at the ceiling, feeling embarrassed about her actions, about her mistakes. "I hurt her. I betrayed her. My parents wouldn't even talk to me for weeks after that. My whole life I've been pushing, testing. I finally pushed them too far."

"So you ran away?"

"Yeah, I couldn't live with what I did so I ran away to forget. I was a coward."

"I don't see it that way," Ben said as he swept his hand over her hair. "You taking some space wasn't a bad thing. Look at who you've become. You're a wonderful mother and thoughtful and kind and you are the best friend I've ever had."

"How can you say that? You've barely know me."

"I'm very smart, you know. And I've got excellent taste in women." He gathered her closer. What she had done was distasteful, but it didn't make her a bad person. It didn't change how he felt about her; if anything her extreme guilt made him care for her more. "I think it's time you stopped beating yourself up. It's time to let your family love you again."

"I'm not sure I know how to do that."

"Let me help you."

"Can you start by staying here with me like this tonight?"

"You couldn't drag me out of this bed if you tried."

"We're going to need a ladder to get the angel on top of the tree," Dina said to Ben as they admired their handi-work three days later.

They had left the tree farm treeless, but Ben had come through and had four trees delivered yesterday. They had spent the last two days decorating, Ben even going out with Dash so they could pick out a special ornament to mark his first Christmas.

"I'm sure there is a ladder somewhere in this house." Ben looked at her, frowning. "I'm just not sure where."

"I bet you're kind of regretting sending your entire staff away for three weeks."

"Nope." He looped his arm around her and pulled her into his big body. "Do you know how many people work here full-time? Twelve. I feel embarrassed to have twelve people doing things for me that I can do for myself. I've had a lot of fun these past two weeks with you. I've felt normal for the first time in my life."

"Normal?" She smiled up at him. "Do I bring out the normal in you?"

He kissed her forehead. "You bring out a lot in me." He was quiet for a moment. "You think this house is too big?"

"It's bigger than Disneyland."

"Yeah, but is it too big for us?"

She blinked at him. *For us.* Christmas was three days away. He was assuming she was going to marry him. It made sense that he did. Every day they spent together they were growing closer. Dash was getting happier, more attached to Ben. She had introduced him to Ellis as Dash's father and when Ellis asked her about him yesterday she never bothered to tell her sister the truth. Of course he assumed. And of course she should want to marry him. He was kind and loving and giving and stable. And he never used her past against her. She would be nuts to turn him down.

Then why was there that tiny niggle of doubt stuck in the back of her mind?

"As a kid I felt so isolated here. I don't want that for Dash. When Karen and I were trying she had this dream of sending our kids to the best boarding schools and having private tutors. I always thought the point of kids was to enjoy them, but I never said anything to her about it."

"Why not?"

"Because I loved her so much I would have done anything to make her happy even if I wasn't."

She didn't want him to be unhappy. She would never send Dash away. But she couldn't help but ask, "And what if I wanted Dash to go to boarding schools?"

Will you ever love me like you loved her?

He grinned at her before he swept her feet out from beneath her and rolled her onto the floor. "I would wrestle you. Winner gets to make all the major decisions for the rest of Dash's life."

"That's not fair. You're way bigger than me." She wiggled beneath him but made no move to get away. When they were like this, rational thought floated from her mind.

"But you're way softer than me." He ran his hands up

the backs of her legs. "And prettier." He touched his lips to her throat. "And you make me forget myself."

"Ben," she moaned as he slid his hands beneath her shirt to feel the skin on her back. "The door's not even closed."

"There is no door to close in the formal living room." He found the button on her jeans and undid it with just one hand. "Come on, my sweet girl. Wouldn't you like to make love beneath a Christmas tree just once?"

"I might get pine needles in my hoo hoo."

"I'll pick them out."

"Lord Jesus. I cannot believe my eyes." Dovie yelled, "Benjamin Rowe, get off of that girl right this moment!"

"Busted," he sighed, but gave her a long, slow kiss before he lifted his body off hers.

She was surprised that he did so in front of Dovie. They weren't hiding things from her, but they weren't flaunting their relationship either.

He got to his feet and went to Dovie, looping his arm around her shoulder. "It's her fault, Dovie. It's that shampoo she uses. It makes me crazy."

"It makes you fresh." She swatted his arm.

He grinned widely at her. "Despite you ruining my plans I'm glad you're here. Would you mind watching Dash for a few hours? Dina and I and are going to go grocery shopping for Christmas dinner and then I'm going to take her out to eat."

"Grocery shopping? You two?"

"Yeah. We're going to cook this year. It's going to be fun."

"Fun?" Dovie looked at him curiously. "Of course I'll watch the boy."

"Thanks" He kissed her cheek. "Thanks. I'll grab our coats."

"I've never seen him so happy," Dovie said when they were alone.

"Not even with Karen?" Dina hated herself for asking, but his relationship with his former wife fascinated her.

"They married right out of college. He was still a boy. He had blinders on. I liked Miss Karen, don't get me wrong, but she was too cold for my Ben. Ben will love and love and love until he has nothing left to give. Karen left him all loved out. And then there was Virgil. You don't want to know how much Ben did for him. You don't want to know how much life got sucked out of him in the process. But you, my dear, are different. You and your son are bringing him life instead of taking it away. You two are making him happy."

"But he barely knows me."

"He knows enough."

"What if I can't keep him happy?"

"You can try. And he will try. That's what a relationship is. A lifetime spent trying to make each other happy."

Twelve

Christmastime Is Here...

It was Christmas Eve. Finally. And it had been the fastest slowest two weeks of Ben's life. But he wouldn't change a moment of it. He was living life again and nothing could make him go back to the way things were before.

Dina stood beside him in the kitchen leaning her soft body against him as they stared at the turkey defrosting in the sink. "I can't believe we got so much food. Actually I can't *believe you* got so much food. There's enough here to feed twenty people."

"I don't go grocery shopping normally. I guess I went a little overboard. I didn't see you trying to stop me."

"How could I have stopped you? You looked so damn happy with your shopping cart and your little store circular. Who knew two-for-one deals would make you giddy?" She turned into him and lifted her mouth for a kiss. "Who knew I would fall so hard in love with a man who wants to cook?"

He looked at her, not sure he had heard the words correctly. But he felt them. Right in his chest. And it solidified everything for him.

"I didn't mean to let that slip, but it's true. I love you." She looked back at Dash, who was watching them from his high chair. "He loves you too."

"Mr. Rowe," Dovie called. "Your guests are here."

"Guests?" Dina blinked at him. "You didn't tell me about any guests."

He shrugged, not wanting to leave this conversation, not wanting to stop talking about her love. "They're a surprise for you."

She left the kitchen without another word. He pulled Dash from his high chair and followed her to the front of the house.

Dina stood frozen for a moment. Her mother, Phillipa Gregory; her stepfather, Walter Garrett; her sister, Ellis; and her husband, Mike, were all standing in the foyer. For her. One phone call from Ben and they all came to see her.

Looking back at him, she seemed shell-shocked, seeming not to know what to do.

"Your family is here, honey. Go."

"Yes," her mother spoke, her voice cracking a bit. "You haven't seen me for two years and you stand there like a statue. Get yourself over here."

"Mom." She slammed herself into her mother. "I'm so sorry."

"Shh," her mother soothed. "No more apologizing. It's over. We start over now." She let Dina go and wiped her eyes. "Now let me meet my gorgeous grandson."

"I want you to meet Ben too." She left her mother's side and linked her fingers with Ben's. "He's really good to me."

"I know. He's brought us all back together."

* * *

Being around her family was different this time around. There was no tension, no animosity, no reliving the past. They were just happy and together. And she had Ben to thank for it. Her family was in the kitchen, somewhat taking over the prep for tomorrow's meal. Mike and Ellis were baking pies. Dina's stepfather, Walter, was brining the turkey. Her mother was mixing the drinks. Dina felt so stupid for thinking they had turned their backs on her. She could have had them all along. But maybe, she thought, they needed this time apart. She needed this time away from them to grow. It took a lot of time and some help from Ben to make her realize that she wasn't a bad person, that she had something to offer somebody else. She wanted to thank him for that, but when she looked up from her conversation with Ellis she realized he wasn't there.

He had snuck away from them all. She knew how hard this must be for him. He had no family of his own to celebrate with. None besides her and Dash. She needed to remind Ben that they were there for him. That he wasn't going to be alone anymore. That they would be the family they both needed. She could picture future Christmases and family get-togethers and him and her and Dash as a family.

She found Ben in his office, a place she hadn't seen him go in days. It was such a different picture from the first time she saw him there. Long gone were his three-piece suit and supertidy hair. Long gone was that stern expression, and the little bit of unhappiness that floated around him. He was a different man from the one she had met. It didn't seem like she had walked into his life only twelve days ago; it seemed like she'd known him for a lifetime.

"Hey," she called to him, and he looked up and smiled softly at her. "I was missing you."

He placed the small piece of paper he had been staring on his desk and opened his arms to her. "I was just taking care of a little business so I can enjoy the rest of the holidays."

She sat in his lap and immediately his arms came around her, his lips resting on her forehead. "How are you, sweet girl?"

"I've got a bone to pick with you."

"What is it?" He kissed the bridge of her nose.

"You invited my family without asking me. What if I didn't want to see them? What if I wasn't ready? This could have been a huge disaster. You shouldn't do things without consulting me."

He kissed the tip of her nose, then each of her eyelids, before his kiss settled on her mouth. "In the future I won't, but Dash could use all the love he can get. We could use all the family we can get. I quite like having loud holidays."

"Me too." It was extremely hard to be miffed at him when he said things like that. "Everybody seems so happy, but my stepfather isn't fond of Dash's name at all. He said it's a grammar symbol and not a name. He says we should have named him Walter and been done with it."

"I like the name now. Maybe he'll become some kind of track star. Dash Rowe, world's fastest man."

"What a proud papa you would be. I think we need to talk about getting his last name officially changed and all the stuff that comes with it."

Ben kissed her brow. "As soon as the New Year comes. I promise. Maybe we should head back downstairs. Your family is going to notice we're missing. They might get the wrong idea."

"We're not doing anything."

"I know, but if I feel this beautiful bottom in my lap any longer I might get the wrong idea."

"Perv." She stood up, glancing at his desk as she did. There was a picture of his wife there. Just sitting there for Dina to see. That must have been what he was looking at when she walked in. He didn't even bother to hide it from her. That told her a lot. Even after everything, even after all the plans they were making, he still wasn't ready to let Karen go. Her heart sank. As much as she loved him she was never going to more than second or third place in his heart. She had too much pride to live her life like that.

Her decision was made. She couldn't marry him.

Thirteen
And So This Is Christmas...

Ben didn't fail to notice that Dina had been somewhat sub-dued when they returned to her family last night. He knew why. He knew she had seen the picture of Karen on his desk, but in that moment he couldn't explain to her why it was there.

He loved his first wife, a big part of him always would, but she was no longer going to be the person who ruled over his life. It was now time for him to live. To be with the living. He went to explain it to Dina last night, but when he went to her he found her sleeping, or at least pretend-ing to be. He knew that day had been long for her and he didn't have the heart to wake her up to talk about it. But maybe he should have. Today was the day they had agreed on. Today was the day she was going to decide if she was going to be his wife.

She was missing when he woke up that morning, but he knew where to find her. It was the first place he liked to go in the mornings too. She was sitting by Dash's crib, her knees pulled to her chest, just staring at the surroundings. She and Ben had decorated this room too, with a tiny tree and antique train set that traveled around the base. Dash's first ornament hung prominently in the front, along with the one Ben had made when he was just a child.

"When I was a kid," she said without looking up at him, "I used to wake up at six just to see what Santa had brought. I'm well over thirty. I don't believe in Santa anymore and I still can't seem to sleep very long on Christmas day."

"Me either."

She looked up at him. "I can't marry you, Ben. I'll never take Dash away from you, but I'm going to stay with my parents for a little while."

No. He wasn't accepting that. He wasn't going to let her go. He lifted her from her spot on the floor and sat with her on the plush rocker that was nestled by the window.

"I've been very happy since you came into my life."

"Ben . . ."

"I was saying good-bye, Dina. To Karen. That's why her picture was there. I loved her very much, but she's gone now. And I had been so busy mourning the loss of everything we could have had that I stopped living. But then you come along and in less than twenty-four hours made me want to live again. You gave me hope for the future and at first I didn't want to talk about her because it seemed so wrong to think about her when I was falling in love with you, but if you want to know about her I'll tell you everything."

"What?" Her eyes snapped up to his.

"We can talk about Karen if you want."

"No, go back to the part about falling in love with me."

"I love you." He smiled. "It's very foolish and impetuous of me to fall in love so quickly, but I think it's about time I started acting a little foolishly."

"Ben . . ."

"And that's why I don't want to marry you either. At least not yet. I don't want you going in with doubts." He slipped a ring out of his pocket and placed it on her finger. "I want a fresh start for both of us. That means we leave the past and all our old demons and start over together. I know you love me, but I would like you to take a year and really think about if you would like to spend the rest of your life with me. Dina, the only thing I need is for you to be happy."

"A year?" She sat up straight, shaking her head. "I changed my mind. Hell, I'm getting old. I want to pop out some more kids before I dry up. And you expect me to twiddle my thumbs for a year. Screw that. I want the old deal."

He wasn't expecting to hear that, but it was exactly what he needed to hear from her. "Okay, Dina." He gave her a very long, deep kiss. "Whatever you want."

"Okay?"

"Okay."

"But don't expect me to just sit around here and be your wife. I was serious about wanting to open my dance studio. I want to work for something. I don't want you to think I'm marrying you for any other reason than love."

"I know, sweet girl. I couldn't have fallen for you if you didn't."

"Da?" Dash sat up, rubbing his eyes with his fist.

"Good morning, son. Did we wake you?"

"Did you hear that?" Dina looked at him wide-eyed and then rose to collect Dash from his crib. "He called you Da."

"I did." He collected them in his lap, holding them close. "It's official now. We have to be a family."

"We already were," she said. "From the moment we walked through the door."

"Merry Christmas!" Phillipa burst into the room, her family following close behind her. "How is everybody this morning?"

"Great. Do you guys have to rush off tomorrow?" Dina asked.

"No, we're all off this week."

"Good. Because we have a wedding to plan."

"A wedding!" Ellis screamed. "How soon? I need at least two weeks, Dee."

"For what?"

"I have to make your dress. I have one already started down at the shop that we can make over in a few days, but if you want one from scratch it's going to take me two weeks."

"I could buy one, Ellie."

"Over my dead body." She turned towards the door. "Mikey, take me to the shop. I have to get my things."

Her husband sighed as he followed her out. "But, baby, it's Christmas day."

Ellis just blinked at her husband before she walked out the door.

"Don't you think you should eat breakfast first?" he called after her as he followed her out.

"We have to go too, Walter," Phillipa said to her husband. "I need to get my address book. I have to invite Cynthia Silverman. That woman said my Dina would never catch a man as good as her precious Becky's, but I'll show her. My girl has snagged a billionaire."

Suddenly they were alone again. He had his family in his arms and contentment in his soul. And he thought for the first time that this was what it must feel like to truly have it all. "Are you ready to start your life over with me, Miss Gregory?"

"I am." She smiled at him. "And I couldn't be happier about it."

'Tis the season to fall in love...

Don't miss these other delightful holiday e-novellas

Christmas at Seashell Cottage
Donna Alward

The Billionaire Cowboy
Mandy Baxter

Once Upon a Christmas Kiss
Manda Collins

The Mistletoe Effect
Melissa Cutler

A Little Christmas Jingle
Michele Dunaway

Blame It on the Mistletoe
Nicole Michaels

From St. Martin's Press